Out of the Depths

The Jonson Chronicles

Book One

by Antonia Harris

The contents of this work, including, but not limited to, the accuracy of events, people, and places depicted; opinions expressed; permission to use previously published materials included; and any advice given or actions advocated are solely the responsibility of the author, who assumes all liability for said work and indemnifies the publisher against any claims stemming from publication of the work.

All Rights Reserved
Copyright © 2017 by Antonia Harris

No part of this book may be reproduced or transmitted, downloaded, distributed, reverse engineered, or stored in or introduced into any information storage and retrieval system, in any form or by any means, including photocopying and recording, whether electronic or mechanical, now known or hereinafter invented without permission in writing from the publisher.

Dorrance Publishing Co
585 Alpha Drive
Suite 103
Pittsburgh, PA 15238
Visit our website at www.dorrancebookstore.com

ISBN: 978-1-4809-4003-1
eISBN: 978-1-4809-4026-0

Contents

1 Prelude 1
2 Lord Have Mercy 19
3 There's No Place Like Home 45
4 Cravings 55
5 Variations on a Theme 67
6 Thanksgiving – Part 1 79
7 Thanksgiving – Part 2 131
8 Black Friday and Saturday 151
9 There and Back Again 195

Dedicated to

the many wounded warriors on and off the battlefield, and to those who need to laugh but cry far too often.

And

to the memory of my father, one of the wounded warriors, who navigated the murky waters of the VA system at length with grace, dignity, and humor until his death.

1

Prelude

Out of the depths, I cry to you, Lord.
Psalm 130:1

I've just received the worse kind of news a wife could; my husband had been gravely wounded. I am Lettie Jonson, and I am married to Bruce Jonson, a captain in the U.S. Army, currently on deployment in Afghanistan.

My life, though not passing before my eyes, was irrevocably changed. My heart sank. My soul wailed a silent scream more hollow and lonely than the winds that whipped across desolate mesas. The thought of losing my soulmate froze my blood and metaphorically paralyzed my limbs. My chest tightened as I struggled to inhale the very air I needed for existence so I could understand the words being spoken to me.

I was informed while Bruce was leading his squadron on patrol in a remote valley, it got pinned down by enemy gunfire. Bruce did everything he could to protect his men, but somehow, during the fire fight, they got separated and all but three in the squadron were killed. Bruce, Mike, and Preston were captured by the Taliban. For days, Bruce and his men suffered immeasurably. Much of what happened to them was unspeakable, but my husband received the harshest treatment since he was the squadron leader. Bruce was beaten, burned, starved, cursed, screamed at continually, completely deprived of sleep for seventy-two straight hours, and finally, they attached electric wires to his testicles and, in effect, did their best to geld him. If he passed out, they revived him and made his existence such a living hell he wanted to die just to make the torture stop. On the fifteenth day, as near as we could count, he and his surviving men were inexplicably thrown from a moving vehicle, completely naked, near a U.S. checkpoint in the wee hours of the morning. They had cruelly used a rusty nail to pin a note through the chest of young Preston that simply said, *Allahu Akbar*; Allah is "greatest". God only knew how long it took for them to be found. The temperatures were frigid. My man should have died that morning, but thank God, he miraculously survived.

By the time I was notified, Bruce had been at an army hospital in Landstuhl, Germany for over a week. His condition was still touch and go with unfavorable odds on go. I was told in plain terms if I wanted to see my husband alive I needed to be on the next plane to Germany.

Petrified, angry, and overwhelmed, I knew I had to get to Germany somehow, and quickly. If there was a remote chance I could see Bruce one last time, no matter his state, I would be there—period. I first reached out to his unit's family liaison representative and was told the U.S. Military did not pay for dependents to fly to the aid of their wounded sponsor unless it was stateside. In other words, I had to find the money on my own. This month was atypical in that there was too much month left over at the end of our money. I scrounged for every penny I could find. I not only turned over the cushions of all the chairs and the couch, but I went through every purse I owned, and article of clothing with pockets. I took what we had in our savings, but still didn't have the necessary monies. At the eleventh hour, our church and the USO came through and provided a way for me to get to Germany and back without having to ritually fast while being there. After quickly notifying my job and arranging for vacation time, I took a red-eye out of JFK. I wound up sitting next to an attractive young mother named Kirsten and her young son, Martaan. It would be nice to have the distraction on such a long flight, or so I thought.

Kirsten Jungerheld was taking her young son to Germany so he could meet his grandparents for the first time. In an attempt at small talk, I began a friendly conversation with Kirsten.

"Is your husband stationed in Germany?" I asked.

"Oh, no, I am not married," she replied.

"Forgive me, I don't mean to pry.".

"Oh, it's all right. I don't mind telling people I'm a single mother. I came to the U.S. as a high school exchange student, and then decided to go to college here. In my junior year at NYU, I got pregnant. Martaan's father was a sweet guy and (whispering) a good lay, but I didn't love him. I wasn't going to further complicate my life by marrying someone simply because I was pregnant. I was raised to believe in the sanctity of life, so I kept the baby. I thought about giving him up for adoption, but once I saw him," she said, while tenderly brushing the hair from his forehead, "there was no way I could do that."

"He is a handsome lad," I said. "He looks to be about four. How old is he?"

"My baby is just twenty-three months," she proudly said.

"Really!" I replied with a touch of incredulity wondering if the child had Marfan syndrome. "He must take after his father," I added. Martaan looked like he had been spawned by one of the Titans. If that baby was only twenty-three months, I shuddered to see him in high school; he was going to resemble a refrigerator with a mop of hair. As it was, he could suit up for the New York Jets. Martaan was so big he had to have his own airline seat, even though chronologically he should have been able to sit on his mother's lap. It was just as well because Kirsten's legs would have gone completely numb with that boy sitting on them.

"O, ja! Everyone thinks he's large for his age, but he looks just like my papa did at this age."

"Was his father a large man, too?" I ventured.

"No, no. He and I were about the same height and weight. Martaan takes after the men on my side of the family."

"What type of work does your father do?" I asked, thinking surely, he and Andre the Giant must have been roommates.

"Papa is the town butcher," Kirsten said, beaming.

"How nice," I replied. Having a butcher in the family was a really good thing because it would take many herds to keep that boy fed and satisfied.

"Ja! Mama says she cannot wait to stuff him with schnitzel and strudel," she said, smiling.

I smiled back at her, thinking all the while **run piggy, run!** This little boy would suck every knuckle you've got, and he wouldn't need a bottle of hot sauce to help him do it.

Martaan was dark-haired with incredibly long eyelashes that framed hazel-green eyes. Looking at him made one want to get on one knee and hug the stuffing out of him. He was positively cherubic; God's receptacle of pure innocence. His mother, Kirsten, was a study in contrast. She was blonde, blue-eyed, solidly built, but not heavy, with a full bosom that reflected a post-partum mother. I also suspected she knew her way around a few beer steins.

After half an hour more of small talk, we began to yawn and shift in our seats. It was time to sleep. Ten minutes after closing my eyes, Martaan spoke. What I heard jolted me wide awake. I expected to hear a little munchkin's voice; what I heard instead was a deep, husky contralto. I had to look directly at his mouth to make sure I wasn't dreaming.

"Mommy! I hungreeee," he informed Kirsten. "Mommy, want eat!" He then climbed into his mother's lap and unbuttoned her blouse. Kirsten, drowsy, gently pushed his little hams away. He became more insistent. "Mommy, want eat NOW!" he barked.

I gave a sideways glace toward Kirsten, and became horrified at the thought she was still breastfeeding. To my amazement, she calmly unbuttoned her blouse further, like all young mothers who allow their children to feed on demand, unhooked one side of her nursing bra, and commenced feeding her child. In no time, the "baby" was sucking so hard I thought I heard some of Kirsten's vertebrae pop. Martaan grunted with every swallow like a frat boy at *Yung Chow Fat's All-You-Can-Eat* Chinese buffet. Soon, the pint-sized Hoover vacuum started slurping as if he was getting the very last of a thick and creamy milkshake. In his zeal to nurse, he managed to free his mother's other breast and kneaded it like some horny adolescent with his first real score.

Just when I thought the scene could not become any more surreal, Kirsten's kneaded breast began to gush milk. Martaan greedily latched onto the lactose geyser and started sucking like a thirsty man who'd just come out of a desert.

At the same time, he began kneading the first breast. Softly Kirsten began moaning. "Oh, baby…baby."

I quickly caught the eye of a flight attendant and motioned for a blanket, but she was one step ahead and cut the cabin lights till she could reach us with sufficient cover. WRONG MOVE!

Martaan immediately started bawling, "No dark! – No dark!" which woke everybody the hell up! The cabin lights promptly came back on and another stewardess was right beside us with a blanket to cover up the scene.

Kirsten, having been roused from her semi-wet dream, corralled her "girls" and tried to comfort Martaan.

"WAAAAAAAAAAAAAAAAH," he continued at the top of his lungs and voice register.

"Shhh! Shhh! Mommy's here. Mommy's here," Kirsten said as she tried to get him back to sleep.

"No dark! No dark! I scared! WAAAAAHHHHHHHHHHHHHH!" he lowed like a calf with laryngitis.

"My baby, my baby, it's okay. Mommy's right here," she crooned as she continued to rock him while tenderly covering his face with kisses.

Like most children who have stayed up past their normal bedtime, Martaan rapidly de-escalated and quickly fell into a fitful sleep. Seeing the concern on my face, Kirsten quietly explained to me Martaan did not sleep or cope well with darkness. He always required full lighting at night. The average nightlight was too dim for his needs, so when the cabin lights went out, it set him off. Her pediatrician told her it was all a normal part of infant development, and he would soon grow out of his need for light at night.

I merely nodded my sympathies while watching the now angelic cherub slumber in the seat next to me.

My heart started to bruise a bit for Kirsten. Raising children with a mate was challenging enough, but to do it single-handed was so much harder. Soon, she may not be able to get another man in her life, let alone her bed, because Martaan's needs would shortly begin to consume her young life. Maybe while visiting at home, her parents would be able to convince her to move back and give the boy a loving, extended family. Lord knows he was going to need the strength of his grandpa to bring him to manhood.

Presently, Martaan became fitful again in his sleep and started kicking. Kirsten did the best she could to lay half of him in her lap, but "baby" was so long his foot seemed to reach my left ovary with every spasmodic kick. Good thing I wasn't using it. Within forty-five minutes, Martaan had finally reached dead man's sleep. My whole left side was enormously thankful. Only two things would have made the situation better: an ice pack and a stiff drink. I pondered whether or not to summon the flight attendant regarding the latter when my ears picked up the raucous sound of snoring. The gentlemen behind me had a snore that sounded like he was gargling. The deeper he fell into sleep, the louder he became. At one point, I thought he might drown, such was the gurgling. Within rapid succession, all the snorers on the plane came to life.

Across the aisle from me, an older woman started snoring with a high-pitched *pweeeeuuunnnn* sound. Oddly, I giggled to myself because it reminded me of the farts my father would cut when we were kids.

It always started with, "Baby Girl, pull my finger!" *Pweeeeuunnn* – to which we children would laugh until our bellies hurt. Mama would walk into the room, see us in stitches on the floor, and then—the smell would hit her.

"Calvin! That's just nasty! Stop teaching our children such boorish behavior!" she shouted while fanning the air. My mother was the only person I knew who could literally turn her nostril inside out when offensive aromatics assaulted her delicate senses. Later, as an adult, I would often have to privately advise my mother to "fix her face" when we were in public because her nostrils would be going through all kinds of calisthenics.

"Oh, Jewel, you know there's mo' room out than in. Better to fart and take the blame than bust a gut and go lame," he playfully replied. He then rushed across the room and swept her up in his arms. She halfheartedly pushed him away while beating at his chest. Within moments, they were entwined in a deep and passionate kiss. We children stopped laughing and marveled at my parents' love for each other, and by extension, us.

Farther up on the opposite side of the airplane cabin, someone contributed to the nocturnal cacophony with a whistle snore. Behind me in the far rear, someone sounded like a hard substance rubbing against a cheese grater. My initial thoughts were this person needed to have themselves checked out for sleep apnea. Then I began to wonder how they had ever lived this long with that snore. Rounding out the symphony was the best impersonation of a bear in hibernation I've ever heard. Granted, I've never been, nor do I ever want to be that near a bear hibernating, but, I imagined that's what one would sound like.

I was so tired by this time sleep eluded me entirely. Worry and fear for Bruce had now crept back to the forefront of my mind. My belly began to twist and sour with concern for him. What if I didn't get there in time? What if he took a turn for the worst? What if he became an invalid? What if he'd been calling for me? What if? What if? What if?

My sore left ovary and a cabin full of snoring all began to press in upon me until I could feel the sting of tears in my eyes. I needed to get a grip and some fresh air, but that was impossible at 48,000 feet. I reached up and turned the cabin fan onto my face as high as it would go. My tears began to puddle and fall. If I didn't find the strength to contain myself, I was going to become a snotty, blubbering mess in short order. That's when I remembered a meditation exercise I did while an undergraduate in college.

Funny how the things one thought would never be useful in life become a salvation in dire circumstances. I quickly wiped the tears from my eyes and drank chai from an empty cup, only my cup was a king-sized bed and my chai was 800 count pima cotton sheets. I closed my eyes and concentrated on my breathing. Once my breathing had slowed and regulated, I envisioned the bed—its dimensions, its aesthetics. My cup was a dark finished, cherry wood sleigh bed. Oh yes, the kind of sleigh bed that verily said, "Giddy up!" Next, I concentrated on the bedding: crisp, white sheets with plump, soft, white quilted pillows, a high-loft white down comforter, and a white, delicate, lace-edged bed skirt. Finally, I felt myself slipping between the cool, silken sheets graced with the light wafting scent of lavender. My tension melted away into a serene bliss, which made my breathing more regular and deep. Teetering on the cusp of blessed rest, I was jarred into acute wakefulness by a wet slithering in my left ear. Literally, I jerked straight up off my seat. Whipping my head around, I saw Martaan laughing at me with one finger in his mouth. That boy just gave me a wet willy!

"Martaan," I warned, narrowing my eyes with "the look" every mother hoped to master to bring unruly children into submission. Suddenly, as if my calling his name was an invitation, he flew into my lap and threw his chubby arms around my neck for a big hug.

"Hi," he whispered.

"Hi," I whispered back. I gently embraced him, but when I tried to pull him away he resisted. I didn't force him from me, but instead held him closer. My arms needed Martaan, and I could only assume he, too, needed me at that moment. Together, we slept embraced until the pilot announced we were making the final approach into Frankfurt.

"Good morning, ladies and gentlemen. We are now on final approach to Frankfurt International Airport. Please fasten all seatbelts and put trays in the upright position. Crew, prepare for landing."

Martaan, now resting on my bosom, began to stir. First a yawn, then a lazy stretch as he fluttered his eyes. The next thing I knew he grunted, bore down, and his bowels exploded. His pull-ups could not handle the strain and a warm stream of watery poo came down his leg into my lap. My Lord, what a stench! I didn't know what that boy ate in between nursing, but whatever it was, it must have died inside of him.

"Mommy! Mommy! Poo-poo!" he cried.

"Aaaaaaaagh!" I squealed.

Immediately, Kirsten's eyes flew open and she shifted into mommy hyper-drive. In a flash, that diaper bag had opened, changing mat unfurled, a gallon sized zip-lock bag opened up, and she had a diaper wipe in hand.

"Come here, sweetie, and let Mommy clean you up," she cooed.

A flight attendant, on her way to the back galley to strap in for landing, noticed Kirsten and launched into her canned reprimand. Upon seeing, not to mention smelling, the situation and recognizing my distress, she told Kirsten to change the baby quickly. She waited the requisite moment to receive the offending pull-up now contained in the make-shift bio bag all the while giving me as sympathetic a look as she could muster. Then, she resumed her trek to the back galley. Kirsten sheepishly apologized for my predicament, but I also noticed she kept a firm hold on angelic Master Martaan just in case he accidently got some of his own poo back onto him.

We landed with a hard bump that dangerously jiggled the poo congealing on my tunic. Once we arrived at the gate, it was announced that military personnel, seniors, and those traveling with small children could disembark first. No sooner had the announcement been made did Kirsten snatch up her things and her young'un. She practically ran her ass off that plane as *auf wiedersehen* dopplered back to me.

I let everyone disembark before I began to stir because I was a shitty mess! Fatigue had so racked my body it was hard to think, let alone think straight. A hand gently touched my shoulder, which made me jump. I thought I was alone in the cabin. I turned to see not one, but two ladies looking down upon me.

"Ma'am," said the flight attendant, "my name is Susan Hatch, and I saw what happened to you with the baby. My sister Cindy, and I would like to help."

Standing next to her was a woman, not much older, in army camo fatigues, gently smiling down on me. Tears stung my eyes, and try as I might, I could not stop the floodgates this time that commenced to open wide. After a minute of full-on sobs, I regained my composure.

"Thank you so much," I sniffled. "I honestly didn't know what I would do. I've got less than an hour to make the connection that will take me to the Landstuhl Military Hospital."

"Are you going to visit family in the hospital?" Cindy asked.

"Yes, my husband," I said.

"Okay, here's the plan," said Susan. "Give me these soiled clothes and go to the lavatory and sponge with this."

"What's this?" I asked as Susan handed me a bottle of blue liquid.

"It's a shower in a bottle," Cindy said. "It's what we give patients who cannot stand in a shower in order to get clean. Simply wipe down with this. It will gently cleanse and remove any odors on you. There's no rinsing necessary."

"I need to get my bag for a change of clothes," I stammered.

"No time!" snapped Susan. "Get moving!"

As carefully as possible, I removed my soiled clothing, bagged them, and handed them to Susan. I then proceeded to the lavatory and sponged off with the shower in a bottle. True to her word, it did its job. I smelled fresh and clean. Throwing on a set of scrubs Cindy gave me, I came out, collected my bag, and then proceeded to disembark.

"As it happens," Cindy said, "I'm on my way to report to Landstuhl now. Perhaps we could continue together?"

"I would love nothing more," I said gratefully.

Praise God for Cindy Hatch. I would never have made it to my connecting flight if she had not been there to guide me. I could barely comprehend what the boards said, so great was my fatigue. And, to my shame, my high school French was utterly useless.

Appreciatively, I allowed Cindy to lead me like a puppy to the gate of our connecting flight. Once aboard and strapped in, I crashed before the plane's wheels were up and slept soundly until I was shaken awake by Cindy.

"Lettie, Lettie, wake up! We're landing."

I opened my eyes to a foggy confusion. Where was I? Strong turbulence jostled the plane, and then it hit me. Reality sped to my consciousness like a meteorite to Earth, which barely stifled my scream of alarm in time. I quickly looked into Cindy's eyes. Her gaze was calm and her hand on mine reassured me all was well, and the plane would land intact momentarily. Just as I was about to speak, the plane dropped like a roller-coaster at Six Flags. My stomach rose and kissed the back of my throat before hurling itself downward. Thank you, Jesus, there was nothing in my stomach because I would have vomited on the spot. All I could do was gasp for breath and try to stem the terror assaulting my senses. At last, the plane landed with a surprisingly smooth glide onto the runway. With full flaps down, the engines roared as the pilot applied the brakes. In no time, we were at the gate, docked, with cabin doors opened. As the multitudes hustled for their bags, I turned to Cindy and spoke.

"Cindy, I want to thank you for your kindness and all you've done. How can I possibly repay you? May I buy you dinner?" I asked.

"Think nothing of it. No payment is necessary," she said.

"I must do something," I insisted. "Can I at least replace the scrubs I'm wearing?"

"No way! Besides, those are a pair of old scrubs that belonged to an ex-boyfriend. I carry them with me for 'just in case' moments. You truly happened to be that 'just in case.' Actually, I'm glad they were useful to you. Those were the last reminders of a failed relationship, and I'm finally glad to get rid of them," she smiled.

"Then, surely, I can buy you a cup of coffee," I reasserted.

"Done! By the way, do you have anyone waiting to take you to the hospital?"

"No, I'm on my own. I was going to try and hail a taxi," I said.

"Well, today's your lucky day. I've got a buddy meeting me, so simply tag along with us. We can get you through the main gate a whole lot quicker than a cab will," she explained.

Once again, I thankfully agreed to be dragged along like a stray puppy. After going through customs, we met up with our ride. Cindy asked what had happened with Bruce, and I told her my horror story without breaking down or tearing up. As I finished my tale of woe, we were entering the main gate to the hospital. Our ride was kind enough to drop me at the central entrance where I could best be helped. Gathering my things, I took Cindy's hand to thank her again. She, in turn, did her best to reassure me Bruce would not only survive, but also fully recover. I could only nod and smile. I watched them drive away as the cold shadow of doubt began its clammy crawl up my spine.

Silently, I began to pray, *Lord help me!* My spirit wanted to run through the doors, but my legs were pure lead. Slowly, awkwardly, I trudged my way to the front desk. "Excuse me, I am the wife of Capt. Bruce Jonson. Can you please direct me to his room?"

The young man behind the desk gave me his prompt attention. All business and little warmth, he asked to see my I.D. After handing him my military dependent's I.D., he looked at it, then at me, handed it back, and, matter-of-factly, said, "Please have a seat over here. The Patient Advocate will be with you shortly."

Fifteen minutes went by before I was approached by a plump, middle-aged woman and an army officer.

"Mrs. Jonson?"

"Yes! I'm Lettie Jonson," I replied.

"Good morning. I'm Mrs. Haas, Patient Advocate, and this is Maj. Stanley Charles. Please come with us where we can talk more privately," she requested.

The looks upon their faces morphed my doubt into horrible fear. I was rooted in my chair and could only blurt, "Tell me, is my husband still alive?"

The two of them cast a knowing glace at each other before Maj. Charles continued speaking. "Yes, he is still alive. Please, Mrs. Jonson, come with us. We have much to discuss before we can allow you to see him."

It took Herculean effort to get my hips out of the chair. Mrs. Haas took me by the arm while Maj. Charles carried my bag. An elevator ride and two hallways later we entered a consultation room that could only be described as G.I. Jane Chic. Someone had tried hard to make the room inviting and soothing, but they must have run out of investment capital midway through because non-threatening drab was the result.

"Mrs. Jonson," began Maj. Charles.

"Please, call me Lettie," I interrupted.

"Very well, Lettie. As Mrs. Haas has already introduced me, I am Maj. Stanley Charles, and I am Capt. Jonson's attending physician. Ma'am, your husband is still in ICU in critical condition. His vital signs are thready, and, to be frank, he's a mess. I am surprised he's still holding on. I know you're anxious to see him, but I must first prepare you. He has a third-degree burn on his left flank we are still aggressively treating. When you enter his room, know the smell will be pungent. Portions of his body are still quite swollen, so he's not going to look like himself. He was tortured and beaten in ways I will discuss with you later. He is comatose by design, intubated, and on a respirator. It is vital we keep him in as sterile an environment as possible. Therefore, you will suit up, glove up, and mask up. If you feel you are going to vomit or faint once you're in the room, you will indicate that immediately. Tears are natural, but I would ask you do your best to check your emotions while in the room with Capt. Jonson. You may certainly break down *outside*, but not inside his room. Am I clear? Do you understand?"

"Yes."

"I'm sorry to come across so harshly, but your husband is my patient. I'm not only duty bound, but honor bound, to give him my best care. Lettie, what you're about to do, without a doubt, will be one of the most difficult things you've ever done. I must be candid with you. He may not pull through, but the decision rests entirely with God and Capt. Jonson. The patient has to want to live as well. I believe God is the Supreme Physician. If He wills it, Capt. Jonson will not only live, but recover – fully. Now, do you think you're ready?"

"Yes," I breathed.

"Okay. Let's get you suited up," he said.

For the third time in less than twenty-four hours, I found myself being led like a stray. Not a garden variety stray, but the frightened and traumatized stray that's been beaten so systematically a mere shadow sends it into fits of apoplexy. While putting on my suit, I began shaking badly, I needed help getting fastened.

Mrs. Haas, God bless her, gently took my cheeks in her ample hands and with the most compassionate look and soothing voice simply said, "Have faith. God is able. Now, breathe...with me."

Focusing on my breathing, in...out...in...out...in...out, I reached for my mental cup of chai, except this time it was a steaming mug of Jamaican Blue Mountain coffee with two sugars and a generous dollop of cream. In...out...mental slurp...in...out...two mental slurps, my shaking finally subsided. I opened my eyes to see Mrs. Haas's gentle and approving smile.

"I think now you are ready. Let's go and see your husband," she said.

Walking out of the room, we abruptly turned right and went through a set of double doors which led to the ICU ward. Three doors down on the left was Bruce's room.

Maj. Charles, also suited up, met us at this door. "Are you ready?" he asked.

"As I'll ever be," I whispered.

"Remember: the first sign of distress and you're out," he warned.

"Yes, sir."

It was cool upon entering the room. The lights, exceedingly dim, gave the effect of twilight. Bruce had more tubes, leads, and wires coming out of him, more than I had ever seen on TV, or in the movies. Monitors steadily beeped while the ventilator methodically pumped air into his lungs and brain. Being in his room felt more like walking onto some Sci-Fi movie set. It became irrevocably real once the smell hit me. I was so thankful I had not inherited my mother's sensitive nose, otherwise mine would have twisted right off my face. The smell of charred flesh, oxidizing blood, and pus was pervasive. A weaker person would have bolted from the room, but I was determined to stay no matter what. Somehow, I knew deep inside if Bruce should pass away this smell would not haunt me.

Tentatively, walking to his bedside, I looked fully into his face. The bruises on his cheeks were now a rather pretty, turquoise blue/green with tinges of yellow around the edges. Clearly, that was a sign that some of his injuries were beginning to heal. His full lips were a grotesque caricature of his noble face. He had multiple nicks and cuts as if he had been hit by shrapnel or buck-shot. His eyes remained slightly swollen and purplish.

Bruce always kept his hair cut close. As his salt and pepper locks grew in, it was evident Bruce was going balder. The horseshoe was more pronounced and "Le French Bangs," as we called them, were making a cameo appearance. Bruce hated the fact he was balding, that's why he adopted the close cut. I used to tease him that he joined the wrong branch of service.

"If you wanted high and tight, you should have been a Jarhead," I teased.

"You know you're strictly-dickly," he responded with a mischievous grin. "You want a man – not a pussy!" he said with a twinkle in his eyes.

"Careful! You won't want your comrades in arms to hear you," I warned.

"They ain't here, are they?" he replied, chuckling.

Watching his breath mechanically rise and fall, I tenderly lay my hand on his chest. I remember reading sometime back that comatose patients were aware of their surroundings. They could hear and remember words spoken to them. I trusted my man was not some vegetable in that bed, and, on some level, he heard and understood me.

"Bruce?" I softly called. "I'm here with you, baby. I'm right here with you."

Maj. Charles, who was watching Bruce's monitors, caught my attention while I was speaking and motioned for me to continue.

"Sweetheart, I came to be with you as soon as I could. I love you, Bruce Jonson. Don't you quit on me, and don't you dare die…that's an order! I need you to come back to me. I want you no matter what shape you're in. I need you, Bruce. I know you're in pain, but I want you to come back to me."

At that instance, Bruce's eyes fluttered. Startled, I jumped, which caused Maj. Charles to step over to the bedside. Flashing a penlight in Bruce's eyes, he grunted and then dropped some artificial tears in each eye. After wiping the spillage, he slowly closed his eyelids. Turning to me, he saw the wide-eyed look of fear and confusion on my face and began to explain.

"What you just witnessed, although surprising, isn't as uncommon as you'd think. He is still deep in a coma. When you were talking to him, I thought I saw his vital signs increasing. That's why I motioned for you to continue speaking to him. His heartrate and blood pressure have increased."

"Does that mean he heard me…understood me?" I asked.

"That's hard to say," he responded. "I've seen some pretty strange and amazing things in my career. But, I think it's safe to say it's a positive sign."

"How much longer are you going to keep him in a medically induced coma?" I asked.

"If his vital signs continue to improve, then we can bring him out in a few days. His wounds are so extensive I want to give his body as much rest as we can. Once he comes to, the pain is going to kick his butt. Don't worry; we can manage the pain, but he'll probably sleep a lot as a result of the pain meds."

"What can I do? I feel so helpless," I said. Hot, bitter tears coursed down my cheeks unchecked onto my sterile suit.

Fearing meltdown was imminent, Maj. Charles firmly, but compassionately, ushered me out of the room. In the hall, Mrs. Haas gingerly placed a fresh pack of tissues in my hands. I thought she, too, was afraid a tsunami of tears would break forth from my weary, sleep-deprived eyes.

Sighing deeply, Maj. Charles gave me a long sober look before he asked, "How long has it been since you've slept?"

"I napped on the flight over," I said.

"Uh huh! Do you truly want to know how to help your husband, Lettie?"

"Of course!"

"Go to your room. Lie down in a prone position for no less than eight hours. Once you've slept, take a long hot shower. After that, get an old-fashioned German breakfast in you. Then, perhaps, lie down again. You cannot help your husband if you are broken. These are doctor's orders, and you will follow them to the letter, understood? Failure to comply will result in no visitation privileges for you. It would be a shame for you to have come all this way and not spend time with him, yes? I am serious about the care I give my patients, and you are, by extension, now my patient."

Just as I was about to lodge my protest, Maj Charles took my hands into his.

"Lettie, please trust me. I don't believe he'll pass in the night. As a matter of fact, I think we've turned a corner. But I am serious in what I'm telling you. I don't want to see you for twelve hours. Understood?"

I narrowed my gaze at him like a sullen child who suddenly had dessert abruptly taken away before I reluctantly murmured, "Yes."

With the bargain struck, Mrs. Haas escorted me to my hospitality room. It would be my home for the next two weeks. I was informed my bag and belongings were waiting inside, and once situated, I unceremoniously flopped in the bed and slept like the dead and buried.

2

Lord, Have Mercy!

I followed doctor's orders, maybe a little too well, because I found that much needed REM sleep stalked and overcame me. Twelve hours later, I got up, showered, and ate. Thanks to Mrs. Haas, I had room service. No sooner had I finished my last bit of schnitzel, which was quite tasty, did my eyes become heavy and sleep laden again. There was no use in fighting the Sandman because the deck was stacked against me.

When I finally awoke from my slumber, I was rested, alert, and ready to spend quality time with Bruce. I contacted Mrs. Haas to ask for her assistance with suiting up, and she graciously met me within the hour.

Entering Bruce's room was a repeat of my first visit. The lighting dim, the smell still pervasive, the monitors beeped, hummed or thumped, and Bruce was still impersonating a member of the Borg Collective from *Star Trek*. Knowing I would spend many hours in his room, I brought the Bible and one of Bruce's favorite books to read aloud.

I looked fully onto his face and I gently stroked his cheeks, noting the beginnings of a beard growing in. I always liked a man with hair on his face, but Bruce was by-the-book clean-shaven. I asked him once while on R&R to grow a short beard for me. His response was quintessentially Bruce.

"Woman, a man's glory trail is *not* on his face!" he said.

"True," I responded, "but it would make for some nice foreplay."

"Well, when you put it like that, my answer would have to be no, NO, and *Hell-to-the-NO!*" he laughed.

What I wouldn't give to kiss him right now. The urge to nibble and nuzzle was born out of a raw hunger for his physical touch. How I missed his embrace, the tightness of being enveloped by his muscular arms. I yearned to inhale the aroma of his musk, to taste the saltiness of his nipples. I craved to feel the weight of his body on mine, and I longed for the urgent, hungry kisses he would bestow on my neck, my breasts, and my belly. My reality check came to the forefront. I may need to prepare myself. Bruce's body was so broken, and I didn't know if his mind was keeping pace. *Lord, have mercy on my husband*, I prayed as I gently brushed his lips with mine. Before I could straighten up one of the ICU nurses entered his room.

"Oooooo! I'm gonna tell!" she said with crinkled eyes and smiling voice. "I'm gonna trust since you both have swapped spit before your unmasked kiss won't hurt him. Do not let Maj. Charles see that kind of action. He'll have you out of here so fast it'll make your head spin. I'm Annie, by the way, but everyone just calls me *Sketty*."

"Sketty?" I asked.

"Yeah, like spa-sketty. It's a joke everyone started playing when I first got stationed here because my last name is Pasto. Annie Marie Pasto. Annie Pasto, get it? I didn't want to be referred to as 'salad', so we settled on *Sketty*."

"Is that what you would prefer to be called?" I asked.

"Oh, I really don't mind. It's all in good fun," she answered. "You know you've been accepted around here once you get a handle – a nickname."

"All right, then, Sketty it is. I would be obliged if we kept my lip nuzzle between us," I said.

"Girl, that ain't nothin' but a word! I am going to have to ask you to have a seat in the corner until after I've finished checking Capt. Jonson's vitals, okay?"

I nodded. Deftly, Sketty went about her duties checking, rechecking, and recording. Once all of Bruce's vital signs and monitor settings had been recorded, she changed the burn wound's dressings. That's when I asked if I could see the wound and observe her practices.

"Certainly, you may observe as long as you stand right here, and do not attempt to help. I've got to warn you, the sight isn't pretty, and the smell will be worse. Do you have a strong constitution? If you don't, then stay in the corner until I'm done. I don't want you passing out or throwing up on me."

"I'll be okay," I assured her.

Sketty positioned herself where I could clearly see everything. She slowly peeled away the dressings, which was a macabre collage of blood, serous fluid, and dead skin. The wound itself was not as deep as I had expected, but it still looked quite angry. There was necrosis around the edges that was turning a greyish-black.

"Will that dead skin need to come off?" I asked.

"Yes, we're going to have to debride him again," she answered. "Burns as extensive as these usually need multiple debriding before the wound grows healthy flesh. He's going to need a skin graft as well. All-in-all, Capt. Jonson's come a long way from when he first got here. I'm gonna wait until after Maj. Charles has completed rounds before we begin debridement." Looking directly into my eyes she added, "He truly is improving, but I'm not going to sugar coat this for you. Capt. Jonson can recover, but it's going to be a long and hard road to travel. He's going to need a lot of therapy – both physical and mental. He's going to need you. He's going to need your strength, your love, your patience…but more than anything, he's going to need your support. Do you understand what I'm saying?" Her eyes pierced mine searching for that kernel of lucidity, that seed which grows true mental clarity and awareness of a difficult and serious situation.

"I believe I do," I said.

"No…I don't think you do, but you will," she responded. "Your man is going to need you 25/7!"

"But, there are only twenty-four hours in a day," I scoffed.

"Exactly! That's how much he's going to need you, and that's how much he's going to rely on you," she reaffirmed.

I wanted to throw a snap-back at Sketty, but caught myself when I realized she was trying to communicate with me on a more profound level. I wisely chose to open my ears and close my mouth.

Sketty returned her attention to the wound's dressing. Once completed, she then inspected the more superficial wounds. Silence hung like a gossamer curtain floating between us. Finishing her tasks, Sketty once again turned to me. Though masked, I could see her eyes had softened, and I assumed she was smiling. "If you would like someone to talk to, Lettie, I would be honored if you called upon me," she offered. "My duty schedule is at the nurse's station, and I'll leave a phone number by which to reach me."

"Thank you, Sketty. I would like that very much," I said.

Sketty then turned, exited the room, and went to attend to her other patients.

Alone with Bruce, the beeping of monitors, and whooshing of the respirator, I pulled the chair to his beside. I opened one of Bruce's favorite books and animatedly began to read the saga of *Dune*. Not long after I began reading, Maj. Charles came to check on Bruce while performing his rounds.

"Good morning, Lettie. I can see by your eyes you were able to get some long-needed sleep and rest. May I also assume you've eaten, too?" he asked.

"You will be pleased to know I've followed doctor's orders to the letter," I replied.

"Excellent! Now, give me a few moments to check on patient No. 1," he replied. Maj. Charles read Bruce's charts, checked his vitals, and rechecked the charts before returning his attention to me. "Now that you've gotten some rest, we need to schedule a time to talk. I know you have questions, and I have much I need to share with you regarding Capt. Jonson's condition. My evening is relatively free. Will you join me for dinner, and afterwards we can talk?"

"Yes, I welcome that."

"Good," he said. "I'm going to go out on a limb and assume you're going to be here most of the day, correct? Why don't I swing by and collect you around 18:00 hours? Sorry, that's 6:00 p.m."

"That will be acceptable. I'll make sure to write down my most pressing questions," I said.

"Until 6:00 p.m. then," he said before departing.

Maj. Charles came for me promptly at 6:00 p.m. Instead of going to the hospital cafeteria as I expected, he took me to the base Officer's Club. We were seated in a well-lit, but secluded, part of the dining room. I suspected he pulled some strings to make that happen. Maj. Charles was a handsome man in an average kind of way. His appearance wasn't enough to make a woman make a double-take, but he wasn't forgettable either. He was a dishwater blonde with the most expressive brown eyes. His eyes were like windows to his soul. One could believe they saw in him a person of great compassion and humanity. Some vets would call him a *"good* guy" because he was a doctor who bothered to know the whole person. He wasn't interested in treating a nameless, numbered face. He wanted to know the man or the woman as much as possible before giving long term orders. When off duty, he was a pleasant and affable man with a gentle spirit and ease about him.

After having placed our orders for drinks and food, Maj. Charles lazily crossed his legs and shifted into a comfortable position before he said, "Okay, Lettie, hit me with your easy questions."

"Will Bruce always be on dialysis?" I asked.

"We hope his current renal failure is transient in nature. That means we hope it is temporary. Capt. Jonson took a viciously brutal beating which caused his kidneys to fail. We're hoping his kidney function will fully return."

"Do you know if he has any brain damage?"

"We believe there is some damage, but again, we won't know the extent or severity until he regains consciousness. He may have only sustained a bad concussion, or he may have more serious issues. We just don't know yet."

"I saw the burn on his left side doesn't have a skin graft. Will he need one?"

"Yes, he's going to need a skin graft, but right now, we're still debriding the wound. We're doing our best to stem the necrosis, but only time will tell."

"How much longer must he have all the tubes and wires attached to him? He looks like something out of a Sci-Fi movie."

Smiling, Maj. Charles answered, "Well, once he regains consciousness we'll begin releasing him from a majority of the tubes and wires." Looking at me with a more serious face, he said, "Tell me about your husband, Lettie."

"What would you like to know?

"Let's start with simple things: his likes, dislikes, habits, favorite pastimes, did he play sports? Etcetera."

"Bruce is very athletic. He played football in high school and college, but he knew he wasn't talented enough to turn pro. He always said he just liked hitting people and having the opportunity to vent his frustrations out on the gridiron. As long as a ball is involved, Bruce will play it, or watch it on TV. Football, basketball, baseball, tennis, soccer, bowling, racquetball, volleyball, broomball, cage ball, stickball, handball...you get my drift. He is exceptionally competitive. He's a man's man and a woman's friend. He genuinely loves people," I said.

"What do you mean by a woman's friend?" Maj. Charles interrupted. "Does he have a history of infidelity?"

"To my knowledge, Bruce has never strayed outside of our marriage. No, what I mean is Bruce knows how to make a woman, any woman, feel needed and appreciated. I don't care how young or how old, he can apply his charm and make a woman open like a budding flower. He is extremely charismatic, chivalrous – the epitome of a fine officer and gentleman. He's intuitive and sensitive, but not in a mushy sort of way. He can read people like no one else I know. He instinctively knows when to push or pull back; when to stroke the ego, or challenge a person, and he always does it in the most non-threatening way. It's uncanny and remarkable at the same time. Bruce pushes himself hard. Failure is not an option in his book. We're always our own worst critic, but Bruce seldom beats himself up. He gives his absolute best effort, and then he'll say, 'The rest is in God's hands.'"

"Is Capt. Jonson a religious man?"

"Bruce is a man of great faith and spirituality. Sometimes, I believe his faith carries the both of us. He loves God with a passion that almost rivals his love for me. Personally, I think God won out with the rival stick, but I'm not complaining. No man has ever loved me the way Bruce Jonson has, and no man will ever be able to take his place. That's why I'm here. If these are Bruce's last days on Earth, I need to be here. Maj. Charles I swear to you I will do whatever it takes to help him get healthy again. I would give my life for him."

"How long have you two been married?"

"It's been a little over eleven years."

"Any children?"

"No. We were in no rush. We wanted to wait until we could comfortably afford children, and then, before we knew it, we were complete within ourselves; we just never got around to having any. Why?"

"Ah! Our meals have arrived. I don't know about you, but I'm famished!" he exclaimed.

"Yes, I'm feeling rather peckish myself," I added.

We dived into our meals with gusto. Maj. Charles ordered steak, and I chose the wurst platter with a stein of beer. I must say, these Germans know their way around a brat. Maybe I should have exchanged contact information with baby Martaan's mother, Kirsten. After this dinner, a butcher hook-up would be most desirable. Even though I cleaned my plate, I made sure to leave some room for dessert. I had heard so many wonderful stories about German cakes that incorporated eighteen eggs or more into them that I had to taste one. After the final coffee had been served, our conversation started again at a leisurely pace.

"Did you enjoy your dinner?" Maj. Charles asked.

"Yes, I did, thank you. I always thought wurst was just a pretentious wiener. Boy, I sure have been deliciously educated this evening."

"I'm glad you enjoyed it. It's no secret that Germans know their way around a hog," he chortled. "And how about the beer?"

"Oh, my goodness, it tasted nothing like the brews in the States. I'm so glad I ordered it."

"As long as one doesn't make a steady diet of this food, one can stay healthy. Otherwise, be prepared to let the clothing out." Maj. Charles' demeanor changed from light and casual to somber before he continued the conversation. His brow furrowed, and his look was one of a doctor giving serious information, if not bad news. "Lettie, I've asked the questions I did to get a better picture of who Capt. Jonson is because we need to treat the whole man. Learning he's not a quitter is good. Learning he has a deep and abiding faith, is even better because he'll need those resources to help him with his journey back to wellness. I'm going to discuss a few items at a time with you because I don't want to overwhelm you. You'll also need time to process what I'm saying," he began.

"First, and foremost, you need to understand your husband was brutally tortured for no other reason than they could. According to the surviving members of the squad, the Taliban never asked a single question. These men were tortured for sport. Capt. Jonson received the lion's share of it because he was the squad leader. Your husband was relentlessly beaten. You see the bruising on his face is beginning to heal. What you don't know is his spleen was ruptured and had to be removed. During surgery while removing the spleen, we saw his liver had taken a real pounding as well. His kidneys were ruthlessly beaten causing failure. Since arriving at Landstuhl, we put him on kidney dialysis and catheterized him so we can determine if or when his kidney functions begin again. His right femur is broken in two places. His x-ray looked as if four or five people stomped the hell out of him."

He continued, "Lettie, your husband's testicles were grossly abused via electric shock. He received some serious burns to both. Most of the swelling has gone down, but we don't know if he's lost reproductive function. If he is able to produce and maintain an erection, there may be a good deal of pain associated with it. And, we won't know how much difficulty there will be achieving orgasm and ejaculation. His prospects, hypothetically, for siring children may be sharply reduced. Or he may not be able to sire children at all. As you know, all sex begins in the mind. The state of Capt. Jonson's mind will be the greatest determining factor on whether his, and subsequently your, sex life comes back fully."

With one hand on my breast and the other covering my mouth, I listened intently to all Maj. Charles said, nodding at appropriate times to assure him I understood. My world spun and the room seemed to grow appreciatively dimmer until I realized the lighting had diminished as the wait staff began lighting candles on all the tables. After measured moments of silence, I asked Maj. Charles how to proceed.

"I can pretty much guarantee Capt. Jonson's military career is over. Beyond the physical, he's going to need your strength to help him transition into civilian life. One of the first things you need to do is establish your support systems, especially a spiritual support system. This will be for the both of you. Being a primary caregiver is no small task. As devoted as you are to him, you will need a respite and some well-deserved "me time." Without it, you will break. Do not fall into the trap of feeling guilty because you're not there with him 25/7. You are flesh and blood, not some—Borg," he smiled.

"Secondly, be patient. I can't stress this enough. Your journey is going to be hard and long. This is a marathon, not a sprint. Expend your energies carefully so you'll have something for the finish line."

"Third, once Capt. Jonson is state-side, establish family counseling. They will help you both build and use coping tools for the challenges ahead. When the period comes where you can resume intimacy, go slow and take your time. Rome wasn't built or destroyed in a day. You will not be able to pick up where you left off. Sometimes that can be a blessing, but most often, it's a dreaded curse. Understand this before going back into the bedroom. Strongly consider seeking sexual therapy to ease the transition and mitigate any frustrations."

"My last recommendation, for now anyway, is pray. I firmly believe God is able to do far above and beyond anything we could possibly imagine. He didn't bring you this far to leave you. He'll see you through and give you the means necessary to overcome every obstacle. Believe me, you two are going to have one hell of a testimony when this is all said and done."

"Thank you, Maj. Charles," I said while fiddling with my napkin. Suddenly, I stopped fiddling and locked eyes with him and whispered, "I'm scared." Tears dropped into my waiting napkin.

Reaching across the table for my hand, Maj. Charles waited until I gave him my full attention before speaking. "Lettie, most army wives do not move Heaven and Earth to be with their wounded husbands. You've already shown me you're cut from hard wood. I'm giving this to you straight because I've seen too many wounded warriors go home to a spouse who thinks she can fix everything if she just loves him hard enough. Hear me and hear me clearly: YOU CANNOT FIX THIS! All you can do is be there for him when he needs you. I believe you're strong enough, but you're going to have to dig deeper, become tougher, and resilient enough to let him fall."

Those words made my head jerk up as I gave him a queer look.

"You heard me correctly. A man like Capt. Jonson needs to make it on his own. That means letting him fall so he can pick himself back up. His masculine identity will hinge upon that. You just told me he was a fighter. So, when he literally falls on his ass **do not** help him up. Let him struggle and fight until he asks for help. Encourage him, but don't coddle him. When he gets angry—let him be angry. He may swear, scream, cry, and even break shit. Whatever it takes — let him vent. Once he's calmed down, gently remind him that you love him, and you honor him, but you **will not** take his shit! Make him aware that even though he may no longer be in the army, he's still an officer *and* a gentleman. The two don't cease to exist just because he's been discharged. Tell him he must *choose* the high ground. He'll understand what that means."

I nodded my understanding and muttered a weak "Thank you" while drying my eyes.

"Oh, and one last thing," he added, "Don't be kissing on my patient until I say you can. I saw you through the window before the nurse exited the room. Next time look behind you. What am I saying?" he sighed, rolling his eyes. "There better not be a next time, capisce?"

I could only give him a chagrinned smile, then I bowed my head in surrender for getting caught. Knowledge is power. I'll sure know better next time, and there was definitely going to be a next time.

My first week in Germany seemed to drag interminably. Each day was a dull repeat of the other. I was greeted or dismissed with the beeping, humming, or whooshing sounds of Bruce's machinery. Every day I read to him from *Dune* and *Proverbs*. On day six, Bruce was taken off the ventilator, the dialysis machine, and the coma inducing drugs. Immediately, he was breathing well on his own. The doctors and nurses waited. I prayed fervently. On day eight, the first of my many prayers were answered. Bruce's kidneys began to produce copious amounts of urine. I praised his efforts by singing to him the line of an old Parliament song:

> *Make my funk the P-funk,*
> *I want my funk funked up!*
> *Make my funk the P-funk,*
> *I want my funk funked up!*
> *I said, owwwwwww, I like the P-funk,*
> *I want my funk funked up!*

Make my funk the P-funk,
I want my funk funked up!

Lord knows, I butchered that song, but I believed Bruce would have laughed if he could. Thinking of those lyrics took me back to when we were babysitting the son of Bruce's friends, Ray and Mary. They needed to take care of some banking business and asked Bruce if he would sit with the baby for an hour or two. I've never been one to swoon over babies, but somehow, Bruce talked me into spending time with him and his little friend. Timothy must have been about thirteen or fourteen months old. He was comfortable with Bruce, but wanted nothing to do with me. Bruce bounced Timmy around, cooed, danced to music playing on the radio, and played with him because he was fussy while carrying on a conversation with me. When the baby started to become cranky, I made a verbal observation.

"Bruce, when's the last time you've checked his diaper? He might be fussy because he needs to be changed."

"Huh. Never thought of that," he said, looking at me with a goofy "duh" expression. "Is that what's wrong with my little man?" Bruce cooed, looking into Timmy's face.

Laying him down on the sofa, Bruce pulled out a clean diaper, wipes, and powder.

As he knelt and cracked Timmy's diaper, I felt compelled to warn him. "Bruce, you might want to get a towel or something to cover his privates before taking his diaper completely off. Trust me, I know from the many experiences of changing my baby brother's diapers, you're taking a great risk of getting peed on."

"Woman, I got this! Stand back and let us men work," Bruce boasted, waving me away with his hands.

Just as Bruce pealed back Timmy's diaper, the radio started playing Parliament's song "P-Funk." Timmy was right on cue as if he could understand the lyrics. When they sang, *Make my funk the P*, he peed. Talk about a hose out of control, Bruce got pee on his shirt, his face, his mouth, and in his eyes before he managed to cover the baby's pee-pee geyser.

"Aaack, it's in my mouth," Bruce groaned, "and all over me. Man, I've nothing to change into."

"Oh my, it definitely looks like you're going to have to go back to your barracks and clean up when Ray and Mary get back. Would you like to postpone our dinner plans?" I asked.

"No, no, it won't take me long to shower and dress. I can be ready in ten minutes once I get to my barracks. Will you wait for me in the car?"

"Don't forget mouthwash, please," I reminded him. "I know you're going to want that good night kiss and under the circumstances, you'll understand my reticence." Bruce gave me a dour look that was one of many I would soon learn and love.

On the evening of the ninth day, I decided to grab an early dinner. I was in the cafeteria reading a magazine and taking my time with a lovely cobb salad. When I returned to the ward, the whole ICU was atwitter with activity and excitement. The entire floor was a party in full tilt.

"What's happening?" I asked Sketty. She was pulling the late shift, and her smile was brighter than any lighthouse on a stormy night as she approached me.

"A miracle is what's happening. Lettie, Bruce woke up about half an hour ago," she informed me.

I felt guilty because I had taken my time with dinner and completely missed him waking up. Hurriedly, I suited back up and dutifully waited for my turn to enter his room.

"Lettie, it will only be a few more minutes, then you can go in to see him," Sketty said.

A few minutes seemed like half a lifetime. The longer I sat, the more nervous I became. I felt like I did on our very first date. My friend,

Veronica, set me up on a blind date with a "really nice guy", which was code language for someone having the personality of a turnip, and the looks of a rube needing a good dental plan. I didn't even know why I said yes. I was perfectly happy leading a quiet, single life. My biological clock wasn't ticking, and I was never the type of woman who needed a man to validate my existence. I must have been bored or hungry. Come to think of it, I was hungry and broke.

I had agreed to meet my blind date at a little bistro that served a wicked sweet potato gnocchi in sage butter just around the corner from my apartment. I said I would be the one wearing Delta red, as in Delta Sigma Theta Sorority, Inc. I chose to wear a red with white polka dot, full-skirted dress with a sweetheart neckline piped with a narrow lace. To accentuate the décolletage, I wore a black, velvet ribbon choker with a Mother of Pearl cameo pendant, drop baroque pearl earrings, and peep-toed four-inch patent leather stilettos. To complete the look, I kept my make-up minimal and fresh, applied ridiculously expensive perfume, and wore a natural toned French manicure. No one could tell this sister she wasn't cute. I wanted my date to know I believed in looking good, smelling good, and I enjoyed every aspect of being a woman. As we agreed to meet early, I was the only one in the bistro wearing red, so it wasn't hard for Bruce to spot me.

I had positioned myself at a table facing the entrance. When Bruce walked through the door, all I could do was mentally shout, *Lord, have mercy! This brother is as fine as frog's hair! Please, oh please God, if there is any justice in the Universe, make this specimen my date.* Truthfully, I expected a dog to come my way, but to my surprise, and sheer delight, Adonis himself stopped at *my* table and asked for me by name. Thank you, God!

"Do I have the pleasure of addressing Miss Lettie Stanton?" he asked.

"I am she," I coyly responded.

"Good evening. I am 2nd Lt. Bruce Jonson," he said as he politely shook my hand, then kissed it.

"Very pleased to make your acquaintance," I grinned.

"I hope you won't think me too forward if I tell you how dazzling you look this evening."

"Why, thank you," I said, smiling shyly. "You, too, have exceeded my expectations."

Laughing with zest, his twinkling eyes locked onto mine, and against my will, I was soon laughing as enthusiastically as he. A waiter presently brought us water and menus. While he perused his menu, it afforded me a chance to surreptitiously inspect him. Bruce truly was Adonis in the flesh — handsome was an understatement. He was casually dressed, and the cut of his clothes accentuated his muscular build. I guessed he stood at six feet five or six inches, and weighed maybe 225 lbs.

His skin tone was a warm café au lait with emphasis on creamy-dreamy. His hair was cut in a tight fade. He was clean-shaven with a well-groomed mustache that proudly occupied space above the most sensuous pair of lips the Good Lord ever created. I was positive these lips never lacked for attention. Bruce's eyes were the color of caramel candy with the clarity of Baltic amber. Sunlight refracted through his eyes in such a way one could not help but stare. His eyelashes were so long they should have been illegal. His smile was like lightening; when he flashed it, the world lit up. The cologne he wore smelled almost as expensive as mine, and I know I sacrificed a quarter of my monthly rent to smell this luscious. Before I knew it, I was admiring God's handiwork. Yes, God knew *exactly* what He was doing when He made this one.

Dinner was phenomenal, and the company was incomparable. We had so many things in common with each other. Our taste in music, our love of movies, and most importantly our love of church. We were both raised in solid Baptist homes. In short, the evening was an unparalleled success; we got along swimmingly. So much so, we exchanged phone numbers and the rest, as they say, was history.

"Lettie?"

Wrested from my nostalgic reverie, I looked expectantly at Maj. Charles.

"We're almost ready for you to go in, but I have a few ground rules before you enter."

"Of course you do," I sparred.

"He's only been off the ventilator for two days. His throat is sore, so no talking. Make your words statements not questions. Do not let him speak. Do not let him move unnecessarily. *Do not* kiss him! Keep that mask on. He's still got a lot of tubes and leads on him, so no hugging either."

"Exactly what can I do with him?" I asked with annoyance clearly in my voice.

"You can hold hands," Maj. Charles grinned. "And if you're especially obedient, I may let you stay past visiting hours tonight. We clear about the ground rules?"

"Crystal!"

"Okay, then let's go see your husband."

Maj. Charles ushered me into Bruce's room. It was still dim and cool, but it was much quieter without the ventilator. He remained attached to various monitors that randomly beeped, but nothing like before. Bruce lay with his eyes closed. I stood at the left side of his bed, and softly called his name. He opened his eyes and looked at me for the longest moment. I wasn't sure if he recognized me or if he thought I was a ghost. Finally, his eyes registered he knew it was me and he raised his left hand enough to reach the guard rail of his bed. I took his hand and gently held it. His eyes never left mine, not even for an instant.

Maj. Charles kindly brought a chair for me to sit in, and Bruce and I simply drank each other in. No one else existed in our world for over half an hour. We were finally together again, complete within ourselves reclaiming our old familiar comfort zones. After a little while longer, I tried to release his hand, but he would not release mine. I searched his eyes, willing him to convey to me what was wrong. One large solitary tear began a slow and lonely trek down his cheek. His grip became tighter when I realized he was struggling not to weep. I wiped his tear away, and rules be damned, lowered my mask to lightly kiss his brow.

"Welcome back, Bruce Jonson," I whispered. "I've been praying for you and for this moment. I hope you know you can't get away from me just yet. I do give you props for working this hard, but I love you too much to let you go," I said, smiling.

Knowing he shouldn't try to speak, Bruce mouthed, "I love you."

I furtively looked behind me and saw Maj. Charles coming back toward the room, so I quickly adjusted my mask. I wasn't getting busted again.

Making his way to the bed, Maj. Charles looked at us suspiciously before he said, "All right, you two, cool your jets. Keep this up and you'll have to get a room."

"*We* have a room," I interjected. "You're the third wheel here."

"I mean a room that *you* pay for and not the US government," Maj. Charles spat.

"Technically, I *am* paying for this room. I pay taxes, which supports our government, which provides for our military personnel. Have I missed something here?"

"You know what I'm talking about. I do not want Capt. Jonson's heartrate to increase any higher than where it is right now. So, pull up, pull back, calm down, and quietly spark with each other," he said, winking at Bruce. "Capt. Jonson, give me a thumbs up or down sign to let me know your level of fatigue, please."

Bruce gave two thumbs up.

"All right. Lettie, I'm going to let you have two more hours with your husband then you're going to have to see him in the morning. Good night, Capt. Jonson, I'll see you at 06:00 hours," Maj. Charles announced before leaving.

During the next hour, I recounted my story to Bruce how I got the news about his capture and release. I spared no details with what it took for me to get over to Germany, including the episode of exploding bowels. The last hour I read aloud from *Dune*, and watched Bruce drift off to sleep. I stayed past my allotted time, watching my husband peacefully sleep. Sketty finally threw me out, and teasingly admonished I should come back tomorrow only if I was fully fed and watered. Sighing, I reluctantly left Bruce's side. Silently, I thanked God for today because, indeed, it was a good day.

The next morning, fed and watered as directed, I suited up, and made it to Bruce's bedside by 7:00 a.m. Rounds had been completed early, so Bruce and I were alone for the greater part of three hours. At 10:30 a.m., an ICU nurse, whom I had not met, came in.

"Good morning, Capt. Jonson, Mrs. Jonson. My name is Nancy. Captain, how's your pain right now?" she asked.

Bruce motioned for something to write with. Nancy speedily figured out Bruce's request, and produced a mini white board and marker. With little difficulty, he wrote three words: OK, cold, and water.

"I think we can take care of this pronto. We're going to keep the temp of the room the same, but I will bring you a warmed blanket to help with the chill. Glad to hear your pain is managed. As for water, I'm going to give you some crushed ice to suck that way we can determine how hard it's going to be for you to swallow. I'll bring a cup and leave it with your wife, all right?"

Bruce ably nodded. I gave him a scant spoonful of ice, and waited to see how he handled it. I noticed swallowing was a challenge, but soon he motioned for more ice. At the rate he was going, he would be taking nourishment by mouth in quick fashion. After exhausting the cup of ice, he gestured for the white board again and wrote, *missed you.*

"I missed you more," I replied.

He continued to write, *Scared I die without seeing you once more.*

"Me too," I said. "Apparently, God is not through with you yet."

Next, he wrote, *No more Army. Ready to go.*

I gently squeezed his shoulder before saying, "Yes, I believe they are going to discharge you from the service."

Bruce closed his eyes for a moment before he continued, *Tired. No more war. Want peace.*

I could only nod in affirmation to the obvious. Patiently, I waited for him to continue.

Sighing deeply, he wrote, *How R my men?* and he fixed on me with a penetrating gaze.

"Baby, I've been so focused on you, to my own shame, I haven't even inquired about Mike or Preston. But I promise I'll find out and get some news for you."

A look of horror and disconsolation etched itself across his face. Rapidly he scribbled, *Only 2?*

As tenderly as I could, I told him only three men in the squadron survived: Mike, Preston, and himself.

From the depths of his soul, Bruce began to breathe life into his despair and he howled. He reached an apex with a bloodcurdling scream of "No – no – no!" Then he thrashed his head and limbs as best he could. Monitors quickly responded to his actions, and in a flash his room was a blur of nurses in motion.

"What happened?" asked one nurse.

Before I could answer, another nurse shouted at Bruce to calm down while a third pushed a sedative into his I.V. As quickly as the kerfuffle erupted, the room fell into silence sans beeping monitors. Maj. Charles strode in, and in true military fashion, demanded his nurses' report.

"Capt. Jonson was in the company of his wife when his monitors detected stress. Upon entering the room, we found the patient thrashing and extremely agitated. We tried to calm the patient verbally, but feared he would rip his lines, so we immediately sedated him," Nancy reported.

"What happened?" Maj. Charles barked, looking squarely at me.

Mustering all my courage, under his baleful eye, I told him, "We were talking via the white board when he asked me about his men. I explained as gently as I could only three men survived. That's when Bruce lost it."

Maj. Charles looked at me hard, and then curtly nodded. He dismissed the nursing staff, and wrote explicit orders he be paged the moment Bruce woke up. Turning to me, he ordered me to sit. This Maj. Charles was formidable, and I dared not test his resolve, so I hastily sat in the chair by Bruce's bed.

"Lettie, I'm not happy about what just happened in this room, but it wasn't unexpected either. I am not blaming you in any way. What you witnessed is just the tip of the emotional storm you and Capt. Jonson are going to have to weather together. This was the easy part; it gets progressively harder from here on out. When Capt. Jonson awakens, *I* will update him on the disposition of his men, and I'll read to him the official field report from the attack in Afghanistan. Then, I will discuss his current physical status. I normally do that one-on-one, but I'm going to make an exception and give you the opportunity to be in the room with us if you want."

"I choose to be here," I hastened to respond.

"Until that time, I will allow you to stay, but you may not disseminate any more information to Capt. Jonson before filtering it through me. Understood?"

"Yes, sir."

Four hours passed before Bruce woke up. In that time, I was able to take a nap myself, and read a few ladies' magazines. Maj. Charles came into the room, and quietly waited for Bruce to fully awaken. Once he had Bruce's full attention, he began the arduous task of disseminating requested information by reading the Afghanistan field report, then moving on to the current update of Mike and Preston. Mike was already back with the unit in Afghanistan. Preston's psychological injuries were so severe he had been shipped back home. Throughout the whole report, Bruce had no reaction, not even a mumbled word or sound. He looked at Maj. Charles the whole time, but his face was devoid of emotion. When Maj. Charles updated

Bruce on his own condition, a spark of life took ahold in his eyes. Addressing the more serious issues first, he explained the transient nephrology was proving the assumption it was indeed temporary. His kidneys began to function again, and the blood tests revealed he was almost back within normal parameters. Bruce would need to be kind to his kidneys, and choose his food and drink with care so they would not become over taxed in the following months.

His burn was a third-degree wound, and it would need a skin graft. For the interim, cadaver flesh would be used until they could harvest his own skin. The broken femur, though healing, would become a thorn in his flesh. It was broken in two places. Bruce would not be able to be as physically active in the future as he had been in the past. He might develop arthritis in that leg as well. Either way, the prognosis promised frustration, pain, and anticipated weight gain. Maj. Charles suggested Bruce consider turning to water sports to help keep his weight down and increase his physical stamina. The other less threatening wounds would completely heal in time, and give him scars to brag about. At this point, Maj. Charles took the time to ask Bruce if he had any questions thus far, or if he wanted any further clarifications. Bruce nodded and wrote one word on his white board—*NUTS*.

Maj. Charles reached for a sip of water, looked at me, took a deep breath, and jumped into the pool. "The electrocution of your testicles burned them and caused much swelling. We don't know yet the extent of any internal scarring. I believe that you will, in time, be able to produce an erection along with the ability to ejaculate. I suspect, at the first, this activity will be painful, but I think that, too, will subside. What we have not tested to see is whether you can produce any sperm."

Bruce quickly scribbled, *I have Lettie. That's enough.* Then he looked at me with a fire in his eyes.

My throat tightened and my vision became blurry. Tears of joy welled in my eyes, and I reached for his hand and held it tight.

"Physically, you may be capable of performing the sex act—but your mind may not let you. I want you to know this is expected and completely normal under these circumstances. Your sex drive may diminish drastically. This, too, is normal. Just as the body needs an allotted time to heal, so does the mind."

"In another week or so, once we've down-graded you from critical, you will be transferred stateside to Walter Reed. There, you'll finish your convalescence and begin your physical therapy. You will also undergo psychological evaluation for PTSD. There's no getting around it, so don't even try. You're intelligent, so be smarter; take advantage of every offering available." Maj. Charles looked pointedly at me before he continued with, "You have a fine and outstanding woman here, Capt. Jonson. Please don't let me hear you've been making her life hell, or I swear I will find you and open up a can of extra-strength whoop-ass."

Bruce scrutinized Maj. Charles, sizing him up before he wrote, *"You may try, but I am THE Master Ass-Whooper."*

Maj. Charles blustered, laughing loudly, and Bruce genuinely smiled as both men sat, and metaphorically admired each other's hard-on. Honestly, the testosterone began to suck the air out of the room.

"I bet you were a frightening S.O.B. in battle," said Maj. Charles.

Bruce responded writing, *"You know it."*

More laughter ensued. They truly were a band of brothers and comrades in arms. Maj. Charles finally asked Bruce if he had any other questions or requests.

Bruce wrote, *May I speak?*

"If you feel up to it, you may certainly try."

"Please—brush my teeth," he croaked.

Grinning, Maj. Charles asked, "Anything else?"

"Steak—rare—I'm starving," Bruce said.

"I was wondering how long it was going to take you to ask for solid food," he chuckled. "We'll get you started tomorrow morning on some broth, and maybe even a bit of custard pudding. Don't give me the hairy eyeball; you know you've got to crawl before you can walk. Besides, last I looked, you were still sucking on ice, right?"

To that, Bruce merely stuck his tongue out at the major. Suppressing a guffaw, Maj. Charles informed me I had only one more hour then I was to take my leave. He would check back at that time to make sure I left, and Bruce was settled for the night.

Alone once more, Bruce turned to me and rasped, "I love you, and I meant what I said. You are my everything. As long as I have you, I'll be all right."

The next five days flew by. Each day, Bruce got measurably stronger. He had a slight setback of a low-grade fever when the cadaver flesh was applied. His spirits, however, did not seem to dampen. Every waking moment of his day, I was with him. When he napped, I coffee-klatched it with Sketty, or one of the other nurses. The night before I was scheduled to leave, Bruce and I had an extremely emotional discussion. By that time, his voice was much stronger and held up until late evenings.

"Lettie, I want to talk to you about something."

"Okay. What's on your heart?" I asked.

"When I was in that hell-hole, I almost gave up. I *almost* lost hope. They never even asked me a single question. They stripped me naked, and strung me up like some hog for slaughter. I did what I was trained to do. Name, rank, and serial number was all I said. When I stopped speaking, they beat me harder. When one man got tired, another one took his place. It got so bad I couldn't take it anymore. I asked them, 'Why? Why are you doing this? What do you want from me?' Somebody must have been able to understand English because that's when they cut me down. A day or two later, they tied me spread eagle to a chair. Just when I thought it couldn't get any worse, they brought in a car battery and hooked me up to it. They poured cold water all over me and made sure my feet were sitting in pools of water before they flipped the switch." Bruce stopped talking, visibly shaking with eyes scanning the room, but seeing nothing. "For the first time in a long time," he whispered, "I was terrified. I…I…tried to be a man, but I could smell my own nuts frying—and the pain," he uttered with a strangled voice. He looked at me with wide eyes that were slightly wild; he was visibly shaking harder now. "I would have done anything — said anything — to make that pain stop. I screamed until I had no voice left; just slobber and spit, and still they just kept on flipping that switch. I tried to pray, I did! I kept repeating to myself, 'Lord help me – deliver me – make it stop!' I know I passed out, but when I came to I was strung up again, and they hit me with a blow torch," he said fully crying. "A *blow torch*, like I was some side of meat!" he rasped.

"Baby, don't tell me anymore, especially since it's upsetting you," I tearfully pleaded.

"NO! I gotta tell you – I can't hold this in no more! They *hurt me for no damned reason*! I prayed harder and asked God to give me strength. But, Babe, *I hate them*! I hate them for what they did to my men. I *hate* them for all they did to me. And I *hate* them for what they've done to us! I *hate* them…I…*hate*…God, forgive me, **I hate them!**"

Angry, stinging tears mingled with racking sobs washed over my husband. I wanted so desperately to hold him, rock him, and assure him that everything was going to be all right. But, Maj. Charles' words haunted me. Could I be strong enough to let him fall? I cried along with Bruce, but I remained silent otherwise.

Hearing Bruce's cries, one of the ICU nurses came into his room. I held my hand up for her to stop. She astutely assessed the situation and quickly retreated.

Tearfully, Bruce continued to speak. "Lettie, I need you to promise me something," he cried.

"Baby, anything. Just tell me how I can help you."

"I need you to pray for me. I want you to pray every day and every night. Get Pastor Wilson and our church family to pray for me 'cause I don't want to be this hate-filled man. I don't *want* to live like this. I can't live like this. Will you do that for me?" he pleaded.

"Yes, yes, you know I will. As soon as I get back home, I'll get you on the prayer list as well as the prayer chain. I'll meet with Pastor Wilson and let him know as much as you want me to share," I assured him.

At length, Bruce finally cried himself out and was reduced to the post-cry hiccups. He waited for those to subside before he spoke again. "I've started having nightmares about being back in *that place*. I wake up dripping wet and shaking. One night I wasn't sure where I was. It took me a few moments to understand the beeping was my monitor. It scares me. I don't want to be like one of those old crazy coots who needs medication for the rest of his life. I can't be some mental cripple!" he emphatically spit. "Lettie, I know you love me, but I hope you don't think less of me because of what I've told you. I don't think I could bear the thought if you did," he said with fresh tears spilling from his eyes.

"Bruce Jonson, you listen to me and you listen well," I said with real anger. "Nothing you could do would ever make me love you less, or think less of you. You are my hero and always will be. I am incredibly thankful you came back to me, and I will not allow you to wallow in self-pity or self-doubt. You and me, we're going to make it. We're going to make it! You hear me?"

With that, Bruce started crying hard again, and his hiccups returned with a vengeance. I cried right along with him, and held his hands as tightly as I dared. The hour was growing late, and I knew I needed to be at the airport early in the morning, but I couldn't leave him just yet. I suspected I was going to have another rough crossing of the Atlantic, but I was much more at peace about the whole prospect. At 11:15 p.m., we said our last good-byes. Unfortunately, the ICU nurses were in the room, so I couldn't kiss Bruce. But before leaving, I reassured him I would be at Walter Reed as soon as I knew he had arrived. Bruce blew me a kiss, and I dramatically caught it and held it to my heart before leaving.

The trip back, thankfully, was uneventful. After getting home, I dumped my things and took a long, steaming, hot shower. Afterward, I slept until the bright sunshine in my eyes made it impossible to stay in the bed any longer. My first order of business was to contact Pastor Wilson. It was a Saturday, and I didn't want to interrupt his family time, but I knew he was anxiously awaiting any news of Bruce. Our phone conversation was intense, but productive. Immediately, after hearing all I had to say, Pastor Wilson said he would put Bruce on the prayer chain, prayer list, and a few internet prayer list serves. We had him covered seven ways to Sunday. I made it my business to be in church the following morning so I could thank our church family for all their help and to give an abbreviated update on Bruce's condition. Bruce was a well-respected serving deacon of the church. When they learned how far he had come physically, the congregation erupted into spontaneous praise complete with dancing and shouting a la Pentecostal style. Their demonstration of praise and faith warmed my heart and gave me the assurance I needed Bruce and I would receive all the support and assistance necessary.

3

There's No Place Like Home

Bruce came back to the States three weeks from the day I left Germany. I was advised to give him two days of adjustment before visiting, and they were an agonizing two days. When we were finally reunited, I could fully kiss him with no rules or masks.

His skin graft was healing well, and his face had less discoloration. He somehow managed to bribe someone to cut his hair and shave his beard, much to my disappointment. He still was unable to stand on his own, but he could sit up with some assistance. He was now eating semi-solid foods, but he still talked a great deal about that steak.

Walter Reed Military Hospital was not as accommodating as Landstuhl had been. I did not have the same level of unrestricted access to Bruce's doctors, and I'd swear, the nurses had been teleported from some World War II gestapo unit. The best comportment I received from nurses Hilda, Gretchen, and Kratchet was a chilly civility; no warm, nor fuzzy from these women. Even Bruce said he made sure he was a perfect gentleman with Nurse Gretchen.

I knew these women didn't play when Pastor Wilson came to visit Bruce not long after he returned stateside. Pastor told me of his experience when he arrived a mere ten minutes after visiting hours had expired and asked if they would make an exception for clergy.

Nurse Hilda's response was, "When the good Lord sends me a wet fleece along with a dry one, calls me via a burning bush, and then uses a *different* jack-ass to speak to me, that's when I'll think about making an exception for you!"

Nonplussed and smiling, Pastor Wilson tried to out maneuver her assault with, "My sister, I only wish to pray with my congregant."

She parried with "How marvelous! Then by all means, please enter your prayer closet—at home. Otherwise, come back at the posted visiting hours and *not* before or *after*!" Nurse Hilda then assumed the defensive position of legs spread, both hands on hips with the *I wish you would* expression on her face. Pastor Wilson, although a fearless warrior for the Lord, was not a stupid warrior. He gracefully bowed, lifted his hands in holy surrender, and slowly backed away.

"Sister Lettie," he confessed, "That woman scared me!

Bruce progressed with his convalescence and various physical therapies at an accelerated pace. He said he was working hard so he could get out of the hospital and sleep in his own bed. I encouraged his resolve because our bed was far too empty without him. Four months from his capture, Bruce could finally come home. Up until his last two days in-house, I was a nervous nester. I cleaned and re-cleaned, organized and reorganized, redecorated and rearranged the furniture twice. I wanted his homecoming to be perfect.

I drove Bruce's old, beat-up truck to bring him from the hospital. Brewster the Rooster, as it was duly christened, was what some would term vintage if it had been in better shape. To me, it was simply an old bucket of bolts. In its heyday, I'm sure its color was red, but now it had oxidized into a sad, matte rust color. When he was home, Bruce was forever tinkering around with Brewster. He never polished his truck either. He always said he liked Brewster's character just the way it was. The truth to that story was the more you rubbed on Brewster, the more the paint came off. One certainly didn't want to wear good clothing while in it, or around it because the outcome was always the same; rust smudges everywhere. Brewster was a three-speed column stick shift with a clutch that was heavy-duty industrial strength. One had to aggressively stomp it in order to shift. Bruce had modified the engine and exhaust system to where it now sounded like a monster truck complete with the most incongruent *ahh-oo-ga* horn. It had newly upholstered thickly padded, beige pleather bench seats with shoulder harness seat belts. The cab itself was otherwise sparse and utilitarian in appearance. Bruce made driving Brewster look cool. I, on the other hand, must have appeared to the unsuspecting public as Mrs. McGoo, instilling fear in every defensive driver on the road.

I wanted Bruce's homecoming to be a joyous one, so I thought bringing Brewster to the hospital would give him a chance to get reacquainted with his old friend, and it would be much easier to transport his wheelchair. I made sure to put the step stool in the truck bed just in case Bruce needed it to get into Brewster. The look on his face affirmed my decision when the staff wheeled Bruce out to the curb. One would have thought his long-lost sister had just shown up unexpectedly on his doorstep. After getting in and buckling up, Bruce took my hand to say thanks.

"Babe, thank you so much for this. I've missed Brewster. And listen to him sing," he said, stroking the dashboard.

"Sing? More like cough," I said.

"That's only because he hasn't been on the open road in a while. Why don't we take the long way home so you can open him up, and let him stretch his legs," he said with shining eyes.

"Under the circumstances, I think Brewster can wait a little while longer before getting on the open road. Besides, you know how hard it is for me to drive this old rust bucket." I said.

"Pay no attention to her, Brewster! She doesn't mean it," he laughingly shouted. "Well, if you won't go the long way home at least take the interstate and push him up to 75 mph."

"Happy to take the interstate, but the speed limit is 70 mph. Brewster will have to get opened up at a later date. You know, you ought to thank me for keeping Brewster. I almost sold him to get to Germany," I confessed.

"I'm glad you didn't do that. How could you even entertain the thought? Brewster is a part of the family! We stopped being sold 150 years ago," he indignantly replied.

"Baby, why is it a *he*? Every worthy vessel has historically been a *she*," I pointed out.

"It's a man thang; you wouldn't understand," he scoffed, falling silent.

The entire drive home Bruce hung his head out the window more like a bald Golden Retriever instead of my husband. Occasionally, he would grunt when he noticed something new or unusual about the scenery.

Pulling off the interstate onto the city streets, Bruce murmured, almost as if he were speaking to himself, "I missed this place. Never thought I'd say that about here."

Pulling into our driveway, I saw a small crowd gathered by the front porch waiting for us. I had invited Pastor Wilson, but he took the liberty of bringing the entire church's deaconate with him.

"What's this?" Bruce asked. Turning to me, he screwed his eyes up and asked, "Did you set this *surprise* up?"

"I'm just as surprised as you are," I honestly replied.

"Welcome home, Deacon!" Pastor Wilson bellowed while opening Bruce's door. Helping him out, he gave Bruce a big bear hug as some of the other brothers took the wheelchair and step stool out of the truck's bed.

Each deacon took their turn welcoming Bruce home with words, handshakes and hugs. Deacon Wilbur Brown was so overcome with emotion he not only hugged Bruce, but kissed him, and then started shouting "*Glory – Glory –Gloooraaaaay*" while holding onto him. Pastor Wilson quickly disengaged Wilbur before he could hurt Bruce. I hustled everyone into the house before they broke into speaking in tongues in the front yard. Once inside, the joy levels continued to increase. I forgot I had given Deaconess Simms a copy of my house key before leaving for Germany. She, and as many of the other deaconesses who didn't have to work, had come in and prepared a sumptuous repast. They were setting the table buffet style as we entered.

Limping into the dining room, Bruce engaged his indomitable charm and loudly exclaimed, "My, my, my, my. To quote Psalms 118:25; this is *sho' nuff* the Lord's doing and it is marvelous in my eyes!" Looking up at the ceiling with arms spread wide he vociferously continued, "Thank you, Father, for allowing me to see my other favorite women once again and for the bounty of their labors!"

Those old sisters started sniggling like little school girls, then they queued up like bees going to the hive for honey; each eager to kiss Bruce and hug his neck.

Sister Simms quietly approached me, after getting her hug and kiss first, and gently pressed our house key into my palm. "Lettie, I hope you don't mind, but I held onto the key specifically for this occasion," she said.

"I am most grateful to you and the other deaconesses. I don't really know how to thank you all," I replied.

"Honey, it's simple – you just open your mouth and say the words. We all know where your heart is," she smiled.

"Yes, ma'am," I nodded. "I'll be sure to send my formal thanks in a day or two, but until then, thank you, Sister Simms, so very, very, much," I said, hugging her tightly.

Watching the last of the bees suck up their honey, I saw Roland Matthews, Rallo, enter through the patio door with a platter of steaks fresh off the grill.

Placing the platter strategically near Bruce, Rallo loudly proclaimed, "Hail to the sick and A-fflicted, our wounded warrior, brother, and friend. God has answered our prayers and has safely returned you to the bosom of our affections!" Concluding his proclamation, Rallo strode over to Bruce and shook his hand, slapped it, dapped it, and then he gently gathered Bruce into his arms, and embraced him like the brothers they were. Pulling back and smiling widely, he guided Bruce to a chair at the table and motioned for Pastor Wilson to step forward and speak.

"Brothers and sisters, we've gathered today to welcome home our beloved brother and deacon, Bruce Jonson. We are only going to tarry long enough to break bread with Deacon Bruce and Sister Lettie. We will have plenty of time later to visit at length. Now, let us bless this amazing spread. Rise Peter, slay and eat – him who reaches gets the meat! Amen."

Everyone broke into riotous laughter at Pastor Wilson's irreverent blessing as the feasting officially began. Bruce sat as Master of his table. His every desire was immediately fulfilled and piled high upon his plate. My admonitions about eating lightly was an exercise in futility, and furthermore, wasted breath. The honeybees knew exactly what they were doing as each one had taken great care to prepare a dish they knew to be one of Bruce's favorites. They made sure he ate like a condemned convict. Complete satiation was their only aim. A few of the dishes they prepared I loved myself, like Sister Roberts's whole pickled peaches. That woman could make one hurt themselves. Sister Taylor's light bread stuffing was so fluffy and savory it could make one cry. Sister Brown's rolls were a mile high — light, airy, buttery, and baked to perfection. Sister Collins' greens were extraordinarily awesome. She *put her whole foot up* into those greens! And, don't let me get started on Sister Simms's sweet potato pie; it was legendary.

The honeybees busily buzzed, but there was one drone within this good company who deserved special recognition; that was Brother Rallo. He sure knew his way around a grill. Rallo could season meat better than anyone I knew. He was passionate about his grilling, and it showed. He took great pride and care in his cooking, and lived vicariously through others as they enjoyed the meats he prepared. Bruce's rare steak was grilled with precision and liberally seasoned with Rallo's secret steak rub blend.

Bruce's first bite elicited a sigh that could only be conveyed as a state of TBO; taste-bud orgasm. His eyes literally rolled to the back of his head. The second bite brought head bobbing and grunts of extreme approval. The third bite caused Bruce to lock eyes with Rallo and point his knife at him. The bromance was rekindled!

The whole surprise repast was a delicious cornucopia of gastric delights. My only complaint was that these saintly folk, who would give the very clothes off their backs to someone in real need, were *stingy as hell* when it came to sharing their recipes. Sister Roberts had already informed me her recipe for pickled peaches was going to the grave with her.

Approximately ninety minutes after the feasting began, Pastor Wilson announced it was time for everyone to leave. "Y'all don't have to go home, but you do have to leave this house!" he said, jokingly. "We need to let Deacon Bruce and Sister Lettie get re-acclimated to being together at home again—alone."

In no time the honeybees had found storage containers for every unfinished dish and placed them in my somewhat bare refrigerator. At the twenty-minute mark, folks were walking out of our door. Before leaving, Rallo told me he would be back over tomorrow afternoon to deal with the grill. Waving farewell to all, I closed the door as the last person departed. Walking back into the dining room I burst into laughter as I caught Bruce unbuttoning his pants to breathe more freely.

"I don't know about you, husband," I said, "but I could stand to take a nap."

"Whew! I thought you'd never ask," Bruce confessed.

Together, we slowly walked down the hallway to our bedroom. I helped Bruce completely undress, and then assisted him to the bed where he could make himself more comfortable. I slid out of my slacks and laid down next to him content to hold his hand as we both fell into a glucose induced sleep. As I drifted off, I mentally thanked the Lord for another day's journey.

Sunday morning, bright and early, Bruce awoke anxious. He wanted to get to worship services early, but wasn't sure if he would be able to get himself *squared away* in time. I managed to convince him he had plenty of time to shave, shower, dress, and have a decent breakfast before getting underway. Moving into the bathroom, Bruce began to fret about what he could wear, certain none of his current clothes would properly fit him now. His personal aesthetics would not allow him to attend church looking anything less than GQ sharp. I told him to go ahead and get started, call me if he needed help, and not to worry about a thing.

Bruce had several classic-cut suits that had gotten a bit snug on him in the past year. He was going to give them to charity, but I took them and put them into storage instead because I knew from experience Bruce's weight tended to fluctuate, especially when he was on deployment. He always came home thinner than when he left. Fortunately, I remembered to take one of his more favored suits out of storage to the dry cleaners. While he was showering, I began to lay out his clothes. I placed on the bed his chocolate brown wool suit, a new white dress shirt with French cuffs, a pair of neutral silk brocade braces, a matching set of abstract silk tie and pocket hankie that complimented the braces, a new set of gold-filled cufflinks and tie tack, a pair of pinstriped nylon knee-high socks, and his most comfortable pair of square toed Stacy Adams dress shoes, well-polished and near spit-shined. Finally, I placed one of his favorite colognes, John Varvatos Vintage, near his cufflinks so he'd be sure to see it. I couldn't wait to see Bruce's face with my choices. For myself, I chose a classic black knit wool jersey chemise with expensive looking costume jewelry accents, a simple neutral wrap, and a pair of La Perla seamed stockings with my five-inch leather pumps.

Bruce managed to shave and shower without any help from me. Upon opening the bathroom door, he stood transfixed in the doorway looking at the clothing arrayed on the bed. I turned to him, while still dressing myself, and drank in with appreciation the look of wonder and amazement on his face.

"Woman," he hoarsely croaked.

"You may be the sick and A-fflicted," I interrupted, "but this morning you will look every bit the conquering hero."

"But how did you…when did you…where?" he sputtered.

"If I tell you, then I'd have to kill you," I teased. "I know it's been a while since you've sported braces, but I took the liberty of having a tailor make the adjustments in light of your wounds. Did I do all right?"

My question was answered with eerie silence and the next thing I knew Bruce was swaying, trying desperately to hold himself upright within the door frame. Rushing to his side, I helped to stabilize him, then guided him toward the foot of the bed. I knelt next to him to make sure he wasn't ill or ready to pass out.

"What's wrong, beloved?" I asked with worry drawn across my face.

"I just got a little woozy there for a minute. I think the shower may have been too hot. I'm okay, promise," he assured me. Reaching down he gently took my face into the palm of his hands. He fixed me with a loving gaze and asked, "Have I told you today how dear you are to me? How much I love you?"

I caressed his hands with mine and tenderly nuzzled his palms.

"I don't know where I would be without you," he stated, "and I don't intend on finding out."

"You smoothie, you. Come on, let's get you dressed or we really will be late," I said.

Fully dressed and finally ready to go, I stopped Bruce at the door leading to the garage. There was one last thing needed to complete his look. I went to the closet and produced a sleek ebony wood cane with a highly-polished brass handle. I saw the cane in a boutique near work and impulsively purchased it thinking Bruce might be willing to use it. He quizzically looked at me and then the cane.

"I know you, Mr. Jonson. You're not going to let me take the wheelchair with us this morning, and you cannot stand long unassisted. So, I'm giving you a little bit of stylish assistance. But even this won't aid you for any length of time, so you must promise to sit down, or we leave when you get too fatigued. Deal?"

"Deal," he chuckled wryly.

While on our way to church, we ran into traffic. There was a multiple vehicle accident on the interstate which slowed our progress. Once we could get off the interstate we took back roads to the church, but by the time we arrived we were truly late. The worship service had not only started, but the choir was already into their first selection when we entered the sanctuary. They were enthusiastically singing *I'm Going All the Way* by André Crouch as Bruce and I walked down the center aisle to sit near the deacons. Upon seeing us, the Mt. Pisgah family rose out of their pews and raised the roof in loud and *undignified* praise! They were shouting so joyously the choir sang louder. The harder the choir sang the more boisterous the congregation praised until the Spirit of the Lord descended upon the church body like an atom bomb. Even the stoic ushers, who normally aid others overtaken in the spirit, were shouting, jumping, and crying in praise. Several of the congregants were violently possessed by the Holy Spirit where hats, and a few wigs had become dislodged. So loud was the cry of the church that the organist kicked open all the presets, and still she could not drown out the shouts and cries of exuberant praise. Bruce, too, was emotionally caught up. As he lifted his arms in praise to the Lord, tears streamed down his face. For thirty solid minutes, the church was in a Pentecostal accord. From the youngest to the eldest, all were uttering praises for Bruce's safe return. The congregation began to gradually settle down as the Spirit of the Lord lifted off His people. Pastor Wilson ably began preaching a fiery, uplifting message of God's hope.

After the benediction, Pastor Wilson asked Bruce to join him at the main doors so he could greet the church family. A protective look must have passed across my face because Pastor Wilson immediately amended his first request and asked that I join Bruce. He motioned to another deacon that a chair be brought for Bruce to sit in. I smiled, mouthed my thanks, and dutifully took my place next to Bruce. He was the most secure and the most content he had ever been before his deployment. Little did we know this Sunday was going to be a defining measurement for normalcy in our lives.

4
Cravings

Bruce was home for good. He had received his discharge papers and was slowly acclimating himself to civilian life. At first, his days were spent keeping a myriad of therapy appointments at Walter Reed Hospital. His routine soon leveled out to a Monday-Wednesday-Friday schedule; Tuesday-Thursday he either worked around the house or tinkered on Brewster. Saturdays, yard work, and Sundays, church. By the ninth month of his convalescence, Bruce had completely finished all physical therapy. He walked with a limp when the weather started turning cold, and only slightly limped the rest of the time. Otherwise, one would never have known he'd been physically wounded.

The nightmares began to resurface for Bruce, but now he confided about them to his therapist, Lloyd Wrightman. Lloyd insisted he maintain his Monday-Wednesday-Friday schedule, and participate in a PTSD support group twice a week, along with his weekly private sessions. I never asked Bruce about his therapy sessions. I always believed he would confide in me as he did before. I was wrong. Bruce's nightmares became worrisome and, at times, frightening. He thrashed about, kicked, screamed aloud, and often woke up crying, dripping wet with sweat.

"Uhmm, no!" Bruce mumbled in his sleep, his breathing quickening. "Don't do that! Stop!" he shouted. Bruce thrashed and became entangled in the bedcovers. Before I could get him untangled, he screamed a loud, blood curdling scream and sat upright as if a spring had snapped and propelled him forward. "Aaahhhh!"

I turned my light on and saw Bruce dripping with sweat, heaving for air. "Baby? Baby, it's alright," I said, reaching out to assure him with my touch.

He slapped my hand away and stared at me like I didn't belong in our bed.

"Bruce? Baby, are you okay?" I asked.

"Don't touch me!" he roughly answered. It was his only response before springing from the bed in to the shower.

I waited for his return, but I fell back to sleep. The alarm was what woke me. Looking over at Bruce, he slept soundly, oblivious to the alarm clock. I rose and went about my routine.

As I was dressing for work, he awoke.

"Morning, babe," he murmured.

"Good morning, Bruce. How are you feeling this morning?" I asked, waiting to see if he would talk about last night.

"Okay, I guess," he yawned, and that was the end of his commentary. "I'll see you when you get back this evening." Then he rolled over and went back to sleep.

Getting in to work, my day was typical, and I stayed busy until quitting time. Arriving home, Bruce had already prepared a light dinner. I was thankful because I was tired, and all I wanted to do was vegetate.

"Wow, baby, thanks for preparing dinner," I said, kissing his cheek.

"It's the least I could do for my woman," Bruce responded, pecking me back.

I didn't bother to change out of my clothes. I took my shoes off, washed up, and came back to the kitchen to fix my plate. Joining me, Bruce sat and ate sharing small talk with me. After dinner, I rinsed and stacked the dishes in the dishwasher before heading to the shower. I took a long, relaxing, hot shower. After drying off, I put my nightgown on.

"Babe, are you going to bed already?" Bruce wanted to know.

"Yeah, I'm really tired. I didn't sleep well last night, and 5:30 a.m. came too soon. My day was nonstop, and quite frankly, I'm bushed," I said.

"What can I do to help you feel better?" Bruce asked.

"Come hold me and cuddle with me till I fall asleep," I requested.

Bruce quickly hopped in and out of the shower, slipped into the bed, and held me from behind. He tenderly and lovingly wrapped me in his arms as I fell fast asleep. I was later jarred awake by Bruce screaming in horror. The noise scared me so badly, I squealed. Bruce woke himself up and cried like a frightened child. I scooted over to him, and that was when he turned on me and lashed out.

"Don't touch me!" he recoiled as if my touch burned his flesh. "Leave me alone! Just…leave me alone," he railed as he shoved me backwards – hard.

"Bruce?! It's me! It's Lettie. Don't you recognize me?" I pleaded.

"Stay away from me," he said with a cold, dead affect, no longer crying. "I don't want you near me," he continued with an emotional coldness that stunned me.

I expected him to get up and take a shower, but instead he rolled over and turned his back to me.

I was beside myself and confused. What had I done to receive such treatment? I moved to the furthest corner of my side of the bed and literally racked my brain for hours pondering upon any clear-cut mistakes or missteps on my part. After what seemed an indeterminate amount of time, I could find no fault. Bruce continued to moan or cry out in his sleep, occasionally thrashing. When I finally began to drift off back to sleep, the alarm went off. Oh, Lord! Another night of no appreciable sleep. Today was going to be rough.

I got up and went through all the motions. Got myself to work on time and put in my eight hours. Driving home was difficult. I was so tired I literally drove like a timid, old lady and crept on the city streets to the house.

Coming inside, Bruce greeted me effusively. "There you are!" he said, coming over and gathering me in his arms. "Babe, you okay?" he asked, searching my face.

"I don't feel well, Bruce," I replied, which wasn't exactly a lie. "I need to lie down and sleep for a while. Will you be okay without me cooking dinner?"

"Don't worry, babe. I'll go out and get something for us both," he said, feeling my forehead.

I wanly smiled and staggered to our bedroom. I barely hung up my clothes before collapsing in the bed, reaching a dead sleep within minutes. I woke up some four hours later, acutely aware of my hunger. It was nearly 11:00 p.m. when I got up and went into the kitchen in search of food. Bruce was nodding in his reclining chair with the TV watching him. I did my best not to disturb him, but he awoke anyway.

"Hey, babe," he yawned. "How are you feeling now?"

"A little better. I'm still sleepy, but I'm hungrier. I'm going to grab a bite, and then go back to bed. You don't have to wait up for me if you're tired."

"Yeah," he yawned again, "I think I'm gonna hit the sack now." He rose from his chair, came and lightly pecked me on my cheek, then schlepped to our bedroom.

I took my time eating. I caught the late news and a good portion of the Jay Leno show as well. I wanted nothing more than to return to my bed, but I also wanted Bruce to be good and asleep before I got there. I'd be keeping to my side of the bed tonight, doing my best to rest before his nightmares took over.

At 12:30 a.m. I gently slipped into my side of the bed until awakened by the feeling of someone or something watching me. I slowly opened my eyes. I was facing where I should have seen Bruce's figure, but he was no longer in the bed. I rolled over and turned on my lamp. Standing above me with a vacant, but malevolent, look on his face was Bruce. He was stark still except for the clutching and flexing of his fists. His presence scared me to death! I screamed and scrambled to the edge of his side of the bed and had one foot on the floor in case I needed to lock myself in the bathroom. My breathing was near the point of hyperventilation, and I began to shake badly. Bruce never moved nor did his eyes track my movements. I suspected he might be sleepwalking. My fear had not lessened by that thought, but instead was weighing on my bladder. I quickly went into the bathroom to relieve myself. Averting that near accident gave me time to collect my thoughts and wits. I apprehensively returned to our bedroom.

"Babe, you okay?" Bruce asked, coming over to me acting like his old self.

"Yeah, yeah," I stammered. "I just needed to use the bathroom," I said edging to the bed.

"Wait a minute, babe. Come here," he gently pulled me by my arm. "You're sweating," he observed as he wiped my brow. With true concern in his eyes, he asked again, "Are you sure you're alright?"

I nodded vigorously, avoiding his eyes, and said, "I just need a bit more rest is all." He let me go but kept watching me with suspicion. I got back into the bed, turned the light off, and pulled the covers up around me. I lay down with my back towards him, but I couldn't close my eyes for love nor money.

Bruce slipped back into bed and spooned closely behind me. "Woman, your heart is racing. You're beginning to concern me," he commented.

"Umm, I'll be better come morning," I mumbled, all the while shouting in my head, *You're concerned?! You're scaring the **hell** out of me!*

A quick peek at the clock revealed it was only 2:00 a.m. If I was lucky, and God was willing, I had another three and a half hours of sleep ahead. Fortunately, God was willing, and I slept undisturbed until the alarm clock went off at 5:30 a.m.

A month went by with the same nightly scenarios. The strain began to wear on me. Every night I went to sleep with the man I knew and loved, sometimes tenderly wrapped in his loving and protective embrace, only to wake up to a stranger who was unresponsive, distant, and/or emotionally cold. By the light of dawn, that stranger would be *my* Bruce again. I selflessly exercised long-suffering and patience with my husband, but tucked away, deep down, I was scared and hurting. We had not shared any physical intimacy other than hugs and short kisses, and I missed him. I missed his touch, and I was getting hungry—really hungry. I felt like a woman adrift at sea who was surviving on captured rain showers while wishing for a gully-washer to come along. Rain showers kept one alive, but it surely didn't satisfy in any way. I kept reminding myself I had promised to love this man in good times and bad. This was a marathon, not a sprint, and currently I was in the bad times.

One year to the day he was captured and tortured, Bruce's nightmares dramatically intensified. Adding to the list of demonstrative behaviors, Bruce now became more physically violent during his dreams.

One night, he began screaming, and when I tried to wake him, he slugged me hard in the stomach. I immediately crumpled and slid to the floor. It took a long moment to catch my breath, meanwhile, Bruce continued to scream and thrash. After about two more minutes of hell, Bruce woke himself up. He leapt out of the bed, and I knew by past experiences he was dripping with sweat and shaking badly with fear. Straight away he jumped into the shower without even checking to see where I was, let alone if I was all right. I didn't hold it against him; my husband was suffering. Bruce took a long, long shower. Every fiber of my being wanted to check on him to make sure he had not harmed himself, but I knew *my* Bruce wasn't in the bathroom; the changeling was taking a shower. I decided instead to lay back down and will my stomach pain to cease. I would confront Bruce in the morning.

When I awoke, he was gone. It was Veteran's Day, so I knew he had no VA appointments. I was thankful, too, my offices were also closed in observance of the holiday because my gut was still in quite a bit of discomfort, and I would have hated calling in sick. Rising, I went to take a shower to start my day. Lifting my nightgown I saw my reflection in the bathroom mirror. I had a massive bruise the size of a salad plate in the first stages of black and blue. No wonder I was still in pain. Staring at the ensuing riot of colors, I realized this was going to take a while to fade. The good news was I would have no problem hiding the bruise from view, even from Bruce, because he showed less and less interest in any form of intimacy. Once dressed, I went in search of my husband. He was, predictably, in the first place I looked – the garage. For whatever reason, he was under Brewster's hood.

"Good morning, Bruce. What 'cha doing?" I asked.

"Morning, babe. Just giving Brewster a tune-up," he replied as if last night never occurred.

"I got a little nervous when I woke up and you weren't in the house," I continued.

Bruce leaned over, stuck his head out from under Brewster's hood and cocked an eyebrow at me before grunting, "Uh huh."

"Would you like something to eat?"

"Nah, I'm good. Maybe later," he replied before going back under the hood.

"Well, then, I'll leave you to it," I said before going back into the house.

Bruce stayed in the garage working on Brewster all day. He neglected breakfast and lunch, and the dinner hour was rapidly approaching. Any other Veteran's Day, the grill would be smoking, and our house would be filled with men from Bruce's unit. There would be some beer drinking, and much loud talking, laughing, and the never-ending one-upmanship war stories. This year was quiet because Bruce's unit was still in Afghanistan, but I knew he would be going down his own private memory lane. I didn't feel like firing up the grill, so I put some brats on the Foreman grill instead, made some coleslaw, and a quick fruit salad. I hoped the aroma would entice Bruce to share dinner and a movie with me. Whoever said a man's heart was through his stomach did not lie. No sooner had I removed the last brat did Bruce appear with a smile, eagerly washing his hands at the kitchen sink. Normally, I would have had a major meltdown about washing car grease and grime in my kitchen sink, but today I decided to pick my battles, and I let it go. We had far more serious issues to be concerned about.

"Woman, how did you know?" he asked, drying his hands.

"Oh, I took a well-educated guess," I said, laughing. "I even have a cold beer from the micro-brewery for you, too."

"You're far too good to me," he said, giving me a strong bear hug.

Eye-blinding pain shot through me, but I did not flinch or cry out. This secret was mine to nurse and mine to protect. Breathing slowly and shallowly, I steadied myself at the kitchen island.

"You okay, babe?" Bruce asked with real concern on his face.

"Yeah, yeah. I'm just…cramping a little," I replied.

"Do you want me to get the hot water bottle for you?"

"No, no, baby, you fix your plate and sit down. I picked up the latest Sci-Fi flick, *Dark Metropolis*, from the video store. Would you like to watch it with me?"

"Sure. You know, I was meaning to catch that flick when it was in the theaters. I'm glad you rented it."

We watched the movie together, made small talk during the slow portions, and hooted and hollered during the action scenes, especially when the annoying, helpless female got devoured by the aliens. At the end of the movie as the credits rolled, I collected all the dishes, and took them into the kitchen to be cleaned. Bruce decided to watch the late news while I finished up. Half an hour later, I found him fast asleep in his reclining chair. I hesitated to wake him, unsure of *who* would appear, so I left him, and headed for bed. Ten minutes later, Bruce came into the bedroom, yawning and sleep heavy.

"Babe, why didn't you wake me when you got ready to go to bed?" he asked.

"Oh, I didn't have the heart to disturb your rest," I lied.

"Man, you left me in the dark and everything," he said, almost whining. "Next time, please wake me, okay?"

"Of course."

"Now, bring yo' fine self up in this here bed, and let me hold onto you for a while," he smiled, patting the mattress.

"I'll be right there. Let me turn off the bathroom light."

Once in bed, I carefully turned my back to Bruce so I could protect my massive bruise while we spooned. I was anxious because I didn't want a repeat of the previous night. Surprisingly, we both slept well, and I was quite rested when the alarm clock went off at 5:30 a.m.

Now that Bruce was retired, we no longer had to jockey with each other preparing for work. I could take my time, but old habits die hard. I sped through my make-up regimen anyway. I took great pride in the fact I could go from bed to fabulous – meaning make-up, hair, dressed well, coffee in hand, and backing out of the driveway – in under forty-five minutes.

Slipping into my shoes, I turned and saw Bruce was soundly sleeping, so I silently exited our bedroom and headed for the kitchen where I filled my travel mug with my favorite Jamaican Blue Mountain coffee, and headed off to work.

Several weeks passed, and they were, remarkably, uneventful. Bruce had been himself from evening to morning with no sweats, no nightmares, no thrashing or screaming in the night, just blissful, sweet spooning. One night, two weeks before Thanksgiving, we had gone to bed as usual, only this time I felt a tingle of life in Bruce's manhood. I smiled broadly even though he couldn't see it, and I pressed a little harder against him.

"What?" he asked.

"Someone's glad to see me," I playfully jibed.

"You so nasty," Bruce whispered, holding me closer.

"You know you like it," I said while slowly grinding, enticing his manhood to fullness.

"Slow down, woman! Where's the fire?"

"Right here!" I said, now facing him and guiding his hand toward my garden of delights.

"I...I...don't think I'm ready. I don't know if I...can," he stammered.

"We'll go slow, baby. Nothing needs to happen until you're sure you're ready," I reassured him.

Bruce hesitated for a long moment before returning to my garden. I was scared he would stop all together. Fortunately, he never wore bottoms to bed, so my access to him was rarely encumbered; tonight was no exception. I reached to gently stroke Bruce's manhood. It felt silky smooth, and then it began to lengthen and finally swell within my grip. Our breathing quickened, and my hunger pangs manifested themselves evident as my moans became more like demands. Bruce began to tend my garden like the master gardener he was. For all his fear and uncertainty, our love-making was like riding a bike. He instinctually knew when to push on the hills, and when to coast. He knew when to pedal hard on the straightaways, and when to lean in and out of the curves. Bruce didn't simply open my garden's gate, he flung it wide and majestically strolled through, not with an appetizer, but a main dish that was a veritable feast for my senses. I greedily supped at his table, begging for seconds, thirds, and any leftover crumbs. At the apex of our congress, Bruce released a deep, guttural cry as he shook with spasms of orgasmic relief. Not to be outdone, my own orgasm felt like the Fourth of July complete with brilliant multi-colored fireworks behind my eyelids. Bruce was, once again, dripping with sweat, but on this occasion *I* was the culprit—which felt pretty damned good!

"Woman, you've bewitched me," he moaned.

"Not yet I haven't, but give me time," I teased.

"My god, that was amazing," he breathed.

"That, husband, was worth the wait," I said, "but let's not go another eighteen months to see if it was a fluke," I added.

Grunting his assent, Bruce got up to shower off. As he ran the water, I stripped off the bed linens. Once I knew he had stepped into the shower, I slipped in behind him, and deftly began to soap up his nether regions from behind. As I hoped, he responded immediately.

"Woman, do you know what you're doing?"

"Yes...yes, I do," I purred.

In the blink of an eye, he picked me up and spun me facing the shower wall away from the stream of water. Pressing hard against me, he held my wrists firmly over my head against the wall, and then he kicked one leg aside. Had he not been against me, I would have lost my balance. I was in a vulnerable, if not precarious, position. Bruce took me again right then and there only this time it was rough, primeval—almost brutal. Every pelvic thrust felt as if he were stabbing at me. He swiftly escalated from thrust to piston action. Just as I began to cry out, Bruce withdrew and spun me round to face him. He effortlessly picked me up and impaled me to the hilt of his joy stick. My pain was exquisite, but still he was not satisfied or finished. I locked eyes with Bruce and became acutely aware this was not *my* Bruce making love to me. *This man* generated a burning heat and had a menacing air about him. *This man* had an insatiable hunger, and his erotic assaults seemed to emanate from some place of deep seated anger. *This man* could easily hurt me with no remorse demonstrated or uttered. I felt nervous, wanton, yet morbidly curious in wondering if *this man* could take me over the edge, and make me beg for more like some bitch in heat. No sooner had that thought crossed my mind did *this man* hit my sweet spot. I gasped sharply, and before my lungs could take in more air he hit it again... and again...and again until I thought I was going to pass out or lose my mind from such deliriously delicious intercourse. So hard and violent were our communal orgasms that we blessed each other with *jus d'amour* which flowed in rivulets unhindered down both our legs.

Once Bruce and I were able to catch our collective breath, he lowered me to my feet, and pulled me to him in a strong and possessive embrace. The water had gone from hot to pleasantly warm as it washed over us rinsing off the greater portion of love residue. With no words, Bruce began passionately kissing me. He started on my forehead, then eyelids and cheeks before lingering on my lips. He moved on to my neck and then down to my breasts. There he kissed, nibbled, and sucked until my breathing increased again and tiny moans escaped my lips. He then slowly pushed me back against the wall before he traveled down the road well known to my *garden of delights*. In the garden, he kissed every valley and nook and was soon testing the gate with an ever-seeking tongue. Content to simply ring the bell at the gate, my now hypersensitive clitoris had me writhing, but unwilling to surrender or cease activities. If Bruce had hair, I would have been pulling it by the handfuls so intense were the orgasmic sensations. At last, I gave my final strangled cry of surfeit, now wholly spent. Shaking from lover's fatigue I clung to Bruce. Minutes passed before he tenderly began lathering me up with soap, then rinsing me off. Once I was squeaky clean and steady on my feet, he gently guided my hands to perform a reciprocal act. Gazing deeply on his face, I knew *my* Bruce was with me again. Gently, he toweled me dry in perfect silence and I him.

After showering, we put fresh linens on the bed together. Slipping under the sheets, we faced each other, and drank each other in to our fill without uttering one word. Bruce fell asleep first, and I followed not long after the light had been turned off. Lord, have mercy, how this man knew me. Three earthshaking orgasms in less than one hour. Here I had been wishing for a gully washer to come along, and now I was floating in the ebb of my tsunami of love. There was no doubt about it; I would sleep *well* this night.

5

Variations on a Theme

It was official; the holiday season had begun. Lights and decorations went up all over our neighborhood. Our L-shaped cul-de-sac was a pitiable, sad, dull, and dark section of town. There were only seven houses on our street, and we lived smack-dab in the middle at the end. The two houses on either side of us were currently empty. Since the nation's mortgage meltdown, four neighbors lost their homes, and the others lost their jobs and had to relocate for better work prospects. Our closest neighbor occupied a home one thousand yards to our north at the beginning of the street. They had elected to burn one solitary electric candle in their front window and no more.

I asked Bruce if he would string outdoor lights this year for me. His response was atypical. He just stared at me, then slowly arched one eyebrow, cocked his head as if he were looking over make-believe glasses, and gave me the look that said *read my thought bubble*—which meant, no.

"Oh, baby, come on, let's make our street look merry," I cajoled.

"Woman, no!" he snapped with the continued look of incredulity.

"Bruce, don't be such a scrooge!"

"Lettie, let me break this down so you can clearly understand," he said.

Uh-oh, he's calling me by my given name. This can't be good, I thought.

"Our street looks empty, because it is! Us putting up lights does not say we're in the Christmas spirit as much as it says we're the only inhabitants on the block. Please, do come rob us blind; no one will ever notice. You know how these people are around here. Let's not tempt fate. Let these sleeping dogs lie, and let them continue to believe no one lives back here, all right?"

"Well, when you put it like that, I guess I can see your point," I conceded.

"If you'd like to string lights inside, as long as they can't be seen from the outside, then I'm happy to oblige," he said.

"Bah! Humbug!" I spat.

"My pleasure," he retorted as he walked into the garage.

Bruce always had flawless logic. That was one of the most annoying things about him, and in this instance, he was spot-on. But I wanted Christmas this year. I was deprived last year, and come the current, albeit sporadic, hell and high waters, our home was going to be joyful whether he liked it or not. So, I went to the kitchen, poured myself a mug of Mountain Joe, sat down with pen and pad, and planned every lighting scheme I wanted to put in place. I was going to have a fantasy winter wonderland inside. Since I had installed blackout blinds and curtains, at Bruce's insistence, four months ago, having light spill to the outside was not going to be a problem. Once I finished with my plans I grabbed my purse and keys, got in my car and drove straight to Home Depot.

At the store, I aggressively latched onto Dale, a sales associate in the lighting department. I explained my plans, gave approximate dimensions of rooms, and with calculator in hand, he rapidly helped me figure out how many strings of lights I needed to accomplish my goal. Dale kindly steered me toward energy saving lights because creating a fantasy wonderland and paying the subsequent light bill were two different things in my book. Besides, I did not want to hear Bruce's mouth on the matter. Picking up a few extra extension cords and the requisite temporary light clips, I made my way to the check-out. The lines weren't too long, but the impulse merchandise was tempting. I did the mental math in regards to my cart's contents when some nice woman gave me a handful of extra coupons she wasn't going to be using. What a boon; only one item in my cart did not have a coupon associated with it. Try as I might, there was one impulse item that caught my eye and wouldn't let go—The Clapper. It seduced me into putting it in my cart. I was *uber* victorious at the check-out having $135 worth of merchandise, but paying only $75. I was a fiscally-triumphant woman on a mission.

I drove straight home and got Bruce's attention the best way I knew how: I backed into the garage. Whatever he was doing with Brewster came to a screeching halt once he saw I was backing in. I could see the concern and borderline terror on his face in my rearview mirror. He was always afraid I was going to scrape some paint off Brewster by backing in, which, in my opinion, might improve the looks of that old rust bucket. Come to think of it, he never voiced any concern about *my* car losing paint. I parked, perfectly I might add, engaged the garage door to close lest any thieves casing the house were nearby, popped the trunk, and then casually walked past Bruce into the house.

He stood rooted, looking perplexed. I quickly returned with plans and diagrams in hand, gave them to Bruce, who still looked confused, nodded to the trunk of my car, and simply said, "Hit it."

I then walked back into the house and shut the door behind me.

Good soldier that he was, Bruce hastily finished up with Brewster and began the involved task of creating my envisioned fantasy winter wonderland. I, meanwhile, rearranged the den to make space for the tree. Last year during the Christmas clearance sales, I purchased a five-foot pre-lit artificial tree that snapped together in three easy pieces. Now I would see if I had made a good purchase. I dragged the tree from the back guest bedroom and opened it up. It was the model of truth in advertising. 1 – 2 – 3 it was together and standing proudly. I plugged it in and, *voila*, instant holiday ambiance. The domestic goddess hit another one out of the fiscal ballpark.

Bruce had finished the lighting above the kitchen cabinets and had moved on to the bathrooms. By the time he had completed his list of rooms, I was almost done with our bedroom.

"Yo! Woman!" Bruce bellowed. "I'm tired, and I'm hungry, so I'm going to go and get some pizza. Think you'll be ready to eat when I get back?"

"Sure thing. And, baby, bring some salad back, too. All pizza is too many carbs for the both of us."

"Yeah, yeah," he muttered as he left.

By my calculations, it was going to take Bruce a good forty-five minutes before he returned with dinner, so I went into warp speed getting the lighting done in our bedroom. At the thirty-minute mark I had everything plugged in including "The Clapper".

CLAP – CLAP

The bedroom ceiling came to life twinkling soft starry lights. The glow was enough to see and navigate in the room, but not enough to be glaring or bothersome. With about eight minutes to spare, I hastily showered, prepared my surprise, and then alluringly laid in the middle of our king-sized bed with nothing but my birthday suit. Bruce came home right on cue.

"Woman, I'm home!" he yelled. "Babe?"

Hearing no response, he sauntered down the hall to our room. Pausing in the darkened doorway he called, "Lettie?"

CLAP – CLAP

"Oh, sweet Jesus, no she didn't!" he mumbled.

The look on Bruce's face was truly worth all my efforts. His eyes rolled over the entire circumference of the room with his mouth slightly agape. I couldn't decide if it was a look of amazement or disbelief; it was funny either way. When he finally noticed me in all my glory on the bed, his ability for speech gradually returned.

"You startin' some mess now, aren't you?"

"I never start anything I can't finish," I replied.

"Babe, you know I'm hungry."

"Yes, and I intend to feed you well. Do you like my surprise?" I asked.

"Woman, do you remember what happened the last time you surprised me?"

"I'm trying to imagine the sequel," I purred.

"If I come over there, I won't be responsible for what I may do," he warned.

"Baby, you go ahead and eat some dinner. I understand how it is when you're weak from hunger," I baited.

CLAP – CLAP (off)

"See, there you go again writin' checks yo' behind can't cash."

CLAP – CLAP (on)

"Sir, I would have you know my account is abundantly in the black," I cockily jabbed.

"Just so you know, for working me like a slave today, I'm taking every penny you've got!" he growled.

The transformation from Mr. Jonson to Mr. Hyde was remarkable, and a bit frightening. Bruce shucked his clothes in what seemed like one complete movement. The veracity by which he catapulted onto the bed straddling me was startling. Looking into his eyes, even by twinkle light, I knew *my* Bruce was not in this bed. Instead of being frightened, I was aroused all the more. Once again, holding my arms above my head, pinning my wrists to the pillows while impressively planking above me, Mr. Hyde whispered in my ear.

"It's a good thing I like cold pizza."

"Let the games begin," I breathed.

The sequel eclipsed the pilot episode. *This man* superseded all my expectations. He flipped me seven ways to Sunday, and took me in every position possible. In a small corner of the back of my mind, I envisioned myself walking bow-legged into church on the morrow. The master gardener packed his tools away and lay panting on his back, glistening in hard earned sweat. That's when I, the ever-resourceful goddess, unpacked my arsenal for the next round of the games. Reaching for a warm, moist towel I had placed underneath the bed, I wiped down Mr.

Hyde. Afterwards, I trickled warm, edible lubricant down his torso, to the glory trail, past Apollo's Belt, to the long-neglected regions of the hinterlands. Slowly, my tongue swirled and licked until I reached my ultimate destination—joy. It took some intensive coaxing, but joy soon became a joy stick again. Mr. Hyde moaned and jerked until I had milked all the joy from his stick. Taking a second moist towel, I wiped us both down then laid my head on his chest to cuddle. He, in turn, wrapped me in a strong and protective embrace.

"Woman, what has come over you?" he asked.

"Me? *Who* is coming out of you?" I fired back, looking directly into his eyes. I could see by the way he avoided my gaze he was holding something back. I could also tell it was bothering him to withhold from me whatever it was he was thinking. He grunted and absent mindedly stroked my left flank and hipline. I knew not to press; he had gone into mental lock-down mode. I would just have to be patient and wait for him to open up to me. Truthfully, I was getting weary of this waiting game. I kept anticipating the Bruce from Landstuhl to return and talk to me. I began to mourn I wouldn't see that Bruce ever again. My thoughts commenced turning bitter, so I got up and took a shower. Bruce did not follow; he stayed in the bed staring blankly at the twinkling ceiling.

"Bruce, I'm going to put the pizza in the oven now."

"Okay. I'll be there in a few," he said, unceremoniously.

Twenty minutes later, the pizza was warm, and I sat down to eat alone. Tears of despair welled in my eyes. It was hard to comprehend how I could be so sublimely happy one minute and feeling so alone and emotionally destitute the next. I desperately wanted someone to please stop the roller coaster because I was ready to get off. Without realizing it, I was literally crying into my salad. It wasn't until Bruce engulfed me in an embrace from behind that I comprehended I was crying.

"Babe, I'm so sorry. I've been careless and insensitive in understanding how hard all this has been on you," Bruce gently spoke in my ear.

Hearing his words did nothing to make me feel better. If anything, they made me feel worse. My tears morphed into racking sobs. All my buried pain and fears rushed to the surface like oil from a derrick. My tears flowed uncapped, and I didn't care or attempt to control them. For well over a year, I had to be the strong one who held everything together. I was tired and weary to my core. For the first time, I entertained the thought of taking a break from everyone and everything, including Bruce.

"Lettie? Babe, please, talk to me," Bruce quietly asked while on one knee looking up into my face. Clearly, I must have had *that look* on my face because he quickly added, "I know I don't have the right to ask, but I'm asking anyway."

"Bruce, what can I possibly say to you that would not hurt you?" I snapped. "Talking is a two-way street that you seem to think is one-way – your way. Are you going to do me the honor of talking with me if I talk to you?"

Chagrined silence and darting eyes were my answer. I pushed myself away from the table in an attempt to leave the dining room, but Bruce held my hand and wouldn't let me go.

"Babe, please, give me a chance. This, this is hard for me."

"And you think it's not hard for me?" I yelled.

"No. I know it's been hard on you," he choked. "It hurts me to see you cry like this. What can I do?"

"What can you do?" I sarcastically asked, wiping the tears from my face. "What you can do is **TALK** to me, that's what you can do! What happened to the man who was in that hospital bed baring his soul to me? Where did he go? Can you bring him back? Where is the man who told me I was his *everything*? Can you summon him here? And who the hell is this Mr. Hyde who makes unbelievably mad love to me? Where did *he* come from? Can you tell me?" I railed.

"I am guilty as charged, and I deserve your anger," Bruce said, eyes downcast.

Before either one of use could say another word, the phone rang. I shook with anger amid fresh tears streaming down my face. I just looked at the phone, and my lack of movement made it clear

I had no intention of answering it. It could roll to voicemail as far as I was concerned.

For whatever unknown reason, Bruce answered the phone, but put it on speaker, probably, I reasoned, to annoy me further. "Hello."

"Hey, son! How y'all doing?" chirped my mother's voice.

"Hey, Mama! You caught me just getting ready to sit down for dinner. How're you and Pops?" he asked, masking his voice as best he could.

"We're doing well. I don't want to hold you up, so I'll make this quick. You and Lettie *are* coming for Thanksgiving this year, right?"

"Eh...well...I..." he stammered.

"Oh, no you don't. You're not getting out of this one, young man. We haven't seen you in almost three years. We miss you, and I want to see you with my own eyes. So it's settled; we'll expect you and Lettie this Thanksgiving. Oh, and don't worry about a place to stay, you know we have plenty of room. The whole family will be here including Chester and his brood. Is Lettie nearby?"

I frantically motioned with my hands and shook my head in the negative.

"Uhmm...she's indisposed at the moment. Would you like me to have her call you back?" he asked.

Turning to look at me, I gave Bruce the stink-eye.

"No, no, just let her know I called, and make sure you tell her that you and she are both coming for Thanksgiving. Love you, son."

Click. Silence.

"Now, I *really* am not happy," I stated.

"Babe, your mother's right. We need to go. Let's just bite the bullet and make our plans," he said, matter-of-factly. "Besides, your parents are the only parents I've got now, and I'd like to see them, too. It will be good for us to get away together."

"Bruce Jonson, the last place in the world I want to be is incarcerated in my parents' house with Chester's brood no less," I shouted.

"Babe, you don't mean that. You're just upset. It's your anger talking right now, not you," he said, trying to soothe me.

"The hell I don't!" I snarled, stalking back to our bedroom, slamming the door behind me.

Sunday morning dawned as a bright, shiny day. Too bad my mood was still cloudy. Bruce arose well ahead of me and wisely stayed out of my way. Showering and dressing was an auto-pilot activity for me. Donning my jewelry, I went in search of the rich coffee I smelled wafting down the hallway.

"'Morning, babe. I heard you coming and already poured your mug of Mountain Joe," Bruce volunteered.

"Good morning," I mumbled.

"This is the day that the Lord has made. Let us rejoice and be…."

My stink-eye cut the remainder of that scripture reference off at the neck.

"Okay, I'll let you drink your coffee in peace. Holler when you're ready to go," Bruce said, seating himself in his easy chair.

Great. It was going to be one of those days. I remembered those times during my childhood when my mother and I would argue right before church for whatever stupid reason. Daddy would be driving us to church and Mama would emphatically blurt out of nowhere, "I hate going to church mad. I hate it!" Now, I could truly empathize with her. My fluttering stomach did back flips once Mountain Joe hit it. There was no getting around it, I was going to have to make this situation right if I was ever going to have peace in my life this day.

"Bruce?" I called, sitting next to his chair.

"Yes, babe," he answered, giving me all due attention.

"I'm sorry. I apologize for being psycho-bitch last night. I'm truly sorry for the way I yelled at you, too. Please, forgive me?"

"Before I can forgive you, I need for you to talk to me," he said calmly.

Rage resurfaced and flashed in my eyes, but I caught myself and wrestled down my indignation before opening my mouth. "All right," I calmly acquiesced.

"Tell me—tell me honestly. Do you love me?" he asked with all seriousness.

"With all my heart," I softly answered.

"I know we have some more hills to climb together, you and me. Since you love me, will you hang in there with me a little while longer?"

Now it was my turn to be perplexed. I quizzically cocked my head to the side and narrowed my eyes in confusion. "What, exactly, do you mean?" I asked, suspiciously.

"First, will you visit your parents with me for Thanksgiving?"

"If it means that much to you," I exhaled deeply, "then, yes."

"Second, will you be nice to your brother Chester, his wife, and brood?"

"I'll do my best," I sighed.

"No, ma'am – I don't want your best, I want your promise. Do you promise to be nice?"

"Yes!" I hissed through gritted teeth.

"Third, when we come back from Thanksgiving with the folks will you go with me to a Christmas party being thrown by Lloyd? He says it's time for him to meet our spouses."

"If that would please you," I said, guardedly.

"It would," he asserted.

"Anything else?" I asked.

"Nope," he grinned, "I accept your apology and forgive you."

It took every ounce of self-control not to lean over and demonstrate to Bruce the sound of one hand clapping. All I wanted, at that particular moment, was to slap the fire out of him.

I suspected he felt my vibes because he gingerly leapt out of his easy chair, grabbed his keys, looked back at me, and said, "Raise up! Don't want to be late for church."

Help me, Lord!

We drove to church with music from the stereo as the only sound between us. I felt Bruce's eyes sliding over in my direction several times, but I would not give him the satisfaction of knowing I knew he was looking over at me. Half way there, my conscience was ferociously whipping me. The Holy Spirit convicted my bull-headed, stubborn nature, and I didn't like it, not one bit. I had the quiet—I just wanted some peace. The Spirit kept saying I knew what to do in order to have peace. Finally, I surrendered and yielded up my demon of contentiousness. I had asked for Bruce's forgiveness, but I had not asked for the Lord's. Once I mentally asked God for His forgiveness, I could feel the weight being lifted from me as if some damp shroud had been inexorably removed.

The worship service was exactly what I needed to put me on an even keel. By its end, I felt centered, relaxed, encouraged, challenged, invigorated, and loved. For the first time since Bruce came home, I was not focused upon *his* responses to the service, but upon my own. The singing and the music was a balm for my weary soul. Sister Parker sang *How I Got Over* the old traditional way. The words struck a chord with me because truly, my soul did look back and wonder how we got over —how Bruce and I have managed to survive all the trauma and hell we're going through. My tears flowed, and I could only raise my hand in agreement, in praise. If sister girl went back for that chorus one more time, I believe I would have flipped the pews shouting.

The preaching was better than ever. Pastor Wilson broke the Word down in such a way, an idiot could understand with clarity. His text came from I Corinthians 10:13

> *No temptation has seized you except what is common to man. And God is faithful; he will not let you be tempted beyond what you can bear. But when you are*

> *tempted, he will also provide a way out so that you can stand up under it.*

It seemed as if that sermon was prepared for me and me alone. Pastor Wilson explained how we all had problems in our lives that seemed insurmountable. Problems and situations that kicked us down to the ground, but we were to have hope. Jesus was tempted just like we are. He underwent pain, rejection, disappointment, joy, fear—he selflessly endured the human experience in order to provide a way out for us. Then the pastor centered in on *he will not let you be tempted beyond what you can bear.* That was a mini revelation for me. I was going through my personal hell with Bruce because I was strong enough to take it? I wasn't wild about that prospect, but I was beginning to understand the journey. God's word said I may go through some fire, but He would make a way out for me. That thought gave my spirit ease; hope could continue to grow.

The fellowship of the saints was the frosting on my cake. I was thankful Mt. Pisgah was a charismatic church. My tears never needed to be explained away nor were they looked upon as something awry. My praise was also my catharsis. I could cry, shout, or dance in the spirit, and no one would bat an eye. If I were to speak in tongues, or roll down the aisle, the only thing that might be said would be something along the lines of: "Sister Lettie got a double anointing from the Lord today!"

Thank God for a religion I could feel. All my anger, my tensions, and stress had been liberated through cathartic release. On the drive back home, Bruce and I held hands; we were good once again.

6
Thanksgiving (Part One)

Bruce and I planned to spend all of Thanksgiving week with my parents. I was dubious I could honor the commitment, but I was going to give it my best efforts. My parents, Jewel and Calvin Stanton, live in Hertford, N.C., were staunch Baptists, but also surprisingly progressive in their thinking. My hometown was a backwoods, at least in my mind. Long ago, Hertford was known for growing rice, a bit of indigo, and sweet potatoes. Nowadays, Hertford's claim to fame is being known as the hometown of the late James Augustus "Catfish" Hunter, the pro baseball pitcher, and the CIA training center, Harvey Point. To this day, African-Americans comprise over fifty percent of the town and over sixty percent of the county. Historically, Hertford has always been well below the national average for unemployment. Jobs were plentiful, but I always looked upon Hertford as a sleepy, provincial, backwater.

Mama and Daddy live on our ancestral grounds of three thousand acres in our unusually large family home. Grandpa Ernest made sure his home met the anticipated needs of his growing family. There are six spacious bedrooms, three large bathrooms, a newly remodeled country kitchen with a walk-in pantry, a full attic, a full basement, which has now become Bucket's living space, and a great room we call "the den".

It was high-living, especially back in Grandpa's era. Some of the white folk took exception to his house. They called it "The Manor", and capitalized at every opportunity to comment on what an uppity nigger he was. Grandpa was well-respected in his community, but he was a hard man who didn't take smack from anybody—white folks included. He had a unique way of putting people in their place without raising his voice or causing great offense.

Often, to those voicing their opinion about his house, he fired back, "If you would save yo' money and do the work yo'self, you could have a grand house, too." That retort usually shut the jealous naysayers up.

Grandpa Ernest and Grandma Zinnia had thirteen children—a baker's dozen. Two died not long after birth, a set of twins were stillborn, and three others died from disease when they were school-aged. That left them with six children who made it to adulthood; four boys and another set of identical twin girls. My father, Calvin, was the third eldest surviving child. Uncles Benny, and Thadd were ahead of Dad, then Uncle Thomas and finally the twins, Peaches and Cherry. Uncle Thadd and Aunts Peaches and Cherry were the siblings I knew; the other two passed away long before I was born. Uncle Benny died during World War II, and Uncle Thomas died in a car accident in the early 1960s. Daddy also served in the army during World War II, and when he returned from Europe, he came back home to help grandpa, and to marry his sweetheart, Miss Jewel Thigpen.

Daddy is a farmer, and Mama is a school teacher. Daddy loves working with his hands in the dirt and watching green things grow. I've never known anyone else who gets so much pleasure from seeing a tiny, green sprout grow into something large and, preferably, edible. That is not to say Daddy dislikes the ornamental—on the contrary. Daddy was known far and wide for his ability to grow prize-winning flowers and shrubs. If it was green, he was going to try his hand at it. Once, someone offered to give him a Corpse Plant. Praise God, Mama stepped in to intervene. She absolutely would not hear of it. When he tried to sweet-talk her, she put her foot down backed by her ample hips. That discussion died a quick death. Daddy still works the land with my brother William. They grow soybeans for a local oil distributor. Daddy has what he calls a small patch for a garden. His "small patch" was actually an acre or more of ground. Traditionally, he would raise tomatoes, green beans, a variety of legumes, sweet corn, zucchini, summer squash, ice potatoes, sweet potatoes, cucumbers, okra, collard greens, turnip and mustard greens, kale, broad leaf spinach, melons, and berries, not to mention the orchard of peach and pecan trees. He even put in some sugar cane this year to try his hand at making syrup and molasses. Mama lovingly canned a great portion of the harvest, and either sold or gave the remainder away.

My mama has been a grade school teacher for the past thirty-five years and was scheduled to retire at the end of this academic year. She loved children, loved teaching, and made sure all her own children were well-educated. We all went to college and graduated near, if not at the top, of our respective classes. Besides being a regular teacher, a farmer's wife, and a Sunday school teacher, Mama loves to quilt, sew, and knit. Somewhere along the line, a man who owed Daddy money asked if he could pay him in kind, and Daddy said yes. Two days after that deal was struck a pair of alpacas appeared on the farm, to the delight of my mother. Daddy didn't know what to do with those animals. He was expecting hogs or chickens, but Mama was Ellie Mae Clampett when it came to critters. She wouldn't let Daddy get rid of them. She dutifully did her research and learned everything she could about cameloids. She even made connections with other alpaca farmers in the area. Before they knew it, their pair had turned into a herd. Mama was a savvy business woman who could wheel and deal when she wanted, and through some questionable backroom deals, she acquired an alpaca whose stud fees would keep them living comfortably throughout retirement. She would also have more than enough fiber to spin, dye, and knit for the rest of her natural life.

Mama and Daddy had four children: Anthony, AKA: Tony, me, William, AKA: Chester, and Brett, AKA: Bucket.

Tony became a corporate lawyer and lives in New York City. He is a confirmed bachelor in every aspect of the meaning. He prefers his tea sweet; he's gay and lives in the back of the closet. I heard from him usually once a month, or whenever he'd won some kind of prominent award. I knew he had a partner named James, who is about five years his junior, but I'd never met him. I had no doubt when he was ready, he'd inform the family of his life choices. Until then, my lips were sealed.

Chester, who majored in agriculture, lives in Hertford and is currently a third-generation farmer. Chester has an easy-going personality, and he got his nickname as a kid. Daddy loved to watch westerns, and *Gunsmoke* was his favorite program. When Chester was ten years old, he broke his leg falling out of our treehouse. It took longer than usual to heal, and when he came out of his cast, he limped a lot like the *Gunsmoke* character, Chester. Daddy started calling him that, and it stuck. Chester is a hard worker who lives for his family. He married a local girl, Clarissa Barnes, and in short order commenced to repopulating Hertford. To date, they had seven children, with another one on the way. Every one of their young'uns had a congenital malady of some sort, and still they continued to breed. Clarissa was an attractive girl, but she wasn't the sharpest knife in the drawer, as I remembered. Talking with Clarissa, for me, was like talking to a child; exasperating much of the time. Yet, Chester was totally devoted to her and their children. This was something I was only beginning to understand.

Bucket was the baby who surprised everyone. Mama was perimenopausal when she conceived him. She was so sure she had crossed over the feminine plane into the golden years early she was elated and positively giddy. It wasn't until she picked up significant weight and her belly swelled that she realized something wasn't right. Fearing it was cancer, she immediately scheduled an appointment with her doctor. He performed several tests, including an ultrasound. When the doctor told her she was a good four months pregnant, my mother was speechless, probably for the first time in her life. Daddy, who was with her at the time, was completely gob-smacked when he learned the news. The doctor was worried Daddy would pass out after hearing the diagnosis, but instead, as the story goes, he got a broad, goofy grin on his face and wistfully said:

"Jewel, we're going to have a baby!"

I'm told Mama had tears in her eyes, but I'd bet long odds they weren't tears of joy. I was fifteen when Mama delivered Bucket. He was a fussy, colicky, sickly, squalling baby, who was truly the child of their old age because they spoiled him rotten.

Bucket got his nickname because in middle school he was often afflicted with a nervous stomach, which caused him to vomit—a lot. Whenever he was sick with flu he would, seemingly, vomit non-stop. Daddy would always bring a big bucket to his bedroom during those times because that boy had great difficulty making it to the bathroom before he'd vomit everywhere. This was Daddy's subtle way of saying, "clean up after yourself." Brett hated being called Bucket, and I went out of my way to *only* call him Bucket. In my eyes, they still treated him like a baby, and Mama was forever making all kinds of excuses for his trifling ways. He had a mild learning disability, but it was nothing that hindered him from working. Bucket studied computer programming in college and graduated at the top of his class. He claimed he would be the next computer gamer millionaire. Whenever he was asked to do anything around the house while he was in school, his excuse was he was studying. Now that he has long since graduated, his excuse was he was working, if you could call playing video games all day work. Bucket was a lazy, overindulged, super entitled, no-account, spoiled brat. If he were our child, Bruce would have opened a can of extra strength whoop-ass on that boy long ago. Thankfully, he was not our child, nor our problem.

I was the practical child. I knew as soon as I started high school I didn't want to live my life in Hertford. I vowed as soon as I could leave my mama's house I would not look back, let alone come back. Hertford had *nothing* to offer me, and a whole wide world awaited my discovery. When I went off to college, I majored in business administration and marketing. I landed a pretty lucrative job in a prestigious marketing firm right after graduation. Then, I met Bruce Jonson. I went from climbing the corporate ladder to being various administrative assistants due to the frequent transfers of army life. I am not complaining, nor do I have any regrets because life with Bruce has been a true adventure. I love my family dearly—I just don't like them much; thus, I rarely come back home.

We pulled up to Mama and Daddy's house around dusk the Monday before Thanksgiving. Bruce honked the horn to let the folks know we had arrived. Uncle Thadd was sitting on the porch and vaguely waved in our direction. He was intently watching something on TV.

Mama came rushing through the screen door wiping her hands on her apron shouting back to Daddy, "Calvin! They're here!" Mama met me at the car door, and gave me a quick peck on the cheek and a brief hug, then ran to Bruce and hugged him as if he was the "Prodigal Son".

"My son," she drawled, "it's sooooooooooooo good to see you!" planting kiss after kiss after kiss, and holding him as if he might blow away.

"Mama Jewel! That's right, give me allll yo' sugar," Bruce said, pouring on the charm from his vast reservoir as he picked her up off her feet and held her in mid-air. Bruce could sell ice to Eskimos and dehydrated water to Bedouins. He knew exactly how to charm my mother, and it always began by picking her up and demonstrating his physical strength. Mama always had a weakness for physically able men. I reckon that was why Daddy still had her; for an old man, he could work a young man into the ground.

"Baby Girl," Daddy called before enveloping me in his arms. Then, he kissed me once and held me in his rocking embrace.

"Hey, Daddy." I smiled while letting him rock me like I was his little girl again.

Bruce, meanwhile, had lowered Mama back down to the ground, and kissed her once more on her forehead for good measure before striding over to me and Daddy. "Pops!" he exclaimed.

Daddy, smiling so wide it should have broken his face, initially shook Bruce's hand, and they embraced, beating each other's backs heartily. Daddy pushed away first, and looked Bruce up and down, and hugged him again.

"Son, I'm so glad to see you," he said, looking him over once more. "Boy, you look good!" he cried. "Y'all come on up in the house."

I intentionally packed light, so there was only one bag to bring in the house. Mama directed Bruce to the room we would occupy, and once our bag had been deposited, we all went and sat down in the den.

"Supper will be ready in about half an hour," Mama announced.

In the South, the last meal of the day was supper, and it was traditionally light in fare. In the North, the last meal of the day was dinner, which tended to be too heavy for our own good. Southerners had been slowly catching up to their northern brethren as the meals became increasingly heavier, but the terminology of language remained unchanged; dinner meant lunch, and supper meant dinner in the South.

"Can I help you?" I offered.

"No, no, Baby Girl. You and Bruce catch up with yo' daddy. I'll get Brett to help me."

"Let me help you, Mama. By the time Bucket comes up we'll all have dead lice falling off of us," I sarcastically replied.

"Lettie, you know your brother doesn't like that name," she scowled as we went into the kitchen.

"Yes, ma'am, but if calling him 'Bucket' will irritate him enough to move his ass and contribute to this household, then 'Bucket' it will be for the duration of the week," I frowned.

"Lettie, don't start no mess. Hear me?" she warned.

"Mama, I'm not starting anything. But I promise you this: I *will* finish it if he does."

"Baby, please, play nice. I don't get to see you that often and I haven't had the whole family together in a coon's age."

"Tony's coming for Thanksgiving?" I asked, surprised.

"Yes!" Mama smiled. "And Peaches and Luther, too. Tony said he's bringing his partner, James, with him. I didn't know he had a business partner, did you?"

I quickly found a bowl of vegetables to take to the table to avoid Mama's eyes. I acted as if I never even heard the question. Oh, sweet Jesus, this was going to be a memorable, if not volatile, Thanksgiving. After we had set the table and piled it high with mouthwatering delights, the supper call was sounded.

"All right, everyone," Mama said, clapping her hands together, "food's on the table; everybody come on. Calvin, please bring Thaddeus to the table."

Uncle Thadd had lived with Mama and Daddy since his wife, Jean, passed away ten years ago. His only daughter, Myrlene, died in her late teens from a rare form of cancer, so Mama and Daddy were the only family he had left. Now, in his late eighties, he was slowing down. Uncle Thadd was a prankster when we were young. We kids knew whenever he came over the party was about to begin. He loved laughing and rough housing with us, especially with Tony and Chester. Myrlene was a delicate child. Aunt Jean wouldn't let Uncle Thadd push her on a swing let alone throw her in the air. I was around eight years old when Myrlene died. My heart broke and grieved for Uncle Thadd. It seemed like a light went out inside of him that day; he seldom joked around or rough-housed with us after that.

Once everyone was seated at the dining room table, Bucket came thumping up the stairs from the basement. When he spied Bruce, he nearly sprinted to his side all smiles, handshaking, popping dap, and slapping backs with effusive brotherly hugs.

"Bruuuuuuuuuuuuce!" he croaked like some moose call. Upon seeing me, his enthusiasm waned precipitously. "Lettie," he acknowledged by sucking his teeth.

"Hey, Bucket," I drawled with a saccharin sweet smile.

Brett, unperceptively, kicked his chin at me and I, smile intact, merely fluttered my lashes. It was code language for, "Yeah, you little snot-nosed brat—game on!"

Mama slid her eyes sideways in my direction, and I sat like the stone sphinx; butter would not melt in my mouth. Daddy brought our attention back to the matter at hand and asked for all of us to join hands, for every head to bow, and every eye to close while he said grace.

"Oh, God, our help of ages past and our hope fo' years to come, we thank you fo' yo' blessings, and fo' yo' mercy, and fo' yo' love. We thank you tonight, dear Father, fo' bringing Lettie and Bruce safely home to us. We thank you now fo' the bounty of this table, and humbly ask that you bless this food fo' the nourishment of our bodies. Bless the hands that have prepared and served, in yo' precious son, Jesus', name we pray, amen. Blessed is he who believes, but has not seen," Daddy finished.

It is a custom in the South that once grace has been said, all those gathered around the table must quote a portion, or a complete scripture passage, from the Bible before they may eat. Duplicate scriptures were frowned upon if one was family, but completely acceptable if one was either a guest, or elderly. Daddy always sat as head of his table, and Mama was always at his right hand; an earthly picture of God and Jesus in glory. Next came Uncle Thadd, then Bruce, me, and, lastly, Bucket.

"In the beginning was the Word, and the Word was with God, and the Word was God," Mama quoted.

"He was with God in the beginning," rasped Uncle Thadd.

"He that findeth a wife, findeth a good thing," Bruce said, smiling at Mama.

"Honor thy father and thy mother so that thy days may be long in the land the Lord thy God shall give thee," I said, staring directly at my baby brother.

"Jesus wept," pronounced Bucket as he dived into the mashed potatoes.

Supper was marvelous amid the clatter of utensils on plates. I had forgotten what a wonderful cook my mother was. Bruce ate as if he had only recently been introduced to solid food again. Mama beamed like a full moon on a snowy landscape. Any local would testify a Southern woman's pride comes through empty serving platters on her table of hospitality. The room was filled with much laughter, conversation, and memories.

Mama and I cleared the table while the menfolk continued talking. Between the two of us, we had any leftover food put away in the fridge, dishes, pots, and pans washed, dried, and put away within half an hour. When we returned to the table, Uncle Thadd was in rare form spinning some yarn about Daddy back when they were children. After another hour of laughter and catching up, Bruce and I excused ourselves and retired for the night.

"Oh, babe, I am stuffed," groaned Bruce. "Why did you let me eat so much? Lord have mercy, I had forgotten how good yo' mama can cook."

"No you don't go blaming me," I chided. "You've been an extremely disciplined man your entire adult life. You *chose* to keep eating," I said, "and you did my mama proud. Did you see her face?"

"You sho' right about that," he chuckled, "but I couldn't help myself – it was so gooood."

"Mama put her foot up in it tonight. Imagine what she's going to do on Thanksgiving. Oh, and speaking of Thanksgiving—Tony's coming home."

"Hey, that's great! I haven't seen Tony in – how long has it been?"

"He's bringing his partner, James, with him," I said.

"Oh, Lord!"

"Exactly."

"Do you think he's going to come out to your parents?" Bruce asked.

"I'm sure of it," I said. "Baby, this house is getting ready to blow up! I don't know if I can stay through Saturday."

"Babe, you're worrying over something that hasn't even happened yet. Let's just take things as they come. We've dealt with harder things, you and I."

"But, Bruce, this isn't about us; it's about my folks. You *know* Daddy will get his consecrated oil out and wrestle Tony down to the altar. He might even try and cast demons out of James," I said, concerned.

"Woman, stop it," Bruce said, gathering me up in his arms and kissing me lightly. "By the way—what's up with you and Brett?"

"Nothing. I simply let Bucket know there won't be none if he don't start none."

"Babe, you know he doesn't like that name. Call him by his right name, please."

"I'll call him by his right name when he starts living up to his responsibilities around here and not before," I said with anger flashing in my eyes.

"Lettie, right now *you* are the one inserting drama into the situation. I don't want to play referee, but you know I will. So, cool your 'nothing's happened yet' jets and chill." This Bruce said while holding my chin up with his index finger looking directly down into my eyes.

"You don't scare me, Bruce Jonson," I shot back.

Laughing, he said, "I'm not trying to scare you." Then his face became intensely serious, "But, I am advising you."

As Bruce looked down on me, I could have sworn I saw Mr. Hyde flash behind his eyes. That *did* scare me. I certainly did not want Bruce to cycle into his nightmares while we were here. Some things were still a little too private for me.

"Then, I'll take what you're saying under advisement," I grumpily responded. "I packed your nightshirt instead of your PJs for this trip," I said while rummaging through our bag, "that way your boys can be free, but you'll still be presentable if you have to face family."

"Thank you. Now, can you please tell me why *you* packed so lightly?"

"Mama has a washer *and* a dryer," I deflected. "As you can see, I packed enough undies to get me through the week."

"Uh huh. If I didn't know better, I'd say you've either prepared to go shopping with yo' mama, or you made a back door so you could leave early," Bruce countered.

"Husband, what small faith you have," I said, feigning a look of hurt.

"Wife, what fork-ed tongue *you* have," Bruce said, eyebrows raised.

At that last remark, we both fell in the bed, laughing. I turned out the light, and we tried to comfortably spoon, but Bruce kept shifting and twisting trying to find a comfortable spot.

"Babe, what's wrong with this bed?" Bruce asked.

"It's small and a little soft, that's all," I said.

"Wow. I guess I'm spoiled," he replied.

"On so many levels," I whispered.

Early the next morning, my bladder woke me up insistent. Bruce wasn't in the bed, and as I made my way to the bathroom, I heard him and Daddy talking in the kitchen. It was still dark outside as I padded back to the bed. Daddy was always an early riser; as a farmer, he had to be. This morning, I surmised, he let Chester handle the early chores. The room Bruce and I occupied was close to the kitchen; so close, one could hear conversations clearly if the door was left ajar, which I did. I confess, I was straight up nosey. I wanted to know what they were talking about and if I could glean any gems of knowledge from my eavesdropping.

"Son, let me get you another cup since I'm up," Daddy offered.

"Thanks, Pops," said Bruce. I heard the coffee pot rattle and the chair skooch as Daddy sat down.

"How bad is it, son?" Daddy asked.

"Some nights it's real bad. I wake up screaming, terrified, and dripping with sweat because I'm back in *that place* again," he confessed. "How long did it take you for things to get back to normal when you went through this?" he asked.

HOLD UP! Daddy was captured during the war? How come I never knew this? I didn't remember ever seeing any PTSD manifestations. I had to have a talk with Mama about this.

"Son, my trauma wasn't physical like yo's. Mine was mo' mental. But, I can tell you this, I did my fair share of crazy. If it had not been for my sweet Jewel, well, I might still be," he chuckled. "I was one of the few Negroes that liberated one of the concentration camps. The things I saw…and smelled; I'll never forget. What white folks did—to each other—was enough to drive anybody crazy. But those po' suffering devils willed themselves to survive. I knew then, when I returned home, the Klan couldn't do nothin' to me unless I let 'em. If those prisoners could love life enough to survive that piece of hell, then I was going to be on easy street when I got back home. Unfortunately, that sentiment was easier said than done. I had the screaming, sweaty, nightmares fo' years after that; only in my dreams, I was always the captive, never the liberator. We really didn't have no VA like y'all got now. If we tried to talk to somebody, we was labeled as shell-shocked, or just plain crazy. But, like I say, Jewel was my rock," Daddy concluded.

"Pops, were you ever afraid you'd hurt Mama Jewel? Physically, I mean," Bruce asked.

"Oh, yes. When she was pregnant with Baby Girl, I wouldn't sleep with her for the last three months of her pregnancy. I got pretty wild back then," Daddy said, slurping coffee. "Why you asking, son? Have you hurt Lettie?"

"Pops, I don't know…maybe…I'm not sure. Lettie hasn't said anything. But, a few times I could tell she wasn't acting like herself. However, I never saw any marks or bruises. Man, I'm scared I may have, Pops. I don't know what to do," Bruce confessed.

"When was yo' las' attack?" Daddy asked.

"Almost three weeks ago," Bruce said.

"Nothin' since then?"

"No, sir."

"Why you think they stopped?" Daddy inquired. After a brief pause he continued, "When's the las' time yo' pipes got cleaned?"

"Beg 'pardon?" Bruce choked as coffee went down the wrong pipe.

"Boy, don't act simple. How long's it been since you've had sex?" Daddy demanded.

"It's…uh…been a few weeks, but before that, well over a year," Bruce reluctantly answered.

"What?" Daddy said, astounded.

Bruce then recounted the events: the initial beatings, all prefaced by the sounding of a horn, which was news to me, the burning, and finally being hooked up to the car battery – testicular electrocution. When he finished, I could tell by his voice he was crying. There were a few long minutes of silence broken only by the sound of mugs being set down on the kitchen table and Bruce's sniffles.

"Have you tested things to see if they still work?" Daddy finally asked.

"Yeah," Bruce affirmed.

"Well?" Daddy pressed.

"It was FAN-TAS-TIC," Bruce crowed.

"How long ago that been?" Daddy wanted to know.

"Almost three weeks," Bruce informed.

"Well, that's why you ain't had no attacks lately. Yo' balls was jus' backed up," Daddy laughed. "Make sho' you blow 'em out 'fo' you leave, hear? I don't want Baby Girl suffering no attacks when y'all get back home."

"Okay, Pops," Bruce laughed.

After the laughter died down, Daddy turned the conversation in another direction toward a more serious side. "So, what you gon' to do with yo'self now that you out?" Daddy asked.

"I truly do not know. I feel like I'm stuck; can't go forward and don't want to go back. I know, right now, I can't work in the civilian world as yet, and I'm kind of scared," he murmured, "I may not be able to hold a job at all. I'm still in PTSD therapy and it helps some, but I feel like something's missing."

"That would be yo' wife," Daddy interjected.

"Maybe so, but I need to make some plans…we need to make some plans regardless. My VA benefits will run out in about two more years. I've got to be able to hold a job in order to have health insurance, and I pray I can get some. They may hold my condition as *pre-existing* and deny me."

"What about getting on Lettie's health insurance?"

"I hadn't considered that, Pops. Thanks for the obvious suggestion," Bruce said. After a few moments of sipping coffee, he continued.

"It's a damned shame how our government treats the vets who bleed and die for this country," Bruce said, pounding his fist upon the table. "Do you know that my government has even denied me disability? Can you believe it? If anybody has documentation of proof, it's me, yet they have denied my claim," he said, pounding the table again. "You know, that used to be a life-long contract – we give limbs and life for the protection of this country, the government would at least give us medical care for the rest of our lives. Not anymore. Did you know during Desert Storm if you were discharged, for whatever reason, you had ninety days of medical coverage and no more? The VA literally threw you out onto the street and told you not to come back. I'm blessed, in comparison, because those rules have been amended—now, vets like me get three years, unless I'm documented as being a threat to myself, or others, then I'd get more time at the 'funny farm'. But I don't intend on becoming an emotional cripple. Pops, it makes me so freakin' angry!" Bruce said emphatically.

"I know, son."

"I loved the Army, Pops. I was good at leading men, and I excelled at killing them. Granted, while flat on my back at Landstuhl, I told Lettie I was ready to leave, but I really wasn't. I think I just needed some rest and a break from combat. The Army didn't even give me a chance to come back, Pops," Bruce choked. "They discharged me saying I would never be able to resume my duties as an infantry field commander. They even went so far as to schedule me for PT evals knowing I could barely walk. That wasn't fair, Pops. They took my life from me, and I'm real salty about it," Bruce said, his voice dripping with bitterness. "I was due to be promoted to Major, too."

"Son, I understand yo' pain, and I feel for you, but you got to focus on the future now not the past," Daddy advised.

Bruce took a few moments to calm down before continuing. "I've been thinking about relocating, I just don't know where yet. Our neighborhood has declined dramatically, and the criminal element will soon overrun us. I've done just about everything possible to keep Lettie safe, but I'm more concerned now than ever. I've noticed small gangs casing the empty houses. I think they're trying to strip the piping and wiring for scrap. I call the cops every time I see something, but it's just a matter of time before they hit us. God help them if they do. They're going to *need* God to keep me off them if they hurt my wife."

"You got protection?"

"Yeah, I've got a pistol I keep hidden away. Lettie doesn't know about it, though. You know how she feels about guns."

"Son, what you need is a dog—a big dog like the ones Jewel has only yo' dog would live in the house. Train it so the inside is the territory it protects. Burglars think twice about a place that has dogs," Daddy said.

"Lettie hasn't been one for animals. Do you really think I could talk her into getting a big dog?"

"Ha, ha, ha, ha. Son, I've seen you work. You can charm a woman out her drawers without even trying. A dog should be no problem for you."

"Pops!" Bruce sounded surprised, then succumbed to Daddy's laughter. "You might have a point."

"Now, this talk about relocating, let me guess—you haven't talked with Lettie about this either," Daddy said.

"No, not yet, but I promise, we will get around to it."

"Son, I've got somethin' I been meaning to ask fo' some time now. It ain't none of my bidness, but I'm curious, and since we're talking, I may as well get everything out on the table. How come you and Lettie ain't had no chi'ren? Y'all incapable?"

"Pops, that's a hard question to answer. When we first got married, we wanted to take our time—get to know each other. I started moving up in the ranks, and the transfers became more frequent. Then the wars cranked up, and as much as I envied the other men with their families, I knew all too well that the possibility of Lettie becoming a widow was real. I didn't want my kids to be fatherless. Then, the older I got, the more comfortable I was with just her and me."

"How does Lettie feel?" Daddy asked.

"You know, we've never talked about it. I figured since she never brought the subject up, she didn't want any. Maybe we're both selfish people. I don't know," Bruce mumbled. "When she learned I might not be able to sire children, she said she didn't care; all she wanted was me."

"Son, women say all sorts of things when they scared," Daddy said, sipping coffee. "So, can you?"

"Can I what?"

"Boy, don't make me throw something at you. Can you sire chi'ren?"

"No."

"How do you know?"

"I asked the VA to test me when I first came back stateside and the results came back as *void*. Performing the test was agonizing. I could only give a thimble's worth of semen. The pain was excruciating, and I wouldn't have repeated that test if they paid me. That's why it took so long to have sex. If Lettie hadn't ambushed me that one night I still might not know it doesn't hurt anymore," Bruce said, sheepishly.

"Do you want a family of yo' own?" Daddy asked.

"I *have* a family of my own. I'm content and complete with Lettie. What I don't know is if *she* wants children. If she does, I can't give her any, and I will have failed as a man," Bruce muttered.

"Nonsense! The only thing you've failed at is communicatin' with yo' wife. Son, I recommend you and Lettie sit down and have a conversation soon. Matter of fact, you ought not to leave here before you do."

"Yeah," sighed Bruce. "Pops, you're right. I know I've been distant and closed with her this past year. It's been real difficult for me to confide in her."

"Son, what you scared of?"

"Pops—**it's too much**!" Bruce exploded, banging his hand upon the kitchen table. "I'm supposed to protect my woman, not burden her with my shit! Oh, excuse me, Pops, I didn't mean to disrespect yo' house. Please forgive me. It's just there are times when I feel I'm going insane, especially when the nightmares come. I'd like nothing more than to talk to Lettie about it, but how do I put all that on her? I can't do that to her, Pops."

"Bruce, do you smell that?" Daddy asked, suddenly sniffing the air.

"What?"

"That!" sniffing loudly.

"No," Bruce answered, warily.

"You sho'?" Daddy persisted.

"Yes, I'm sure. What is it you smell?" Bruce asked, perplexed.

"It's strong. I'm surprised you truly cain't smell it," Daddy said, sniffing louder.

"No, Pops, I really can't. What are you smelling?" Bruce asked, now sounding worried.

"**B-U-L-L-S-H-I-T.**"

"Huh?"

"Look here, boy, there're some thangs you need to know and understand. One: ain't nobody gonna love you better than that gal sleepin' in that room, 'cept God. Anybody with eyes can see she loves you, so much so she'd drink yo' bath water. Surely, you got to know this by now. Two: if you don't talk about yo' attacks with her, you gon' break. Now, I'm speaking from experience. Talk to her, confide in her, let her be yo' rock; then let God be yo' anchor. Three: the secret to keeping a good woman is lettin' her be a part of yo' whole life—warts and all. Are you thinkin' she's gon' see you as weak? 'Cause if that's what you think, then you don't know my Lettie at all. You need to start trusting yo' wife, son."

"Anything else?" Bruce asked after a moment of silence.

"Yeah. Sometimes you need to talk to a person in a language they can understand, and I know you understood everything I jus' said to you. On occasion, strong language is necessary to get yo' attention and to get the point across. Besides, this is my house! I do as I please."

"As long as Mama Jewel approves," added Bruce.

"Exactly," Daddy said as they both burst into more laughter.

"Wow," Bruce sighed after the laughter subsided, "I haven't been dressed down like that since I was a Second Lieutenant." Bruce marveled.

"Don't worry, son, I've got plenty mo' where that came from," Daddy said.

With that, I heard them get up then the patting of backs. I could only surmise they had hugged each other.

"Pops, thanks for caring enough to kick my keester," Bruce said.

"Bruce, you are as much my chil' as Lettie is," assured Daddy. "When I see my chi'ren floundering, I'm obligated as a parent to step in. Hopefully to help, or kick keester."

"Do you mean that?"

"I do," Daddy affirmed as they sat back down.

"Then answer me this: when's the last time you've kicked Brett's keester?" Bruce asked.

Yes! Yes! That's my baby. Hit him again! I said to myself as I shadowed boxed in the air.

"Son," Daddy deeply sighed, "that's been my one true regret. I was way too soft on that boy, and now, I fear he's ruin't. I've over indulged him, and Jewel, far too much. It's like shutting the barn door once the horse is out. I'm too late, and I don't think I can fix it now."

"Would you mind if I spoke with him?" asked Bruce.

"No, sir, not at all. I'd be obliged to you if you did," Daddy said.

"Thank you. I'll do my best to talk with him either today or tomorrow."

I heard Mama shuffling her way to the kitchen, so I hastily positioned myself in the bed so it looked like I was still asleep with the door ajar. I even threw in a bit of a snore to seem more realistic. As she was passing, she paused to listen. Pressing on to the kitchen, I heard her address her men.

"Good morning," she cheerily spoke.

"Morning, Mama Jewel."

"Morning, Sweetness," Daddy said.

"Did I hear y'all down here laughing?" she asked.

"Yes, ma'am," Bruce replied.

"What did I miss?" Mama asked, expectantly.

"Nothin'," Daddy snapped. "This was *man* talk.

"Ohhhhh," Mama said, dramatically. "Well, son, I guess you and I will have to have our own *tete-a-tete*." Mama said.

"Mama Jewel, it would be my pleasure. Shall we go out or would you like to take a promenade around the back forty?" Bruce smoothly asked.

"A promenade would be nice; then, I can introduce you to my new babies," she proudly said. "I'd like to talk with you and Lettie together before the rest of the family gets here anyway. Shall we say, nine o'clock?"

"As you wish, Mama."

"Perfect. Now, what would y'all like for breakfast?"

"I'm good till dinner, Sweetness," Daddy answered.

"I'm still stuffed from last night. Mama, you sho' put yo' foot in it last night!"

"Shuh, those were just leftovers. I'm really goin' to break a nail on Thursday.".

"Mama, I don't know if I'll be able to stand it," teased Bruce. "I may die and go on to my just reward if it's better than last night," he gushed.

Oh, my beloved, how you can spin the blarney, I thought to myself. Mama ate Bruce's flattery with two great big spoons.

"Well, what do you think Lettie might like for breakfast?"

"Trust me, coffee is her only friend in the mornings," Bruce said.

"Hmm, still a woman of few words in the mornings?" Mama asked.

"Something like that," Bruce chuckled.

"Why don't you go and wake your beloved and ask her anyway," Mama suggested.

"Yes, ma'am," Bruce replied and immediately came into the bedroom. Sideling over to me, gently tickling my ear, he whispered, "Wake up, Sleeping Beauty."

"I'm awake," I said, yawning and stretching.

"Mama wants to know what you'd like for breakfast," he said.

"Oh, nothing, tell her coffee," I said.

"Nope, you need to get up and tell her yourself."

"Ohhh. You are so mean."

"And now that we have that established, what's your point?" Bruce teased.

"You're incorrigible," I said, now sitting up.

"True dat. Now, come on, get up and get dressed. Yo' mama wants to talk to both of us as she introduces us to her new babies," Bruce informed.

"Oh, new critters," I reasoned.

"Most likely." Bruce agreed.

"Okay, I'm up." I sauntered toward the bathroom to clean up. I made sure to dress down because I knew Mama would drag us over the back forty's hill and dale and through mud and brush. After making up the bed, I slipped into the kitchen for my cup of coffee, then I met Bruce on the front porch promptly at 9:00 a.m. Mama pulled up to the house in the Gator a few minutes after nine.

"Come on you two, climb in," she ordered.

Bruce let me sit next to Mama as he climbed into the back of the Gator. Mama stepped on the gas and off we went. It had been so long since the last time I visited, I'd forgotten how beautiful the landscape was. Three minutes later, we were at the pen and shelters for the alpacas.

"All right children, stay in the Gator until I bring Brutus and Cassius to meet you," she said right before issuing an ear-piercing whistle. From behind the last shelter bounded two robust Great Pyrenees dogs. Both looked identical, but Mama could tell them apart. She brought each one to us separately, and each time she introduced us by making us extend our closed fist so they could smell us. She spoke to them like they were people who could understand every word she said.

"Brutus, Cassius, these are my children. You will be nice to them and not bite, okay? They are my children just like you are. I want you to watch over them and keep them safe, too, okay?"

Mama's dogs had the most human eyes I have ever seen on animals. They were a clear, gentle brown set within white fur, and easily could have been mistaken for smoky quartz crystals when seen from a far. If we seemed suspicious to the dogs, they didn't react as such. These were two of the most relaxed, laid back dogs. When we got out of the Gator and started walking toward the alpaca pen, Brutus was at my side the entire time. He even let me lovingly pet him as much as I wanted. Cassius was clearly Mama's baby because he never left her side. They completely ignored Bruce. I remembered Mama telling me animals were attracted to the opposite sex just like humans. If Brutus and Cassius were an example, then that notion must be true.

As we entered the pen, Mama kept the dogs on the outside. We watched from a short distance as the herd surrounded her. I had never seen alpacas up close. They were cute critters with the sweetest, most expressive faces. She petted each one and called them by name. Then she went to a bin where she kept alpaca feed and motioned for us to come over. She gave each of us a handful and said to feed them. The alpacas were somewhat timid, but once they realized we had food, they soon lost their inhibitions and greedily ate what we offered. Mama told us they wouldn't bite.

"They may not bite, but they do spit," said Bruce warily.

"Son, they only spit on each other. You're safe unless you get in between a squabble, and that usually only happens with the males. Right now, we're in the female pen. They're one big happy sorority. Here, give me yo' hand," Mama said, taking Bruce's hand and placing it on the flank of the nearest female.

"Oh, my," Bruce exclaimed, eyes widening as his hand got lost up to his wrist in fur. "That is thick and mighty soft, Mama Jewel."

"Let me see," I said, reaching for the same flank. "Oooo, Mama, this *is* nice," I agreed. "Can you do something with their fur?"

"Can you do something with it? Wait till we go back to the house, and I'll show you what *I* can do with it. Their fur is called fleece, and it's truly more like hair than fur. It is two times lighter than sheep's wool and eight times warmer. Unfortunately, it doesn't get cold enough around these parts to wear much made from alpaca. Come on over here, and see my new babies."

In the nearer shelter were all of Mama's new babies, five in all: one brown, one dark fawn, one light fawn, one white, and one black. I've never been one to cuddle and swoon over baby anything, but these alpacas were simply adorable. They were somewhat skittish of me and Bruce, but they allowed Mama to pick them up and hold them.

"What is that noise they're making?" Bruce asked.

"They're humming," Mama said.

"Why are they humming," Bruce pressed.

"Because they don't know the words," Mama answered with a twinkle in her eye.

"Ha, ha," said Bruce as Mama and I both giggled.

"It's a corny joke, but it works every time," Mama laughed. "Alpacas communicate in many ways. The most audible is humming. The mommas and babies are always humming to one another, but they also hum when they're curious, content, worried, bored, fearful, distressed, or when they're being cautious," Mama explained. "Why don't y'all help me feed up, and then we can go back to the pavilion to talk when we're done, alright?"

"Sure, Mama," I said.

"Happy to help," said Bruce.

Mama and I fed the hembras (females), males, and crias (babies), made sure their water was fresh and spread new hay in the pens. Mama showed Bruce how to corral their manure, which was an easier job than feeding. Alpacas will only poo in a designated spot. They won't contaminate their eating or sleeping areas, plus, their manure are firm pellets that raked quite well.

Once outside the pens, Mama gave her dogs a Milkbone each as a treat, then we piled back into the Gator and drove to the pavilion, which was about thirty yards from the back door of the house. Mama, always one to be direct, got straight to business.

"Children, I wanted to talk with you both about some things before the rest of the family arrives. Y'all know that Clarissa is expecting again, and I'm asking for your help with the other children. This has been a hard pregnancy, and her doctor's telling her this has to be the last one."

"Finally," I said, under my breath.

"Lettie! That was plain mean and uncalled for. I know I raised you better than that, and I will not tolerate you saying anything disparaging about my grandbabies, hear me?" Mama fumed.

"Yes, ma'am. I'm not trying to be ugly, honest, Mama. But, every one of Chester's kids has something wrong with them. I don't understand why they continue to procreate with that kind of track record."

"Everyone's not like you, Lettie!" Mama said as she wheeled in my direction looking dead into my eyes. "Chester and Clarissa love children. They wanted to have a large family and have welcomed, and celebrated, each addition, even if it meant they weren't physically perfect. Imperfection does not negate acceptance. I've known I would not be getting any grandchildren out of you since you entered puberty."

"Mama Jewel, that's a little harsh don't you think?" Bruce interjected in my defense.

"Truth is often harsh, Bruce," Mama said as she turned her assault towards him. "But y'all know I am not one to, necessarily, sugar coat or mince my words. Lettie has *never* been maternal. This one," she said while pointing at me, "has never liked being around anything baby, especially Brett. I'm not saying anything that y'all don't already know. However, I can tell you my daughter is awesome in her own right. This one," she said while still pointing at me, "is driven, and she tends to be a perfectionist. She doesn't suffer fools, gladly or otherwise. She's sensitive, intuitive, and, I'll wager she's a spitfire in the bedroom too," she said, turning back to Bruce winking.

"Mama!" we both spoke in unison, slightly shocked.

"That apple didn't fall far from the tree. How you think I've kept that man with me all these years?" Mama questioned. "Children, we're all grown folks here."

"Yeah, but…" I sputtered.

"But you've never wanted to see me as anything other than yo' mama. You don't see me as the passionate, sexual, or the desirable woman I am."

Stammering, groping for words, Bruce and I both looked at each other with a little discomfort. Everything Mama said was true, but I was going to have to unpack that particular knapsack later.

"However, let's get back to the matter at hand. Chester can handle his boys for the most part. His girls need some concentrated attention. Suzie is the baby, and she has Down syndrome. Clarissa's been trying to potty train that baby, and I keep telling her it's too soon for that child. I'll make sure she comes in diapers with plenty on hand, but she'll need a keeper. Bruce, in all likelihood, she may latch onto you. That baby may be slow, but she loves her some men. If she doesn't come to you, then she's probably gonna go to Thadd. Carolyn is five and is visually challenged."

"What's wrong with Carolyn?" Bruce asked.

"Her eyes are severely crossed. She sees double of everything and sometimes misjudges the door and winds up walking into walls. She's scheduled for surgery in three weeks. I don't know why the doctors have waited this long, but they said her surgery would be more successful at this age. So, there it is. Carolyn loves to be read to and so do the younger boys. Janine is the eldest girl."

"What wrong with Janine?" Bruce asked again.

"She's got two left feet," Mama said.

"Now who's being disparaging?" I asked.

"No, daughter," Mama said in an extremely exasperated tone, "you know she was born with two left legs from the knee down and has two left feet. She's moved from using crutches to a cane, but walking, as you might imagine, is a challenge. She's never been able to run and play like the other kids, so she's a little shy and withdrawn. Janine is frighteningly bright and loves to play board games. Bruce, if you play Chess, don't be surprised when she beats you. Math is her favorite subject in school, so if either of you can recall your college math, she could use some review with her algebra."

"What about the boys?" I asked.

"The twins, Jesse and Jordan, Brett has promised to occupy with video games. Thomas, who has Asperger's syndrome, is easily kept busy with crayons and coloring books. Don't worry about Thomas, I'll tend to him. I do need to warn you that he has no filter. In mind – out mouth; so if you don't want yo' business in the street, don't engage in his presence."

"What about Willy?" I added.

"When Willy isn't helping Chester with chores or around the house, his nose is in a thick book. He's a non-issue. So, everyone straight? We good to go?"

"Almost. Is anyone other than family coming? Beside James, I mean?"

"Brett has invited his girlfriend, Willa, to dinner; everyone else is family. Peaches and Luther are coming in tonight and will be staying with us through Friday."

"What are the seating arrangements going to be?" I asked.

"I'm so glad you brought that up. Son, I'm gonna need your help, along with Brett, putting some tables together. We're going to have an adult table and a kiddie table in the den. We'll have plenty of room, don't worry," Mama said.

"Will you need my help in the kitchen on Thursday?" I asked.

"Maybe. Stay on deck just in case. Peaches has promised to help and you know how good she can cook. I may just need you to help with the children, but again, I'll let you know in plenty of time."

"So, how's Clarissa really doing?" Bruce asked.

"Well," sighing heavily, "I'm scared they're gonna lose this child," Mama revealed. "Clarissa was ordered to bed rest, but she won't stay down. She breezed through all her other pregnancies right up to and after delivery. But this one is pulling her down. She's losing weight, and is beginning to look poorly. I'm worried about her and Chester. She's due in a little more than three weeks." Mama confessed.

"Doesn't she have any help?" I asked.

"Her mama and sisters go to the house to help, but Clarissa's always been hands on; she doesn't know how to be hands off. Right now, the only thing we can really do is pray for her and the family."

At that moment, Daddy came around the corner of the house in his rumbling pickup truck. Reaching the pavilion, he rolled his window down. "Bruce! Come ride with me, son. I need some help," he yelled.

"Yes, sir," Bruce answered, and then smartly moved toward the truck and climbed into the cab.

"Sweetness, we're going to the barn to pick up the tables and bring them back to be cleaned. We'll be back in a while," Daddy said. Shifting the truck's gears, they ambled off.

"Just as well, I wanted some time alone with you anyway," Mama said, turning to me.

"I'm scared," I confessed.

"No need, but I suspect you have some questions for me." Mama said. "I know you heard everything the menfolk were talking about this morning. Please don't think yo' 'possum playing fooled me," she said plainly.

"How do you do that?" I asked, marveling and goggled-eyed at my mother.

"A mother knows her child, even in adulthood. Now, what's on your mind?"

"How come you never told me about Daddy?"

"How come you didn't tell us about Bruce?"

"That's not fair, Mama. You *know* I've kept you and Daddy abreast of Bruce's progress."

"You haven't shared about Bruce's PTSD, have you?"

"No, ma'am."

"Why not?"

"This has been so hard to bear. I felt I couldn't tell anybody. Nobody."

"Why?"

"Embarrassment mostly. I didn't want people thinking Bruce was crazy. I certainly didn't want anyone to know he'd become violent with his attacks," I said.

"Has he hurt you?"

"Mama!"

"Has he put his hands on you?" she shouted.

"Yes," I whispered, cowering under her scrutiny, "but he wasn't himself."

"How many times?"

"Only twice and I kept it from him. He never saw the worst injury."

"Tell me," Mama demanded with that piercing look she gave us kids when separating the truth from a lie.

I related everything – all the gory details – since Bruce came home. By the time I finished, I was fully weeping. Mama didn't even try to console me. She just handed me a Kleenex and let me cry until I was all cried out.

"Lettie, look at me, and pay close attention. I need my strong, analytical child with me right now. Is that child here? You listening?"

"Yes, ma'am."

"I wish I could tell you that the worst is over, but I don't believe that to be the case. The worst is yet to come. Bruce doesn't share his nightmares with you does he?"

"No, ma'am."

"That much is going to change. If yo' daddy has had any influence in what he told him this morning, Bruce will start to open up."

"How do you know what Daddy said to Bruce?" I asked with great curiosity.

"The air vent in the kitchen joins up with the ductwork that directly passes our bedroom."

"You…"

"Heard every word."

"So, all those times when I would talk privately to Daddy, you were…"

"Listening to everything you said. Yes," Mama confessed.

I was stunned. "So, if you knew, why didn't you ever say anything to me?" I asked.

"Baby, you didn't need me at that moment. You needed yo' daddy. There comes a time in every parent's life when all we can do is advise and point you in, what we hope, to be the right direction. *You* have to make the decision and live with the consequences. We planted what good seed we could into you, and then we had to step back, and see what took root. Failure is the best teacher; we had to let you fall, baby. We were careful not to let you get too hurt, but you needed to bump yo' head for yo'self."

"So, when I was unsure about marrying Bruce, and I was talking to Daddy about it, you…?"

"Was upstairs on my knees praying, 'Lawd, *pleeeese* don't let her lose that man!' And look how the Good Lawd answered prayer," Mama said, smiling widely.

"I don't know what to say," I replied, shaking my head.

"There's nothing to say. Now, let's get back on the subject. Do you know what triggers Bruce's attacks?"

"No, ma'am."

"Once y'all get that figured out, then I believe y'all can begin to heal. Baby Girl, this is a dark patch of ground you're in right now, but it will get better. You've got a good man, daughter; a man worth fighting for. You keep loving him, hold on, and be patient."

"Mama, *tribulation worketh patience*, and I'm tired."

"Yes, I know, and you are about to get your Tribulation Cup filled to over flowing. But, baby, God isn't gonna bring you this far and leave you. No, no, he's gonna bring you through to the other side. Yo' job is to finish the race."

"But it's so hard," I choked as I began crying anew.

"Yes, it's hard, but what doesn't kill you makes you stronger. Anything worth having is worth working for—and dying for."

"Clichés, Mama? Really?" I sobbed.

"There is truth in clichés, daughter. You told me when Bruce was first captured you'd die for him. You still feel that way?"

"I think so, yes."

"Then buck up," Mama said, suddenly grabbing my hands hard, "hunker down, and fight for yo' marriage, hear?"

"Yes, ma'am."

"You and Bruce are at a precarious juncture; if you do not come together – in every way – you *will* come apart. Baby, do you understand me?"

"Yes, ma'am," I said, wiping my eyes. "How did you and Daddy make it through?"

"We loved each other. We were committed to each other. I fought tooth and nail to keep our family together, and to make yo' daddy understand that nothing was going to drive me away from him—nothing. When I was almost six months pregnant with you, yo' daddy had a really bad spell of attacks. One night he beat me, beat me pretty bad. He broke my nose, blackened an eye, and hit me so hard in the belly I just knew for sure I had lost you. Yo' grandpa, Ernest, was still living at the time and heard the ruckus. He busted into our bedroom and pulled yo' daddy off me. I thought Daddy Ernest was going to kill Calvin, but he didn't. He woke him up enough to realize what he had done. Yo' daddy cried worse than a child when he realized how bad he'd hurt me. Back then, doctors made house calls, and didn't report to the po-lice every time a man hit his woman, especially a black man. The long and short of it is yo' daddy stopped sleeping with me, my injuries healed, and you made it here safe and healthy."

"Where was Tony when all this happened?" I asked.

"Child, that boy would sleep through the second coming," Mama laughed.

"How did you explain your injuries to him?"

"I just told him Mama had an accident, and the doctor said I'd get better. Children don't need long, drawn-out explanations. They just need to know they're safe and loved. Plus, yo' grandpa stepped in and spent more time than usual with him."

"How did Daddy change after that? I mean, how did he get better?"

"Well, he started going to church more regularly, studying the Word, truly praying, and seeking God's face. *I* just loved him the best I could, and gave him all the support he needed. By the time you turned one year old, his attacks had become infrequent. When they did come, they weren't much more than a bad dream. And, once Chester came, he'd stopped having the dreams all together. So, you see? Things will get better." After a slight pause, Mama asked, "Do you know why yo' daddy always rocks you when you hug?"

"No. I always chalked it up to wanting his little girl back," I said.

"That's partly true," Mama said, smiling. After another pause, she continued, "He rocks you because when you were born he promised to always take care of you and never let any harm come to you. Rocking you was his way of saying he was sorry for hurting you in utero."

"Oh!" I said as some puzzle pieces fell into place.

"Now, I need to dip in some of yo' other business. How's yo' sex life?"

I started laughing, almost hysterically, before answering with, "It depends."

"Depends on what?"

"On whether we're talking then or now."

"I guess you best tell me about both," Mama demanded.

I recounted everything from the electrocution, to the pilot episode, down to the sequel.

Mama's only comment afterwards was, "Uh huh." She finally asked me the one question I had been anticipating. "Why have you never asked Bruce if he wanted children?"

"He never brought the subject up. I figured he didn't want any. Besides, you're right, I've never wanted any children. Now I know all this time Bruce was afraid to have a family because he didn't want to leave any children fatherless. What if he wants some now? I'm nearing forty. I don't want any babies."

"What about adoption?"

"I don't want any babies!"

"What if Bruce wants a child?"

"I'll let him have a dog."

"Be careful what you throw out to the Universe, daughter," Mama said, pointing her finger at me. "Irony is just *one* of the Lawd's many tools. There is one thing I need you to promise me," Mama said, narrowing her eyes. "It's well within your power to give."

"What?" I asked, suspiciously.

"Before you go home, you and Bruce sit down and talk through all this stuff."

"Mama, you can't make Bruce do what he doesn't want to do," I said. "He hasn't truly confided in me since that last night in Germany."

"All I'm asking is that you try."

Daddy and Bruce returned in an hour's time with the tables and folding chairs in the truck. Bucket was waiting to help unload. Between the three of them, everything had been unloaded, and spread out on the ground to begin the cleaning. I helped by vacuuming away the dust, dirt, and cobwebs from both the front and backs of the tables, along with all the chairs. Any chance of vermin had to be thoroughly negated, especially with Aunt Peaches coming. She was deathly afraid of bugs, no matter the species or size. My aunt had a set of lungs on her that could shame a siren, so we had to make doubly sure there was no cause for alarm. Bruce and Bucket scrubbed down the tables and wooden folding chairs with hot, soapy water and a good splash of bleach. Bruce took the hose and rinsed everything. Afterward, Bucket stacked the tables and chairs at the pavilion in such a way where air could circulate and completely dry them in a matter of hours.

I left Bruce and Bucket at the pavilion. Hopefully, Bruce would take the opportunity to talk privately with Bucket about his trifling ways. I went into the house to see if Mama needed a hand with supper, especially since we were anticipating Aunt Peaches and Uncle Luther's arrival.

"Baby Girl, we're going to go light tonight. We're going to have spaghetti, garlic bread, tossed salad, and pie for supper. I've taken out some meat sauce I had in the freezer and already put it in the crock pot. Once Peaches and Luther get here, we'll put the pasta on and fix the garlic bread. They're driving up from Louisiana so I expect them to be tired when they get here. Why don't you come help me fix up their room?"

"Yes, ma'am."

Together, we ascended the stairs. Mama stopped by the linen closet, and pulled out some fresh sheets, pillow cases, and quilts. We made the bed and lightly dusted around the room. This was my old room, and the light pink patterned wallpaper brought back pleasant memories. I may not have liked living in Hertford, but I did love my bedroom. It faced west, and I always had beautiful light from the afternoon setting sun. In the autumn and winter, the afternoon light would bathe my room in such warmth, I used to hate to see the sun set. I would literally cocoon in here during the winter months. Often, Mama would drag me out and *make* me socialize with the family. I was content to be in my room with my books. After my homework was completed, I read for hours about faraway places and different cultures. I wasn't one for sappy romance novels, adventure was my fancy. I used to dream and imagine living all over the world—anyplace but Hertford.

Mama kept all my old furniture. It was traditional, white French Provincial. I had a vanity with mirror, a large chest of drawers, and a full-sized canopied bed. Since I was the only girl in the family, Mama did her best to try and make me frilly. She labored long and hard with me on her anvil of Southern womanliness, but at an early age my aesthetic was sophisticated, clean, and chic. Mama eventually read those tea leaves, and settled on only making my bedroom girly with every possible shade of pink. I didn't fight with Mama because I knew in my heart, my residence here was temporary. Mama had made one major change to the room: she placed two tufted pink and white striped brocade winged-backed chairs with a small round table between them in front of my west facing window. It was a nice sitting area that didn't block the light, but brought a mature feel into the room. I had to tip my hat to the old girl; she's always had a knack with décor.

"Earth to Lettie," Mama called.

"What, Mama?" I smiled, coming back to the present.

"Where did you go?" Mama asked.

"What do you mean?" I replied.

"I want to know where *my* child is." Mama said.

"Mama, I'm right here," I said, brow furrowed.

"No, only a portion of you is here. I want to know where the rest of you is," Mama continued.

"Mama, I don't know what you're talking about. Would you clue me in?" I asked.

"Baby, come, sit down," Mama said, patting the foot of the bed where she currently sat. "How do I begin?" she mumbled, looking at the carpet.

"Just spit it out," I said.

"Baby, there's been a change in you. I'm not talking about what you're currently going through, I'm talking about a different kind of change. It's as if you're trying to be someone you're not."

"Mama, do you have any idea how crazy you sound?"

"Yes, it sounds crazy, but I'm telling you what I see. I think I've finally figured out one reason why you don't come home so often. When you do come home you turn into an adolescent again, fussing with your brothers, and that bothers you. Am I right?" she asked.

"There's a lot of truth in that, Mama," I reluctantly agreed.

"When you're not here at home, in Hertford, I'll wager you're a much different person. You're sophisticated, polished, professional, and politically correct. Am I wrong?"

"I certainly strive to be," I said. "I don't see how that's changed me."

"You're hiding," Mama said, pointedly. "You're much more than what you're showing. I even see it in the way you interact with Bruce. You haven't always been this—dull."

"Dull?"

"Dull. I know having been an officer's wife was challenging. You had to play a small, but important part in a bigger production. Failure to play your part well impacted on Bruce's career. I understand that, but he's out of the service now. I also know, working in the professional realm, there is a mask we must wear in order to be taken seriously by our peers and colleagues, black folk in particular. I hear the changes in your speech as well. Everything is proper, perfect English; no vernacular for you. What I think has happened is you've stopped taking off your mask."

"Is it a crime to want to do better? You always told us 'to know better was to do better'," I said, defensively.

"Baby, there's no crime in wanting to do better. The crime is losing yo'self to become someone you're not," Mama explained. "You've always had a thirst for knowledge and you've always been a rambling rose. You were spontaneous, had a quick wit along with a quick and witty tongue. The world was your oyster, and you were determined to travel the Seven Seas with Bruce to find yo' perfect pearl. Where is that woman? I believe she's still in there somewhere, but you won't let her come out to play."

"Mama," I said with fresh tears sprouting, "I feel like Atlas most of the time; the world is too heavy for my shoulders. The night you called to invite us for Thanksgiving, Bruce and I were fighting. Well, I was fighting, Bruce was holding my arms. At that moment, all I wanted was the world to stop so I could get off. I've been pouring all my love out to this man, and I'm not getting much in return. I'm trying to be supportive, but it feels like the more I do, the less I'm appreciated. For the first time in my life, I honestly thought about leaving Bruce. I can't take this strain anymore. So, I guess you're right; I haven't been myself in a long, long time."

Mama leaned over, took me in her arms, and stroked the nape of my neck like she did when I was a little girl. "It's time for Lettie to come back. She doesn't have to come home to Hertford, but she does have to come back. It's also time for you to start talking *with* Bruce and not simply to him. Be who you are, baby. I've always told you children that everybody ain't goin' to like you. More's the pity, it's their loss." Pushing back, Mama looked me in the eyes, and then said, "You do you! The

Lord will change what he doesn't like about you. Otherwise, you be true to Lettie. Hear?"

"Yes, ma'am," I sniffled as I wiped my eyes for the umpteenth time.

Mama patted my arm and smiled her signature *you gon' be alright* smile at me. "Since we're up here, help me prepare Brett's old room for Tony and James."

Going again to the linen closet, Mama pulled out sheets and pillow cases for two beds and handed them to me. Then she gathered four of her beautiful scrap quilts. Bucket's old room was down the hall and around the corner from my old room. The décor in his old room was a baby powder blue nautical theme. Mama had separated the bunk beds, and they now occupied space under the north facing window in the room. She had placed between them a square maple finished end table. On it stood a sleek, brass, dual-armed lamp. Each lamp head had its own pull so whoever desired to read in bed could do so without disturbing the other occupant. At the foot of each bed were our old toy chests. They had been refurbished in a matching maple finish, and were now used as additional seating/storage. Instead of a chest of drawers, Mama had a highboy strategically placed in one corner of the room with a silk foliage arrangement on top. The mirror corner held a blue plaid winged-back chair and matching foot stool with a brass torchère lamp on the side of it. On the walls were beautifully framed watercolor pictures of ships, yachts, and lighthouses. Once again, Mama took the childhood décor and transformed it into something akin to a bed and breakfast. The only thing missing was a private bathroom.

The "Blue Room", as Mama called it, needed a bit more attention. It hadn't been dusted or vacuumed in quite a while. After making up the beds, I vacuumed the carpet as Mama dusted and polished the woodwork. We opened the windows while working to let some fresh air in. After bringing the room up to specs, Mama then sprayed everything and everywhere with Febreze. Our task completed, Mama closed the door upon leaving.

"Don't worry," she assured, "by the time Tony and James gets here, the scent will have calmed down. All they'll smell is clean."

"My goodness," I said, looking at my watch, "the afternoon is almost gone. We should get started on the rest of supper."

"Ooooo, you're so right, Baby Girl. Let's get crackin'."

In the kitchen, we moved into overdrive, deciding not to wait until company arrived, but to have the meal ready at their arrival. As I sliced the Italian bread, Mama prepared the garlic spread. While I put the water on to boil for the pasta, Mama prepared the tossed salad. The peach pie was pre-baked and had been thawing on the counter for several hours. Daddy preferred his pie warm, so Mama put it in the oven the same time the bread went in. Aunt Peaches and Uncle Luther pulled up to the house right as I was taking the garlic bread out of the oven. Mama and Daddy met them outside and were escorting them in as I came from the kitchen.

Loud and large, both literally and figuratively, best describes Aunt Peaches. Her voice was like the trumpet that proceeded the town crier. She could take over any conversation if she chose simply by raising her voice. Her personality was bright, vivacious, and almost overwhelming. When she entered a room, there was no doubt the elephant *and* the 300 lb. gorilla were in attendance. But Peaches was a pleasant and gregarious person. She knew no strangers; everyone was her friend. Anyone who met her for the first time always came away believing they'd known her all their life. Peaches was also the kind of person you hated to see leave. Her pleasantness and humorous spirit made one greedy for her company.

Aunt Peaches was cute in the face, in spite of being middle aged. She had a round face with dimples, lively olive green eyes, brown hair with natural auburn highlights and now silver streaks, a charming smile, and a pair of pouty lips with a perfect Cupid's bow. Her complexion was well done biscuit. She was built like the pioneering women of old: stout, full-busted, narrow waist, wide baby-making hips with powerful but shapely legs, and broad sturdy feet. She would say of herself she had *quality fat*. The old Cab Calloway song said it best: *"Must be jelly 'cause jam don't shake like that."* Aunt Peaches definitely did not shake. When she stood her ground, John Deere is probably the only thing that could move her. The fact there was an identical carbon copy of her was an overpowering thought. I barely remembered the last time I saw both sisters together in the same room. I could only imagine the challenges my grandparents had raising those two. Their captivating beauty alone must have caused tremendous grief for Grandpa Ernest. I bet he kept a loaded scatter gun at the ready.

Uncle Luther was the direct opposite of Aunt Peaches. He was tall, wiry to almost skinny, and so black, Uncle Thadd would always tease him by saying, "Luther! Smile, man, we can't see you." Uncle Luther would always oblige and grace everyone with a broad grin. Nowadays, with his false teeth, his smile looked more like the doggie denture commercials on TV, which made it all the more funny. He was an extremely handsome man in his youth, and because he lived a clean life, he mellowed into a fine-looking man in his old age. He was blessed with *good hair*, as the old folks would say, and his hairline never receded. His hair was a straight kind of curly that produced lovely waves when cut short, which was how he currently wore it. Uncle Luther was somewhat shy, but he was also easy going and naturally quiet. He would speak and carry on a conversation, but usually only when he had something worthwhile to contribute. Otherwise, he was content to let Aunt Peaches drive the conversation.

Uncle Luther was a retired railroad worker, and Aunt Peaches was a cook by profession. They were the embodiment of the nursery rhyme *Jack Spratt*, and were totally devoted to each other. They had two children: Doris Esther, a school teacher, and Peter Bartholomew, an insurance salesman.

"Hey, everybody!" Peaches shouted as she entered the house.

She strode straight to Uncle Thadd and hugged him until he croaked he couldn't breathe. Laughing at his remark, she released him, but took his face in her plump hands, and kissed him repeatedly until he began to chuckle. She then hugged him again, and Uncle Thadd did his best to hold on and hold out.

When Uncle Luther came in with their bags, Uncle Thadd greeted him in his customary fashion. "Luther! Smile, man, we can't see you," to which Uncle Luther flashed his doggie dentures.

"Thaddeus, you old reprobate," Uncle Luther said before they both embraced, smiling.

"Brett!" Mama hollered. "Come get yo' Aunt Peaches and Uncle Luther's bags and carry them up to their room."

To my surprise, Bucket appeared like the bellboy at the Ritz—quick, quiet, smiling, and obliging. I looked over at Bruce and all he did was blink his eyes in my direction and smile. Would wonders continue or cease?

"I know y'all must be hungry," Mama said, looking dead at Uncle Luther, "so go wash up and come to the table."

Once everyone had assembled, Daddy said grace and scriptures were recited. Supper was abuzz with lively conversation. Within forty-five minutes, every scrap of food, including dessert, had been consumed. Mama, Aunt Peaches, and I cleared the table and left the menfolk to talk. I washed the dishes, Aunt Peaches dried, and Mama put them all away.

"Lawd, have mercy, I see Luther hasn't slowed down one iota," said Mama. "He still has hollow legs," as we all burst into jovial laughter.

"My man sho' does me proud," crowed Aunt Peaches. "Did you notice? He didn't slow down or loosen his belt." Aunt Peaches said amidst more laughter.

"You reckon he's gonna be all right on Thursday?" Mama asked.

"You watch," said Aunt Peaches, "once he gets his nap, he'll come back even stronger," she laughed.

The kitchen was spotless and ready for the morning's assault in less than half an hour from when we began. The menfolk had moved to the den, and were sitting before a roaring fire when we came out of the kitchen. For the next four hours, we all caught up with Aunt Peaches and Uncle Luther. Uncle Thadd, once again in rare form, told more childhood stories about the twins, and the double-trouble they constantly seemed to cause. It was entertaining to hear the stories, and the denials. Let Aunt Peaches tell it, Uncle Thadd was vastly embellishing certain details to make the story seem more dramatic than it was. At 10:30 p.m., we all said good night and retired to our bedrooms.

"Bruce, what did you say to Bucket today?" I asked. "I couldn't believe Mama only called him once this evening."

"Babe, I'm not gonna tell you everything, but suffice it to say, we had a man-to-man chat," he said, pulling on his nightshirt.

"Will you give me the highlights?" I pressed.

"Tell you what, you tell me what yo' mama said once I left, and I'll tell you what Brett, not Bucket, and I talked about."

"I'll see you and raise you," I said. "I'll tell you about what Mama said if you share with me what you and Daddy talked about, plus, what you and Bucket talked about."

"One, that's a sucker's bet right there. You want more information than you have to give."

"I can raise the ante," I said, as I provocatively twitched naked booty in his direction.

"Woman," Bruce openly laughed, "you can't bet what's already mine, but nice try."

"Oh, come on, baby," I said as I cuddled up next to him in the bed, "I want to know what's going on."

"I'm sure you do," he soberly replied, looking at me. *Mr. Hyde flashed.* "I promise you this, before we leave for home, we will talk. All right?" he asked.

"Okay," I said, and with that he turned out the light, adjusted to a comfortable spoon position, and was soon lightly snoring in my ear. I've waited this long, I guess I could hold out a few more days.

Early Wednesday morning, Mama and Aunt Peaches began preparing for Thanksgiving supper. Mama had purchased a fresh twenty-five-pound turkey, which was brining on the back porch. It would go in the oven late tonight on a low heat to cook overnight. They prepped, chopped, and baked as much as they could before tomorrow morning. Supper would be served early, around 2:00 p.m. They would be up again tomorrow morning at the crack of dawn to finish cooking. Meanwhile, Uncle Thadd and Uncle Luther played checkers on the front porch for several hours. Bruce went with Daddy to help with some farm chores, including caring for the alpacas. Bucket never came up for air from the basement. Who knew when he would come forth? I cleaned the rest of the house by tidying up, changing chair and couch coverings, bringing in and arranging fresh flowers from Mama's flowerbeds, and setting out various candle groupings. Around 3:00 p.m., the menfolk brought the tables from the pavilion into the den for set up. To my surprise, Bucket was in the midst without any prompting from Mama or Daddy.

The tables were handcrafted and made from heavy hard woods. They were unique in design in that struts and cross braces were held in place with removable wooden pegs. It took, at a minimum, three men to assemble one table; two to hold the actual tabletop, while one was underneath assembling the braces and struts. Uncle Thadd was head ramrod with Mama's placement diagram. Daddy and Uncle Luther held the tabletops, while Bruce and Bucket managed the braces and struts. Everything went smoothly until they were assembling the last table. It was placed where the lighting was dim, so Bucket was having difficulty getting the brace holes aligned for the pegs to be inserted.

By this time, Uncle Luther was setting the chairs around the other tables. Daddy and Bruce were holding the last tabletop while Bucket was underneath.

"What's taking so long, son?" Daddy asked.

"I can't find the hole," Bucket answered.

"I bet if you put some hair around the hole, that boy could find it," Uncle Thadd murmured.

"Uncle Thadd, be nice," Bruce chided. "He *is* working."

"I reckon we ought to be thankful for small miracles," mumbled Uncle Thadd.

"Got it!" Bucket said, triumphantly. "We're done!"

Crawling out from underneath, Bruce slapped Bucket on his back and praised him for his efforts. Daddy in turn thanked him profusely for his work. Uncle Thadd just sucked what teeth he had left. Bucket beamed in a way I never noticed before. Could it be, all he needed was more praise to make him step up to his responsibilities? I had to admit to myself, the only thing Bucket heard from me was criticism. Perhaps, I should try sugar instead of vinegar. It was a thought certainly worth investigating.

"Hey! Anybody home?" We all spun around at the greeting to see Tony standing at the threshold of the den.

"Tony!" Bucket shouted and flew into his outstretched arms.

"Hey, baby brother," Tony said as he kissed him on both cheeks and hugged him.

"Hey, son!" Daddy shouted as he went to embrace his eldest child. "Jewel, come out here."

"Thank you, Jesus," Mama squealed. She literally pushed Daddy out of the way as she clung to her child weeping and continuously thanking the Lord.

Tony had to actually peal Mama from his neck before he said, "Hey, everybody, I want to introduce you all to my partner, James MacLeod."

"Hey, James," we all said in unison, smiling, and waving in greeting.

"Where are my manners?" Mama asked, wiping her tears of joy on her apron. "James, welcome to our home," she said before giving him her Mama Bear hug, which startled him somewhat. Grinning, he tightly returned the embrace.

One by one, we all physically greeted Tony and James, making sure to introduce ourselves and mention to James how we were related to Tony. Since the weather was mild, Mama suggested we all sit on the porch to get acquainted. Our porch was regal by any standard, and it wrapped around three-quarters of the house. Mama and Daddy had rebuilt the porch seven years ago with the intent of creating plenty of play space for Chester's brood. It was fifteen feet wide and built with fine cypress wood, which was weathering to a lovely silver. Mama always said no self-respecting house would ever be without a porch or a swing. As our home had always been referred to as "The Manor", Mama made sure the porch reflected the title. She had strategically made several sitting areas with either wicker or cane-backed chairs and tables. Each grouping had lush green potted plants tastefully arranged, and every table had fresh cut seasonal flowers in a vase. Spaced in between these groupings were pairs of identical rocking chairs with a game table in between or loveseat rockers like those one could purchase at a Cracker Barrel restaurant. Three feet from the front door on either side were spring load-bearing porch swings. I could tell which one Mama used most because of all the ruffled pillows on it. I believe Mama outfitted the porch in this way so she could host intimate affairs, yet keep folk outside her house except for bathroom runs. Mama was perplexing and contradictory in many ways. She would never close her door of hospitality, but there were "toxic personalities", as she called them, that she simply would not allow in her home. Serving those particular persons, she would always break out her best china, stemware, flatware, and linens. She was not going to let it be said she wasn't the consummate hostess, even if she didn't like you. Mama was committed to killing you with kindness.

We had congregated around one major sitting area when Mama brought out a tray of snacks, followed by Aunt Peaches who had a tray with two pitchers of sweet tea and glasses. After everyone had been served, we settled in to give James the third-degree.

"James," Mama started.

"Please, mum, call me Jimmy," James interrupted.

"All right then," Mama said smiling, "Jimmy, tell us a bit about yo'-self. It's so rare that Tony comes home to visit, let alone brings a business partner with him. Is that a Scottish brogue I hear?"

"Yes, mum, it is," James replied. "I'm originally from Edinburgh, Scotland, born and raised. I recently emigrated to the U.S. some six years now. I had only meant to visit a while, but the longer I stayed, the more enamored I became with your country and its culture. I'm now considering applying for citizenship."

"Are you married, Jimmy?" asked Aunt Peaches.

"Oh, no, I'm an old bachelor at heart, but I have met someone who is making me much keener on the thought of citizenship," he said, turning to Tony and giving a conspiratorial wink.

"How did you and Tony become partners, if I may ask?" said Mama.

"Well, Mama, Jimmy made me an offer I simply could not refuse," Tony said, grinning, which made Jimmy chuckle as well. "As you know, my law firm handles a wide range of clients and Jimmy is one of them. He has mad entrepreneurial skills. One day, we were talking over cocktails, when he told me about a venture he was entering that was looking for more ground floor capital investors. He sent me the company's prospectus and business plan, which looked incredibly secure, so I came on board as a financial partner. The business took off. I've re-cooped my entire initial investment, and now I'm reaping a shareholder's profit."

"Son, that's great," Daddy marveled. "What's the business?"

"It's a distillery in Scotland," Jimmy answered.

"What?" Mama said, looking at Tony with raised eyebrow.

"No, Mama, I'm not in the liquor business, but I am in the alcohol business," Tony informed.

"Son, you gonna have to help me understand the difference," Mama said with her church lady tone of voice.

"Mama, there is a market for pharmaceutical grade grain alcohol, not only in Europe, but in the States as well. My investments go toward that end, providing hospitals and various institutions of higher learning with quality alcohol for experiments and the cleaning of instruments," Tony explained.

"So, you're not in league with the Devil, leading folk astray with strong drink?" Aunt Cherry queried.

"No, ma'am," Tony laughed. "My intensions are nothing along those lines. But, you do realize that if they wanted to, people could drink the grain alcohol anyway, right? I've got nothing to do with the choices people make, good or bad."

"I know, son. I just don't want to see you sued for wrongful death or something like that," Mama fretted.

"Don't worry, Mama. I'm totally indemnified," Tony said.

"So, Jimmy, is this your first time in the South?" Aunt Peaches asked.

"Yes, mum, and I must say that I am totally fascinated by your culture. I virtually begged Tony to let me accompany him home, and thankfully, he acquiesced," James said, looking a little too adoringly at Tony. "I've heard so much about Southern ways, and especially Southern cooking, I had to have a first-hand experience. I am so looking forward to the feast tomorrow, and solemnly promise not to make myself a pig at your table."

"Son, you gon' have to work hard and long to earn pig status at this table," said Uncle Thadd. "Luther here, can eat any man under the table without unhitchin' his belt a single notch. I swear, he been walking on hollow legs since I've known him."

Everyone burst into laughter at Uncle Thadd's words. Even Uncle Luther had to flash his doggie dentures at that remark.

"Competition's gon' be tough this year, Thaddeus," Uncle Luther quipped.

"Man, what you talkin' 'bout?" asked Uncle Thadd.

"Chester's twin boys. Man, you know them little rascals can eat. Chester *had* to be a farmer just to feed that brood," laughed Uncle Luther.

"Now, don't you go talking about my grandbabies, Luther," Mama playfully warned. "If I remember correctly, Peter made an entire cow disappear one weekend."

"Uh-uh, don't you start lying on my boy," cackled Aunt Peaches. "Y'all know he had hormonal issues back then."

"Gonad issues was mo' like it," guffawed Uncle Thadd. "Luther, didn't that boy keep you in the grocery po' house one year?"

"All y'all need to stop," snickered Daddy. "You know the Word tells us that chi'ren are an inheritance from the Lawd. Imagine how po' we'd be if we didn't have our chi'ren?"

"Imagine how rich we'd be if we didn't have our chi'ren?" hooted Uncle Luther.

James sat transfixed listening to the humorous banter, watching our smiling faces. He was intently examining us like some graduate anthropology student in the midst of field study. He was content to remain on the sidelines observing, but I recognized that look of hunger on his face. It was a look I knew all too well, the thirst for knowledge – an insider's view of knowledge. I was beginning to like James, and made up my mind to learn as much as I could about him before this weekend was over.

Jimmy, as he wanted to be called, was ruggedly handsome. He didn't have the face of a pretty boy or celebrity, more the face of someone who had seen the end of a fist a time or two, and proudly wore the scars as a badge of honor. Jimmy had a thick muscular build, and I could easily envision him in his tartans at the Highland games. He had strawberry blonde hair and a well-trimmed Van Dyke that was more red than blonde. His hair was slightly wavy and stylishly cut to reach the collar of his shirt. His complexion was clear, but he had a few scars that were the result of either the chicken pox or severe acne. His countenance was one of kindness, openness and approachability with a sparkling set of hazel eyes. It was evident he "manscaped" because his eyebrows were too even, a little too precise. There was a rustic element about him, thinly veiled below the surface of his refined sophistication. Jimmy's dress was conservative, but stylish and as I looked from him to Tony, it became clear to me they shared the same retailer, and that meant Brooks Brothers. Tony was a devotee to the brand. Jimmy smelled of self-made money and a lot of it. I surmised he wasn't tightfisted, but he wasn't a spend-thrift either. If he was truly my brother's life partner, he was going to have to demonstrate some aspect of fiscal conservancy because Tony believed in saving and investing for the future.

"Brett, how about you help me take our bags in?" Tony asked.

"Sure thing, Bruh. Mama's got y'all in my old room."

With friendly banter still rolling, I watched my brothers get the bags out of Tony's car. Even dressed down, Tony looked every bit the corporate lawyer. His car, a midnight blue Audi A6, mocked everyone else's car. It was sleek, luxurious, expensive, and detailed to a mirror shine. The interior was titanium grey leather and so clean, it made one afraid to sit down. It was well-equipped, but not the loaded top-of-the-line model. Tony said he only needed enough amenities to impress potential clients, but he still held on to his blue-collar roots of industry, thrift, and philanthropy. He ordered the color in homage to those ideals. I smiled at him on the outside and inwardly cringed at how *bourgeois* my brother had become.

Tony was no slouch. He was always meticulous in his grooming ever since I could remember. Some went so far as to call him prissy. His looks, from a sister's point of view, seemed average, but his peers in Hertford considered him so fine, all the girls, and a few of the boys, were chasing hard after him before he left for college. Looking at Tony now, with age and time between us, he was striking. The grey began to grace his temples, which accentuated his baby-faced looks. Combine that with his professional and financial success, and he was undeniably attractive.

Tony was scarily intelligent, had rapier wit, and was as precise and accurate in his speech and conversation as a surgeon was with a scalpel. Obviously, in order to be the successful, partnered lawyer he was, it was necessary to be precise. I also understood why he seldom came home to visit. It was hard for him to live "Southern". The speech, mannerisms, small-minded customs, superstitious practices, narrow worldview, family values, religious right bigotry—it was all too much for his sensitive soul. He would never admit it, but he truly was his mother's child. He wasn't a mama's boy; that title belonged to Bucket. However, Tony inherited my mama's generous spirit and giving heart, along with her nose for business and olfactory sensitivities. It was going to be quite humorous watching Tony's nose interact with Chester's brood.

"Well, children, this has been lovely, but yo' mama and I need to get back in that kitchen," said Aunt Peaches.

"So right," said Mama. "Supper is only an hour away, so don't fill up on these snacks."

"I won't," chimed Uncle Luther, to which the laughter began afresh.

"So," started Daddy, "Jimmy how do you earn yo' keep?"

At this question, Uncle Thadd and Uncle Luther stopped laughing altogether and gave Jimmy their full attention and scrutiny. Tony shook his head grinning and motioned to Bucket to help him carry their bags upstairs.

Bruce mumbled underneath his breath, "Here we go."

If I didn't know any better, I'd say these old men were acting as if Tony was some bride-to-be and Jimmy had to prove his worth.

Bruce lightly tapped my thigh and surreptitiously pointed to the snack tray. I gave him a questioning look, to which he responded with a motion of his head to please leave. I narrowed my eyes and gave him my *no you didn't* look and that's when Mr. Hyde flashed, and lingered.

Bruce mouthed, "Now – please," where only I could see.

I dutifully rose, made my excuses with as beatific a smile as I could generate, and I picked up the snack tray. Before making my exit, I turned to Bruce, gave him my stink eye and whispered, "We will talk."

"Yes, we certainly will," Mr. Hyde responded.

I was so angry I could have spit, but instead I had to eat my anger. It wasn't easy or pleasant to stuff down. It tasted like some lard heavy, undercooked biscuit that was over saturated and dripping with butter. It left a horrid, greasy, film in the mouth that nothing, short of hard liquor, would cut. When we sat down to supper, my flesh got the better of me and I intentionally quoted Ephesians 5:25:

"Husbands, love your wives just as Christ loved the church and gave himself up for her."

Since Mr. Hyde said we were going to talk, I wanted him to know I was preparing for our talk/discussion/fight. I didn't care if the whole house heard what I had to say because it was coming out via both barrels.

Supper, I'm sure, was tasty, but I didn't remember a moment past grace. I was detached, borderline sullen, and withdrawn. I heard Mama ask me to help clear the table, and I obediently complied. After we cleaned up the kitchen, instead of retiring to the den, Bruce took my hand, and asked me to step outside with him. Before I could answer, we were out the door and down the front steps.

"Bruce, what's going on?" I insisted. Bruce effortlessly picked me up fireman style and started walking toward the pavilion. "Bruce! Put me down!"

"Nope."

"Bruce! This is not funny, now put me down," I demanded.

"Nope."

"Arrrrgh! I am *not* playing with you, Mr. Jonson," I yelled.

"I know you're not," he laughed.

Upon reaching the pavilion, which was now lit, Bruce gently lowered me to my feet. I was livid. Before I knew it, I raised my hand to smack him, but he caught it mid-flight—caught it hard and roughly held both my arms in mid-air.

"Don't! Don't ever raise your hand to me in that fashion again," he menacingly hissed. "In my present state of mind, I will hurt you if you hit me," he said in a low, but threatening, voice. "That is something I do not wish to do. No matter how you feel about me right now, especially after this past year, know that I love you. I love you with my life, but there are certain things I cannot—will not—allow. Do you understand me?"

Angry tears coursed down my face. My lips trembled, working feverishly to keep my sobs in check. I glared at Bruce as if my eyes were laser beams that could vaporize.

Still holding my arms as if I were performing an Iron Cross, he whispered, "Say it."

With chest heaving and nostrils flaring, I refused to speak.

"Say it!" he barked.

Capt. Jonson was present, and his command made me blink as well as jump. Holding my wrists tighter, he lowered his face scant inches away from mine and spoke in a low growl, "Say. It."

My dam of silence could hold no longer. "**WHY?**" I burst forth with open cries and sobs.

"Why, what?" he asked as if interrogating me.

"I'm your wife, Bruce, not some child. You humiliated me!" I screamed. "Why would you treat me like that, in front of company, no less?"

"Lettie," he said, while loosening his grip, but continuing to hold my arms, "sometimes you can be so clueless."

"What the hell kind of answer is that?" I spat.

"G.O.L.F. was fixin' to take place," he explained.

"What?" I spewed.

"Do you remember the meaning of G.O.L.F.?"

"What? No. What are you talking about?" I asked, crying.

"G.O.L.F. – gentlemen only, ladies forbidden. Babe, *man* talk was getting ready to happen. They were just too polite to ask you to leave."

"But you weren't," I blurted.

"That's why I'm paid the big bucks – to implement the hard calls."

"You're unemployed," I sarcastically reminded him.

"A mere technicality," he said. "Let me restate. That's why I *used* to be paid the big bucks – to make sure the hard choices got done."

"You're hurting me," I whimpered.

Slowly, Bruce lowered my arms only to securely pin them behind me.

"Why are you doing this?" I hissed.

"Doing what?" he asked as he backed me up against a supporting pillar of the pavilion.

"Bruce," I whispered, searching Mr. Hyde's eyes.

"Woman, do you know how alluring you look at this moment? If I could, I'd take you right here, right now."

"Stop it. Now you're just making fun of me," I said. "I'm sure I look a snotty mess," I said as I tried to lower my face.

"Yes, but you're *my* snotty mess," he said, gently kissed my tears away.

Gradually, he released my arms and gathered me to him in a crushing embrace. Continuously kissing me, his tongue sought mine and sweetly found it. Whatever anger or resolve I had, melted.

Damn his ways.

7

Thanksgiving (Part Two)

Thanksgiving Day rose bright, shiny, and filled with great expectations. The turkey slowly cooked all night, and the aroma of poultry seasonings, with a good jigger of white wine, filled the house.

We siblings were up, dressed, and ready for coffee by 8:00 a.m. Once fueled, we prepared to man our respective battle stations. Bucket pulled out all his age appropriate video games, I gathered reading books, the coloring books and crayons Mama had set out, and various board games, strategically placing them where I could quickly put my hands on them. The rest of the menfolk congregated around the widescreen TV to watch the first of many football games. Jimmy quickly lost interest and stepped out onto the porch. I decided to follow so I could get to know him better.

"Good morning, Jimmy," I said.

"Morning, lass," he said.

"It's Lettie." I smiled.

"I meant no disrespect."

"None taken," I assured him. "There are a lot of us, and I know how it is keeping names straight."

"True," he admitted.

"Get ready because your name recall is going to be sorely tested once Chester and his family arrive," I warned.

"When do they get here?"

"Probably in about four hours. As you can imagine, it takes quite a bit of organizing to get nine people cleaned up, dressed, fed, and loaded into a vehicle, especially when one is great with child. Did you sleep well last night?"

"Yes, indeed. Your family home is most comfortable and welcoming. I am truly glad I came," he smiled.

"I can tell you've got a lot of questions about the south and Southern living. Anything I can help you understand?" I offered.

"Right now, I'm content to observe. I will say this – I do so admire how comfortable everyone is. No prissy, snooty, stuck-up ways about you folk. You're down to Earth, natural—real. I appreciate that. In my line of work, I tend to be surrounded by brown-nosing, ass-wiping, suck-ups. Forgive me, lass, I meant no offense with my language," Jimmy said, holding his hands up apologetically.

"Again, no offense taken," I smiled. "What line of work are you in, if I may ask?"

"At present, I'm trying my hand at being a head hunter."

"And, how's it going?"

"Smashing success, if I do say," he grinned.

"I get the sense of what you don't like about your job, so can you tell me what you *do* like?"

"I am greatly gratified when I can match up the right person with the right job. On occasion, it tickles me to no end to be able to do a favor for a friend, and it turns into a win-win situation all around. Those are the times it makes gettin' up in the morning truly worthwhile."

"Is there anything special you're looking forward to in regards to the menu today?"

"No, but Tony waxes eloquent when he talks about your mum's cooking. My mouth is already wat'ring in anticipation," he chortled.

"Be prepared to pass out from a food induced coma. Between Mama and Aunt Peaches, your digestive tract is at their mercy."

"Is it true what was said about your Uncle Luther?"

"Oh, my brother, you haven't seen anybody eat till you've seen Uncle Luther in action. I wouldn't wait too long to reach for seconds, were I you. Make sure you put a little bit of everything on your plate, so you can at least say you tasted it. There may be none of what you liked left after the first go 'round."

"Smashing!" Jimmy said, gleefully.

"Would you like to take a walk with me to the pavilion?"

"I'd love to."

Walking to the pavilion, I pointed in the direction of things that might be interesting to Jimmy like the "patch of garden," the road leading to the barn, and further, the alpacas. Reaching the pavilion, I explained this was where the family held summer barbeques.

"Jimmy, how long have you and Tony been a couple?" I asked.

"Told you, did he?" Jimmy asked, somewhat taken aback.

"I've known my brother was gay since high school. It makes no difference to me. He's my big brother, and I'll love him to the end of time. What *is* important to me is the man who may potentially be his spouse. That, I care a great deal about."

"I can respect that," Jimmy said.

"Tony hasn't been home for a major holiday in almost a decade. I can only deduce he plans on coming out to my parents. Is that his plan?"

"He has considered it," Jimmy confessed.

"I won't lie to you, I do not know how my parents will take the news, but know this: Bruce and I support you both."

"Thank you, Lettie. I sincerely appreciate that."

"You also need to be aware that this is hostile territory. Folks around here are not progressive thinkers by any stretch of the imagination."

"Yes, I'm aware, but my curiosity won out over my common sense. What you've told me, I'm sure, is the reason Tony wants to leave early tomorrow. I wish I could convince him to stay a wee bit longer."

"Hold on to your knickers, honey. You haven't met the rest of the family yet. You may wind up in the car, honking for Tony to hurry up come Friday morning," I laughed. "I guarantee this will be a Thanksgiving you won't soon forget."

As Jimmy and I were making our way back to the house, Willa, Bucket's girlfriend, drove up. She got out of her car as we stepped up to the porch. Bucket must have been running on ESP because he shot out of the door like a rambunctious schoolboy.

"Hey, Willa, you're here," he stammered.

"Hey, Brett," she coyly replied.

"Willa, this is Jimmy, my brother Tony's partner," he said, directing her attention toward us, "and my sister, Lettie."

Miss Willa was a mahogany vision of Southern beauty. She was as tall as Bucket, about five feet, ten inches, with a voluptuous pear-shaped figure. She wore a French navy blue belted shirt-waist dress, which she rocked, a three-row graduated pearl necklace with matching drop earrings, and three-inch patent leather pumps. Her make-up was understated, flawless, and her complexion was smooth perfection in sunlight. Willa had an inviting smile in spite of her braces. She wore her hair in a closely cropped Afro that was fiercely lined in a subtle half-moon in the back. Her perfume was a single note—Bulgarian lavender, which spoke volumes to me about her tasteful simplicity. I couldn't posit if she was trying to impress us or not. Either way, she was stunning. I really wanted to like Miss Willa, but I just couldn't understand what attracted her to Bucket.

"Hello, Willa," I genuinely greeted.

"Charmed to make your acquaintance," Jimmy said as he kissed her hand.

Willa gushed.

"Willa just started nursing school," Bucket boasted. Taking her hand in both of his, he held it to his chest and mooned over her.

Willa did her best to look demure and bashful.

"Let me take you inside and introduce you to everyone else," Bucket said, breaking the spell.

"It's nice to meet you both," Willa said before parting.

Jimmy and I resumed our seats on the porch and began a fresh conversation.

"Ah, young love," Jimmy replied.

"Yeah," I said, dryly. "I think I just threw up in my mouth," I murmured.

"Why, Lettie, I would have pegged you as a romantic. You don't seem too happy about their relationship."

"So far, I haven't seen much in the way of intelligence from Willa. Granted, we just met, so time will tell. I don't know what she sees in Bucket."

"Bucket?"

"Brett. Bucket's his nickname," I said, and then explained the history of his name.

"I see," said Jimmy. "Lettie, may I ask you a question?"

"Certainly."

"When was the last time you sat down and had a real honest conversation with Brett?"

"Well…eh…er…"

"I thought as much," Jimmy said with his head cocked to the side. "You're judging him as the boy you remember, and not the man he's become," Jimmy charged.

"Bucket is no man," I countered. "He's a spoiled, snot-nosed, brat."

"And if I asked Brett what he thought about you, what do you believe his response would be?" Jimmy queried.

"I suppose, he'd say I was an evil, hateful, vindictive, bitch."

"And are you?"

"No."

"I've spoken at length with your brother, and let me tell you, there is depth to that young man. He's a dreamer with some great ideas. It's only a matter of time before those ideas come to fruition."

"Are we talking about the same person?" I asked with a hint of incredulity.

"Indeed, we are. May I speak frankly?"

"Of course, I wouldn't have it any other way," I said.

"I suggest you reacquaint yourself with your baby brother and see him through Willa's eyes, for clearly she sees the man, not the boy. And while you're at it, give Willa a fair shake, too."

Jimmy excused himself and went back into the house where the men were celebrating an apparent touchdown. Left with my thoughts, I had to admit I had just been shamed. Jimmy effectively held a mirror to my face, and I didn't like what I saw. It was surprising and audacious how a stranger could feel so free to speak to me in such a candid way, yet, more to the point, how said stranger could so effectively jar me. Bucket had shown several sides of himself this visit I'd never noticed—NO—chose *not* to notice before. This was unsettling because I had always considered myself generous in spirit. I had to own up to my own hypocrisy. I was not generous with my family. All this time, I bristled over my brother's unwillingness to grow up, and now I was faced with my own need to mature, as well as forgive. This visit was proving pivotal in my life. I was going to have to deal with many demons before heading back home. And I would have to bury all my hatchets with Bucket.

At 11:00 a.m., Chester and family arrived at the house. Those of us called into service manned our stations. Cursory introductions were made as the children scattered like roaches. After greeting Mama with kisses-a-million, the twins bolted down to the basement where Bucket and Willa awaited. Suzie, waddled straight for Uncle Thadd. Gurgling, with pacifier in mouth, she raised her arms to Uncle Thadd and grunted.

"Is that my Boodlum?" he cooed. "Come see yo' uncle," he said tenderly picking her up.

She immediately cuddled in the crook of his neck, wrapping pudgy arms as far as she could. Uncle Thadd was back, maybe not rough-housing, but he, nonetheless, was back. He loved him some Suzie, and she loved her some Uncle Thadd.

Mama, true to her word, latched on to Thomas and got him started with coloring books. Willy went to the farthest corner of the porch for a quiet place to read. Carolyn decided Chester's lap was where she wanted to be for the time being. Janine, who was blossoming into a lovely young lady, had come out of her shyness and engaged Jimmy right away in a game of chess on the porch. I had no charges to herd, so I had an opportunity to visit with Clarissa.

My sister-in-law was seated on Mama's swing with all the pillows propped around her and a few behind her back. She was far too thin and appeared sallow, almost grey. Clearly, there was more than fatigue plaguing her. She sat with her arms cradling her belly, laboring with every breath.

"Hey, Clarissa," I spoke.

"Hey, Lettie," she replied with a wan smile.

"Sister, you don't look well at all. Why didn't you stay home in bed?" I asked.

"I couldn't miss this, not for the world. I ain't seen Tony or Bruce in so long. I had to come," she said, weakly.

"Sweetie, can I get you anything?"

"If you don't mind, a glass of water and one of yo' mama's old quilts would be nice."

Straight away, I fetched the water, the quilt, and Mama.

"Daughter, how you doing this morning?" Mama asked, looking closely at Clarissa.

"Hey, Mama Jewel. I'm a little tired this morning."

"And how's my grandbaby?"

"Oh, he's ornery today," Clarissa said, trying to laugh, but not being successful. "He's been rolling all night into this morning. I think he cain't wait to eat," she said, trying to smile.

"Well, he's come to the right table. Looks like we'll be sittin' down before 2:00 p.m., but until then, I want you to rest yo'self and take a short nap, hear?"

"Yes'm."

I helped to lift the glass of water to Clarissa's lips so she could drink, then wrapped her in the quilt. Mama and I exchanged frightened looks before she quietly asked me to sit with Clarissa for a while. Within ten minutes she was soundly asleep, and her breathing had eased. At 12:30 p.m., Mama tipped out on the porch, and asked me to come help set the table.

"Don't worry," she said, seeing me looking at Clarissa, "we gon' wake her in about fifteen minutes anyway. She'll be alright."

Taking a quick head count to see where the children were, I went inside. Mama recruited Miss Willa to help as well, and she started setting the table. I put food on the table as it was handed to me. Mama and Aunt Peaches were steady ladling, spooning, or plating food stuffs. Out of the blue, Willa gave a high-pitched scream, which drew all the football watchers running into the den. There, Willa stood, legs splayed, precariously balancing plates and flatware with a look of shock and horror on her face. Nestled underneath her skirt, was Thomas.

"Mama, it's dark under here," Thomas pronounced.

Chester rushed to Willa's rescue. "Boy! What is you doing? Come out from underneath her skirt," he commanded. "I'm awfully sorry, Miss Willa. He don't mean no harm. The chi'ren play in a tent the color of yo' dress, and I guess Thomas thought he could play underneath you. Please forgive my boy."

As Chester made his explanations and apologies about Thomas, Bruce had relieved Willa of her plates and flatware, and Bucket was already at her side holding her hand to steady her. We all held our breath waiting for Willa's response. One hand covered her mouth, her head was bowed, and her shoulders began the tell-tale bounce of impending tears. To our surprise, she flung her head back and released a juicy, full-throated, belly laugh.

"I must say," she admitted, after collecting herself, "I've had men roll up on me, but this is the first time I've had a little man roll up under me."

"I can be a little man," Bucket said, to which, we all rolled our eyes and groaned. Bruce just shook his head, but Tony picked up the fumble.

"Bruh! We have *got* to work on your game because that," he gestured toward Willa, "was weak."

"Amen!" agreed Uncle Luther.

"Everybody thinks that baby is afflicted when we really need to be looking at Brett," Daddy added, sucking his teeth.

"Need some hair with that, boy?" Uncle Thadd shouted from the other room.

"Uncle Thadd please stop!" Bruce shouted back. "Willa, please don't judge us too harshly," he said, turning back in her direction.

"Judge y'all harshly?" Willa asked. "I like you people, especially this one," she said, staring dead into Bucket's embarrassed and burning face. "I can already tell, life in this family's an adventure," she said, as she resumed setting the table.

As Bruce walked back toward the TV room, he stopped long enough to stroke my cheek. "Round one," I whispered, "bagged and tagged."

Finally, the table was fully laden and the entire family was gathered around.

As patriarch, Daddy spoke, "Family, y'all know our normal custom is to stand, holding hands 'round the table, and each one share one impo'tant thing they are thankful for. This year, we gon' express our thanks at dessert 'cause by the time we get to everyone, our supper will be cold. So, in honor of hot food, let's pray."

"Holy and gracious God, Master of the Universe, we come saying, thank ya. Thank ya fo' my brothers, sister, chi'ren, grandchi'ren, and friends gathered here this day. Bless this food to our nourishment, and keep us from the sin of gluttony. Bless the hands that have prepared and served, in Jesus' name we pray, amen. Come on y'all, let's eat."

Thanksgiving supper was mind-blowing. The sundry dishes with their many complexities, and the wide spectrum of spice combinations were a pleasurable and satisfying assault on the taste buds. Say what you will about French cuisine, I will take my mama's cooking any day of the year. One can always tell how good the meal is by the silence in the room, and our den was mighty quiet.

Uncle Luther was a true railroad man and it showed in how he ate. He came out of the yard slow by tasting the green bean casserole, broccoli and bacon salad, and the Ambrosia. He picked up steam as he rounded the collard greens, baked macaroni and cheese, sausage stuffing and giblet gravy. He hit the plateau on the turkey, cranberry sauce, and Parker House rolls. Then he started to climb the uphill grade with the candied yams, pork roast, and butter beans. Coming down the grade he built up more steam with the shrimp and crab gumbo and the rice pilaf. He finally headed into the station on the cracklin' bread, glazed carrots, and the corn pudding.

"Lawd, lawd, ladies, y'all have outdone yo'selves. I cain't eat another bite, lest I offend and sin against my maker," proclaimed Uncle Luther.

"I always knowed there was a God," Uncle Thadd said, looking up at the ceiling. "I knowed it, 'cause he revealed himself unto me," he shouted, lifting up holy hands. "Today is the first day I've ever seen Luther full. Praise his holy name!" Uncle Thadd went on clapping his hands.

Laughter rebounded around the table and, as expected, Uncle Luther flashed his doggie dentures. Looking over at Jimmy, I saw his head back and mouth agape. Mama beat me to the punch.

"Jimmy, are you all right?" Mama asked.

"Madame, I fear I am about to die, for such gastronomical delights of this magnitude have never passed my lips before this day. And, you say there is yet more?"

Mama and Aunt Peaches swelled up and puffed their chests out like a Frigate bird. They knew they would be going to bed walking on stumps this night because they had surrendered all their feet in the cooking of this meal.

"I have to agree with Jimmy," Bruce said. "I'm ready to sell my clothes 'cause glory cannot be better than this. You didn't lie, Mama Jewel. Do you have any fingernails left?"

"Nope," she grinned.

"Toenails either," chimed in Aunt Peaches.

"Mrs. Stanton, Mrs. Jones, I've never tasted food like this," said Willa with amazement. "And I thought my mama could cook. But I won't say nothing to her if you don't," she laughed.

"Sweetness, Peaches, y'all sho' throwed yo' foots up in this," Daddy complimented.

"Mama, I think I'm going to have to come back home more often," Tony volunteered.

"Lawd, child, if I had known this was all it took to bring you back, you'd have been home long ago," Mama said, beaming proudly.

Everyone, including the crumb-snatchers, complimented Mama and Aunt Peaches on the fine meal. After supper, Willa, Aunt Peaches, and I cleared the table while Mama herded the smaller grandchildren down to the basement for naps. Willy and Janine were allowed to erstwhile occupy themselves. Almost everyone else went to their respective bedrooms to collapse into a tryptophan and carbohydrate induced coma. Chester sank into an easy chair in front of the TV and Clarissa was made comfortable on the sofa. Bucket waited patiently on the front porch for Willa.

I washed dishes while Willa dried, and Aunt Peaches put away. We weren't putting food in the fridge just yet because we knew folk would be coming out of their stupors for seconds in a matter of hours. Our task was to get the dishes and flatware cleaned and ready for the next assault. Once completed, I slipped off to our room and slid in the bed next to Bruce. I had to giggle at the site of him. His pants were on, but they were unbuttoned, unzipped, and half-way off. It looked as if he was in the middle of removing his pants when he simply passed out on the bed. Confident he was breathing, I too, laid down to rest. The house was quiet, the only sound to intrude was the whirr of the refrigerator. Sleep swaddled me instantly.

It was dark by the time everyone rose from their naps. The women began setting all the desserts on the table, along with the appropriate place settings. This was a much easier task than before, and took no time at all to complete. There was the traditional pumpkin pie, the mandatory sweet potato pie, pecan pie, 7-Up cake, jelly cake, Mississippi Mud, peach cobbler, pineapple upside-down cake, the standby six-layered yellow cake with chocolate frosting, three flavors of Jell-O, and two cans of whipped cream, just in case anyone wanted their dessert garnished.

"All right, everybody!" Mama shouted. "Let's gather to say thanks. Choose wisely, children, 'cause y'all can only have one helping of dessert."

"Awwwww," the twins lamented in concert.

"You chi'ren heard yo' grandma," Daddy said. "Come on everyone, gather 'round and hold hands."

As was our custom, we all stood around the table in order of age, except for Clarissa, we insisted she sit.

"I'll start," Daddy said. "I'm mighty thankful that this year was a bumper crop, and I got all my chi'ren home with me."

"I'm thankful to be livin' and surrounded by all my nieces and nephews," said Uncle Thadd.

"I'm thankful for my family and a decent pension," expressed Uncle Luther.

Thanksgiving went on in this vein, including Aunt Peaches and Mama until it was Tony's turn to speak.

"Mom, Dad, thank you for everything you've done for me. I'm thankful for a successful career, and most of all, I'm thankful for finding the love of my life, the one who has agreed to share his life with me." Holding Jimmy's hand over his heart and turning to face him, Tony said, "I'm thankful for you, James."

S – I – L – E – N – C – E.

Tony and Jimmy locked misty eyes with each other, ignoring the stunned assembly.

"What did he say?" whispered Aunt Peaches.

"Said he loved that man," rumbled Uncle Luther.

Bruce squeezed my hand reminding me to breathe. All of us were ogling each other with an unsettling and nervous anticipation.

"Boy!" Uncle Thadd called, getting everyone's attention, "We've known you was queer from the day you could talk. We been taking bets to see how long you was gon' live in the back of that closet," he snickered.

Daddy broke the circle and sighed heavily. I was fearful about what might come next. Daddy bowed his head, as if his heart was heavy and about to break. He slowly walked over to Tony and James. The look on Tony's face said he was prepared to be ostracized and driven out, yet, he held his head high as if to also say this is who I am—take me or leave me. Daddy fell upon Tony's neck and hugged him with all his strength. Tony returned the embrace, but a look of fear and worry crept across his face. A full minute later, Daddy, tearful, pulled away and kissed Tony, square on his forehead.

"My son, I love you for *who*, and not what, you are. Thank you, for trusting yo' mama and me enough with this news. We're proud of you and always have been. We fully support you, and we are so blessed to have another son in the family." Turning to James, Daddy held his arms open, and said, "Jimmy, welcome to our family."

Falling into Daddy's arms, Jimmy broke open and wept unashamedly. Daddy, Jimmy, and Tony, all three stood in a group hug with snot flying. Since the circle had already been broken, I went and brought a box of Kleenex back to the table. Pulling his emotions into check, Jimmy gathered his wits to speak, and haltingly, he did.

"My good people…I cannot express…how thankful I am for this day…and for your love. You have accepted me and made me family, for which I am most grateful."

"Round two," I whispered to Bruce.

Verbal thanks continued apace and then it was Willa's turn to speak. "I have so much to be thankful for, but let me tell y'all how thankful I am to be in your company. The love and understanding y'all have for each other is *amazing*. Can I be adopted?"

"Miss Willa," said Uncle Thadd, "I don't know if you and Brett will ever make it to the altar, but as far as I'm concerned, you in!"

"Amen," seconded Uncle Luther.

Riotous laughter circled the table. Finally, Daddy told the children to shout in unison whatever it was they were thankful for so our ritual could conclude. We took our seats and allowed the children to pass their plates first. With everyone served their choice of dessert, we settled in for another round of lip-smacking.

Excusing herself from the table, Clarissa rose to use the bathroom. Just as she reached the linoleum portion of the floor, she clutched her belly with one hand, steadied herself on the hallway wall with the other hand, and groaned loudly. A great splash hit the floor, only it wasn't water—it was blood. She was hemorrhaging, badly. Bruce catapulted to her side and caught her just as she passed out.

"Chester, bring yo' car around," Capt. Jonson ordered.

Chester flew out the door. Mama ran for bath towels. Willa was instantly on her phone.

"Buddy, it's Willa. We need your help. Need an escort to the E.R. No time for EMTs. We're in route now. Yes, I'm at 'The Manor'."

Mama packed the towels between Clarissa's legs while still in Bruce's arms. Her color was quickly draining, and her breathing had become shallow.

"Let's go!" Willa snapped. "We can make it to the hospital in seven minutes if we move now. Brett, take my car and meet us there," she said all business, throwing him her keys.

"The hospital's fifteen miles away," Bruce said, carrying Clarissa down the porch steps.

"I know, but my brother is a deputy sheriff who's on duty today. He can clear the road by giving us an escort. Let's move! Her life is in danger," Willa said, opening Chester's van doors.

"I'll drive," said Bruce. "Chester, be with yo' woman.

"Chester, don't worry about the children, I got 'em. Y'all just go, quickly!" Mama shouted.

Willa had barely shut the door before Bruce was peeling out of the driveway. When he hit the main road, the police siren began squealing non-stop as it became a distant echo in the night. Bucket dutifully followed, assumedly, at the posted speed limit.

Coming back inside, Mama was bombarded with questions from the four older children. What happened? Where's Mama? Where's Daddy? What's wrong? When are they coming back? Carolyn started bawling and Suzie—well, Suzie was ripe and in need of a diaper change. Mama calmly told the older kids Clarissa was having their baby brother or sister and Chester would be back later. They were all going to spend the night, and everything would be all right. I took Carolyn in my lap to do my best to calm her fears and dry her tears. Showing her some of the books I set out earlier, I asked her which one she'd like me to read to her. She chose *The Wind in the Willows*.

Aunt Peaches had begun cleaning up the blood while Daddy was on the phone with Clarissa's mother, Bernice. Willy and the twins sat with Uncle Thadd and Uncle Luther watching some action movie on TV. Mama had once again managed to occupy Thomas with coloring books and crayons, and Janine had quietly asked Jimmy to play chess with her again. That left Tony, me, and Carolyn at the table. As I began reading about Mr. Toad and Mr. Badger, Tony's face severely contorted.

"What's wrong?" I asked.

"What is—that stank?" he asked with his nostrils almost turning inside out.

"Oh, Suzie needs a diaper change, that's all," I said.

"Uh-uh, that stank cannot possibly be coming from that baby," he countered.

"Tony, it's a bowel movement, and by the looks of things," as little Madame waddled past us, "it's quite a substantial movement."

"Com'ere, Boodlum," Uncle Thadd called. "Are they talkin' 'bout my ba—oh, Lawd—Jewel! Come get this baby. She's stankin' high."

"Honestly," Mama sighed as she came into the room, "Y'all act like you've never smelled a dirty diaper before. Come here baby, let Granny

—WOOOOOOOO! I see what y'all mean," she said looking, askance at Suzie. "This is calling for some bubble bath and tub action." Lifting her shirt, Mama cried, "Good Lawd, it's crawling up yo' back."

At those words, Tony retched uncontrollably. I just laughed, shook my head and softly said, "Rounds 3 and 4."

At 10:00 p.m. we packed all the children off to bed. Daddy left earlier at 8:30 p.m. headed to the hospital, picking up Bernice along the way. Uncle Thadd, Uncle Luther, Tony, and Jimmy sat watching another action movie on the TV. Mama, Aunt Peaches, and I finished cleaning up the kitchen.

At 11:00 p.m., Willa, Bucket, and Bruce walked through the door. It was clear by the looks on their faces the situation was serious, if not grim.

"How's Clarissa? How's the baby?" Mama asked, clearly worried.

"Why don't we all gather in the den so we can tell everybody at once," suggested Bruce.

"Y'all hungry or thirsty?" asked Aunt Peaches.

"Some sweet tea would be nice, thank you," said Willa. Aunt Peaches brought in a tray with tea and glasses as we gathered.

"Well?" Mama pressed. "I can see by yo' faces something's wrong. What's happened?"

"Since Willa's the most well equipped, I'll let her explain," said Bruce.

"Mrs. Stanton," Willa began.

"Baby, I think it's time you started calling me Mama."

"Yes, ma'am. Mama, Clarissa lost the baby and she's barely holding on."

"I knew this baby wasn't gonna make it. I felt it in my bones," Mama sighed. "What happened?"

"Mama, the Lord truly blessed. If we had gotten there five minutes later, we'd have lost both Clarissa and the baby. As it happened, Clarissa's OB/GYN had just finished delivering another baby, so he had the O.R. waiting when we got there. The baby was dead by the time we arrived. The umbilical cord had wrapped around its neck three or four times. It strangled in utero with such force it ripped the placenta away."

"Clarissa told me the baby had been rolling all last night, right up until we sat down to eat today," Mama said, wringing her hands.

"Unfortunately, that's not all. When they opened her up, the doctor found a large tumor on the baby near the umbilical cord—it was cancerous. Somehow the tumor wasn't feeding off the baby, it was feeding directly from Clarissa."

"That's what was bringing her down so low," Mama mumbled.

"She was bleeding out as fast as they could transfuse her. The doctor felt the only way he could save her was to do a total hysterectomy, ovaries included, since cancer was present. It's not the best news, but she's still living, and has seven healthy children. She was given another four units of blood in recovery with no sign of bleeding, so that's good. Clarissa should be screened for the possibility of cancer in the coming months, but I believe she has a good prognosis. Her recovery will take a little longer, and she'll be weak for a while."

"How's Chester?" Mama asked.

"He's a wreck," said Bruce.

"Mr. Stanton and Clarissa's mama are with him. He won't leave Clarissa's side," said Willa.

"You know, they were hoping for another girl," Mama said. "What was the baby?"

"It was a little girl," Willa affirmed.

"Lawd, Lawd," Mama whispered, shaking her head.

"Miss Willa, you was right take charge this evening. How is that?" Uncle Thadd asked after a slight pause in the conversation.

"As y'all know, I'm in nursing school now, but what you don't know is that I'm studying to become a midwife. All I've ever wanted to do was help bring healthy babies into this world. In my spare time, I volunteer in the maternity ward, as well as the neo-natal ward. Plus, my brothers have all told me, I'm bossy," she said, smiling. "When

Clarissa's water broke, and I saw the blood, I knew she was in trouble. I just instinctually reacted."

"Willa, we're glad you were here," said Tony. "Clarissa wouldn't be alive if it weren't for you." We all voiced our affirmations to those words.

"Boy!" Uncle Luther barked at Bucket. "If you mess up, and lose this here woman, we gon' string you up!"

"Amen!" we all said in unison, giving Bucket looks that varied from impatience to the hairy eyeball. Willa simply laughed, taking Bucket's hand in hers.

"Well, children, short of prayer, there's nothing more we can do this night, so I'm going to bed. Miss Willa, daughter, thank you again for all you've done. And, to ride Thadd's coat-tails, consider yo'self officially adopted into this family," Mama said, walking toward Willa to embrace her.

"Here, here," chirped Jimmy.

"That's what I'm talking 'bout," said Uncle Thadd, slapping high-fives to his nearest neighbors.

"Mama, if it's alright with you, Jimmy and I would like to stay until Sunday," Tony said.

"If it's alright? Of course it's alright! I'm glad to have you home any way I can."

Jimmy and I exchanged broad smiles at the news. Once Mama went to bed, others slowly began to excuse themselves. Willa wanted to get home, so Bucket walked her out to her car. Uncle Luther, Aunt Peaches, Tony and Jimmy all retired for the night, but Uncle Thadd went back to the TV to finish his movie. Bruce and I remained at the table.

"Baby, you look tired. Ready to go to bed?" I asked.

"I'm okay. Can we sit and talk for a bit?"

"Sure," I replied, nodding.

Taking my hand, Bruce paused with eyes tracking back and forth over the table, laboring on how to begin. I could sense he was troubled, but waited silently until he was ready to speak.

"Babe, being with Chester at the hospital today did something to me. I'm having some trouble putting this into words, so bear with me," he said, avoiding eye contact. "I've been in heated battle many times, and I've seen my share of scared men, but I've never seen, or felt, the kind of fear Chester had today. Don't get me wrong," he said, finally looking at me, "he held up—didn't crack at all, but I didn't just feel his fear, I could taste it. It was awful," he whispered. "There he was, lost his child, on the verge of losing his wife…I could only imagine what he must have been thinking. That's when it truly sunk in—what you went through with me," he said, tears springing to his eyes. "Babe, I am so sorry. I have taken your strength—I've taken you—for granted, and I am so very, very sorry," Bruce said in a strangled voice. "I tasted a piece of your hell today, and it unnerved me. I've been so occupied with my own crap, I haven't been caring enough, or considerate of what you're going through. Lettie, please, forgive me."

"I forgive you, Bruce," I softly said.

"I want us to talk, really talk, before we go back home, okay?"

"Okay. How do you want to do this?"

"I want to be completely transparent, so let's make a list and work from it. Whatever we don't get around to, we'll tackle once we get home. Deal?"

"Deal." I immediately found paper and pen and we wrote down our list, prioritizing together. Once we were satisfied, we went to bed and started our rest wrapped in each other's arms.

8
Black Friday and Saturday

Before dawn Friday morning, I was awakened by Mama and Daddy talking in the kitchen. Rather than eavesdropping, I got up. Bruce was already dressed and drinking coffee with them.

"Morning, everyone. What's the news?" I asked, rubbing sleep from my eyes.

"Morning, Baby Girl," Daddy said, handing me a fresh mug of joe.

"Clarissa's turned the corner. She's gonna make it through," Mama said.

"And Chester?"

"I made Chester go home to get some rest. Knowing him, he's only gon' nap before goin' back to the hospital," Daddy said. "Bernice stayed behind to be with Clarissa in case she woke up."

"Willa told us the bulk of the report on Clarissa. Has the doctor said anymore?" I asked.

"No. The fact that she made it through the night with no bleeding is the best sign," Daddy said. "Her color's even come up. We should find out today when the doctor says she'll be able to go home."

"Meanwhile, the children will be staying with us for the weekend," Mama interjected. "Be ready to man your battle stations 'cause my grandbabies can be a handful."

"Mama Jewel, Pops, we'll do what we can, but Lettie and I need to do some serious talking today and tomorrow. I hope you don't mind, but there will be times during the day when we won't be able to break loose to help with the kids," Bruce informed.

Mama and Daddy looked at each other, and then smiled. "That's quite all right, son. You handle yo' business," Daddy said.

"That's right," Mama echoed, steady boring holes into me with her laser beam vision, "handle yo' business."

"If you're of a mind to take a stroll, the northwest pasture was fallow this year and is looking right purdy. There might be a few gopher or groundhog holes, so be careful and mind where you step," Daddy said. "Y'all feel free to take the Gator."

"Thanks, Pops. I appreciate that," said Bruce.

"Sweetness, I'm going to lay it down for a while," Daddy announced.

"Be forewarned, Suzie is in our bed. Don't worry, she's double bagged so there should be no cause for alarm. But she may try and mess with you once she wakes up. You know how much she loves looking under eyelids when folk are sleeping," Mama said, chuckling.

"If she messes with me, I'll put her out and close the door," Daddy teased.

"Calvin, you wouldn't dare do that baby like that," Mama scolded.

"No, you right, but I will holler for you," Daddy said, walking towards his bedroom.

"Mama, do you need help with critter chores today?" I asked.

"You know, I'll get Tony and Jimmy to help out today. You and Bruce do what you need to do," Mama answered.

Freed from immediate responsibilities, I finished my mug of joe and cleaned up. Having dressed for the outdoors, just in case we decided to take that stroll, I met Bruce back at the kitchen table. It being early, the children were still asleep. Mama had occupied herself somewhere else in the house, so Bruce and I had the kitchen to ourselves. I suspected Mama was in her bedroom listening to every word we said.

"Ready to begin?" I asked.

"Yes. I'll let you start," said Bruce.

"First, I want you to tell me everything about your torture."

"Babe, you don't want to know about…"

"I said *everything*, Bruce Jonson."

Taking a deep breath, Bruce blew it out slowly. With a faraway look, as if he were back in *that place* again, he began. I hated to make him go there, but I needed to understand, and that meant I needed information.

"I've told you most of what they did to me already. They beat me mercilessly. Every time they got ready to beat me, somebody started playing a horn. I don't know what kind of horn it was, all I know is it was loud and obnoxious. I literally became Pavlov's dog. Every time I heard that horn, it put the fear of God into me. Each beating felt worse than the last, and by the end, all they had to do was blow that damned horn and simply touch me and I would scream. They thought it was funny, real funny, and just laughed and laughed at me. If I didn't scream when they poked me, I would get a swift punch to my kidneys until I did. I was hard and tried not to give them any satisfaction. Consequently, I wound up with kidney failure. They enjoyed torturing me. They did more than try to break me, they wanted to totally rob me of my humanity, and they almost succeeded," he said in a low voice.

"Why did they stop? Why did they throw you out at a checkpoint?"

"Who knows? I honestly can't tell you. Neither can anyone else who was over there. This is one of those circumstances that just doesn't make any kind of sense. I'm thankful they did bring me back to the U.S. lines, but…" his voice trailed off.

"You still hate them, don't you?"

Bruce slowly nodded.

"When you're having a nightmare and start screaming, is it always the same scenario? Or does it change?"

"It's usually the same. I'm being hit with that blow torch."

"Did you know you've started to become violent in your dreams?" I asked.

"I suspected as much. Did I ever hurt you?" he asked, searching my face for possible denial.

"You hurt me in a number of ways," I said.

Bruce, head hung in shame, looked up at me with pain and sadness etched across his face. "I have to know. How did I hurt you?" he quietly asked.

"At first, it was simple rejection. Nothing I did or said would comfort you. Then you moved on to being repulsed by my touch. Often, in the middle of the night, you would slap my hands away, shove me, and sneer or spit at me to leave you the hell alone. Finally, it became physical."

Clenching his jaws to where the vein in his temple became prominent, he closed his eyes and flushed tears down his cheeks. "How bad? How many times?" he softly asked.

"How many times? Twice. How bad? Pretty bad. Your last serious attack, you blew up. I knew you weren't yourself, and I believe you weren't even awake. You hit me so hard in my belly, I thought I was going to pass out. You knocked me out of the bed, and I laid on the floor for a long, long time. You went to the shower. When I finally managed to crawl back into the bed, you were still in the shower."

"When?" he asked with remorse.

"Veteran's Day," I answered.

"Did you see your doctor?"

"No. I didn't want it documented in any way. I bruised badly, to the size of a luncheon plate, but you never saw it because you weren't interested in a physical relationship at that time. You were content to just sleep and wake up next to me."

"My God," Bruce breathed. "Sorry seems such an inadequate word, but I am truly so sorry," he said, crying silent tears.

"Bruce, I'm telling you all this not to make you feel bad, but because you said you wanted transparency. Were you serious? Do you want transparency between us?"

"Yes, I do."

"Then, please, stop crying. What's done is done. We can either learn from it or wallow in it. I don't want to wallow. I want to understand, and hopefully, not repeat any of it."

"Okay," Bruce mumbled, sniffling and shaking his head in the affirmative.

"Let's talk about your hate. You told me back in Germany you didn't want to be a hate-filled man. Is that still true?"

"It is, yes."

"What are you doing about it?"

"As part of my PTSD therapy I talk about it with Lloyd and my group. But, I've taken an extra step. I meet with Pastor Wilson on a weekly basis to try to work through it."

"How do you think you're coming along? Do you think you're making progress or are you status quo?"

"Progress is—slow," Bruce admitted. "I don't know how long it's going to take me to work through all this and be able to fully forgive. But I am committed to doing so," he assured.

"That's good to hear."

"I do need to let you know I'm no longer a deacon. Pastor Wilson sat me down once I confided in him about my hatred. He told me until I've worked through it, I need to serve from the pew, and not in an official capacity."

"How do you feel about that?"

"I certainly understand. I've got no malice with Pastor Wilson. He has to shepherd as the Lord leads, and if this is where he leads, I must follow."

"It's hard to follow once you've been in leadership," I said. "You've commanded whole units and platoons. How are you going to deal with being one of the sheep?"

"The only way I can, with God's grace and help."

"Okay." I nodded. "Now, let's talk about your PTSD sessions. You haven't confided one word in me since Germany. May I have the man who bore his soul to me back? Please? I know this is difficult for you, and I am not insensitive to that fact, but I would like the courtesy of being kept in the loop, especially when it comes to treatment options with you."

"I understand, babe, and you have every right to be included."

"Why won't you talk to me about your nightmares? I know you talk with Lloyd, but why won't you trust me enough to talk with me?"

"From this day forward, I will—I promise. I never wanted to burden you with all my shit. I see now, that was a mistake. Lettie, starting today, I want you to be my rock like Mama Jewel is yo' daddy's rock."

"Bruce, don't blow smoke up my ass if you don't mean what you're saying," I retorted with skepticism.

"Babe, I mean this. I do."

"That means no more embarrassment or humiliation on the sly, right? If you want something from me, you'll come straight out and ask. Yes?"

"Yes."

"Since we're near it, let me ask. The other night at the pavilion, you weren't joking about being hit, were you?" I asked.

"No. I was deadly serious."

"How long have you felt that way?"

"Since I regained consciousness in Landstuhl. I cannot explain to you what happens, but if I feel threatened, especially physically, I feel like I'm sliding down the rabbit hole—losing control. That thought scares me. I don't want to lose control because I don't know if I'll be able to stop beating someone once I start. And I never want that someone to be you. If I have an attack and I get physical with you, get the hell out of the room, out of the house if necessary because I will do everything in my power to neutralize a perceived threat. I am trained to *kill*. I will kill in order to neutralize a threat. Babe, do you understand?" he asked, his eyes pleading.

"I do, but we're going to need to have some kind of containment strategy in place. Bruce, I need to be able to protect myself from you if it ever comes to it. What is the safest way of doing that?"

"Taser," Bruce said, after a moment of thought. "That would be the safest means all the way around. I'll take care of that once we get back home, and I'll train you on how to properly use one."

"So, where do we go from here? You asked if I would meet Lloyd. Does he want to do some kind of group therapy session?" I asked.

"I think he's headed in that direction, yes."

"If you think I'm going to air out our laundry, dirty or otherwise, in front of strangers, you need to think again. I will be happy to work with Lloyd, and you, but no one else. Do *you* understand?"

"Yes."

"What next?" I asked.

"Health insurance," Bruce answered.

"What about it? You've got VA benefits, right?"

"Yes, but not for long. I will only have two more years of benefits, and then I'll have to get private insurance."

"But, how can they do that?" I asked, practicing for my Emmy Award. "You've bled and almost died for this country. How can they just take away your hard-earned healthcare?"

"Babe, when I signed my contract with the army, I signed a binding contract that said my government had all rights and privileges to my body, including, the sacrifice of death. They could do with me what they will, and I have no true legal recourse because I volunteered. So, if they choose to terminate my benefits after three years, they can legally do so. How? My injuries were not sustained during a time of war."

"The hell they weren't," I argued.

"Technically, it is called a 'Peace Keeping Action' not war. Congress is the only body that can declare war, and we *technically* haven't been at war since World War II. If my injuries were incurred during a sanctioned, declared time of war, then I would receive lifetime benefits. Babe, it all comes down to money. Our country doesn't have the revenue to adequately care for all of its military personnel in perpetuity. That's the nature of the beast—part and parcel to the recession."

"That's weak. It isn't right or fair," I argued.

"No, it isn't fair, but who told you life was fair? My concern right now is my PTSD may be considered a pre-existing illness should I try to get civilian coverage now."

"Baby, have you forgotten? You're covered under my medical plan already. We decided two years ago to get you covered just in case something like this ever happened. We wanted a safety net. We discussed this. Remember? Besides, military dependent care sucks at best," I said.

"I completely forgot," Bruce said, giving me the look of a light bulb going off.

Just then, Jesse and Jordan came stomping up the stairs from the basement, "Grandma, we're hungry."

Right on their heels came Thomas, "Granny, me too."

"I'm on it," hollered Aunt Peaches as she strolled into the kitchen. "What y'all want to eat this morning?" she asked, smiling.

"Pancakes!" all three yelled.

"Pancakes? How 'bout some pancakes with some of yo' Granny's berry compote on top? Will that work?"

"Yeah!" all three cheered.

"How about you two?" Peaches asked, looking over at me and Bruce.

"Pancakes and compote? Yeah!" Bruce mimicked. Glancing in my direction he asked, "We good for now?"

"We're good. Round one of Détente is completed," I said.

Breakfast was highly appreciated by all. Aunt Peaches not only cooked pancakes with Mama's berry compote, but she also prepared scrambled eggs, crispy bacon, savory link sausage, and home fries with onions. If anyone left the table hungry, it was their own fault. After breakfast, Mama decided to take all the boys, sans Bucket, out to the Alpacas to do critter chores, and I helped Aunt Peaches clean the kitchen. Once done, Bruce and I went out to the pavilion for the second round of Détente.

"Why don't you start this time," I suggested.

"All right, I want to talk about future work and possible relocation."

"Okay, I'm listening."

"Babe, I've got to be honest. Right now, I couldn't hold a job if I wanted to."

"Why not?"

"I get angry too quickly over stupid stuff. I know I will snap if I have to work with undisciplined people, which are most civilians. It's all a part of my PTSD. Lloyd and I are working on building the tools I'll need in order to cope, but it's going to take time."

"Do you have an idea of what you'd like to do?"

"I'm unsure. There are several avenues I could take, but we'll have to see about market availability once I'm ready."

"What do you think you're good at?"

"Killing the enemy," Bruce said, candidly. "Leading men. Teaching them how to efficiently and effectively kill the enemy." Bruce rubbed his head and face, then folded his hands on the table in silence. "Babe, I am a warrior, through and through. I lived and breathed for the army. I was *real good* at killing. But, I can't do that anymore, and I don't know of any legitimate job openings for hired assassin."

"Baby, didn't you start your army career as military police? Have you thought about going back to that, protecting people as opposed to killing them? Maybe you could even teach others how to protect themselves. Think about finding a position as a security supervisor or security consultant. You have skills that somebody needs."

"That may be true, but we need to supplement our income now."

"Well, we have two things in our favor. One: my car is paid for, so we can start banking those payments. Two: I got a raise this fiscal year, so if we tighten our belts a little, we can survive on my income alone. When do you think you'll be getting your disability?"

"Babe, my petition has been denied."

"What?" I screamed, further preparing for my Emmy Award.

"Babe, calm down. This is typical and the normal process. Every claim is initially denied. It's supposed to weed out those who are running a scam from those who are genuinely in need."

"This is crazy *and* unacceptable. I have half a mind to call our congressman about this," I said, indignantly. "If you, of all people, don't have a proof of claim, then no one does."

"Babe, I'm glad you're in my corner, but I'm gonna ask that you please not contact our congressman."

"Give me one good reason why I shouldn't?"

"Here's the only reason: If you contact our congressman to run interference or curry favor for a speedy resolution, the VA will become hostile, and then they will throw delay, after delay, after delay, causing my claim to run at a snail's pace, or even possibly, come to a complete halt. Once you piss off the powers that be at the VA, you may as well kiss your claim good-bye. They will torpedo any chance I have to the depths of the Laurentian Abyss. Trust me on this."

"That's not right," I lamented frankly, no longer play-acting. "This nation needs to be ashamed, completely and totally ashamed, for how it treats our vets."

"You'll get no argument from me, but the deck is heavily stacked against us, and we are powerless to change the system. So, let's talk about what we can do to save money and spend less."

"We can implement a self-imposed austerity plan," I suggested.

"How, exactly, would that work?"

"We shop small, first of all. Spend only on necessities."

"Like?"

"Clothing is one. We purchase only what we need, not want, during the semi-annual department store sales. If we start having withdrawals—okay, if *I* start having withdrawals—then we shop only resale, consignment stores, or Goodwill. I will make do with my current accessories or I can host jewelry parties to earn free stuff. We can also cut back dramatically on tinkering with Brewster."

"Hold on now," Bruce objected.

"Bruce, you wanted to know how we could make this work. There's nothing wrong with Brewster. You just like pimpin' the ride. You need to go on and be honest about it, so we can move along," I mumbled, waiting patiently for him to speak.

"All right," Bruce said, reluctantly. "I can pull back, a bit, on Brewster."

"We cut back on dining out and eat most of our food stores before buying more. We could play *Chopped* or *Top Chef*, like on TV. Take what we have, create a one-of-a-kind meal, and make a competition out of it. Who knows? We might have fun," I offered.

"Yes, to the dining out, but I'm not ready to sign off on the other stuff just yet. You may need to coax me."

"We can also look at joining a CSA, community supported agriculture, where we'd get fresh locally grown fruits and veggies on a weekly basis by which to cook our meals. Or, we could join a co-op where we volunteer so many hours a week, and get a box of groceries at little to no cost. We'd be participating in community service, and that might help you get more acclimated to working within the civilian world."

"All good ideas, but I'm gonna need to chew on these for a while."

"I could always drop you off at a turnpike on-ramp with a sign that says: 'Will Work for Food'," I joked.

"Very funny," Bruce said, dryly. "Next topic."

"I guess that would be relocation. Do you really want to move? And, if so, where?" I asked.

"Babe, when we first bought that house, you knew there was a real possibility we'd be selling it if my transfer required it."

"Yes, I know, but I like my house," I bemoaned, "especially my shower. What if our next house doesn't have a nice, big, walk-in shower? I won't be able to do—things—in a smaller shower," I said, fluttering my eye lashes.

"You so nasty," Bruce said, stone-faced.

"You know you like it," I reminded him as I lightly stroked his hand.

"Yes, I do like it," he admitted, "but I'm trying to be serious here. Babe, our neighborhood is no longer safe. I see small gangs creepin' weekly. It's just a matter of time before we're hit. The fact we have no immediate neighbors, makes it all the more likely. We need to keep our options open."

"Rallo is housesitting for us. Do you think they've busted in on him?" I asked, truly concerned.

"No, he would have called by now if there was any trouble."

"Okay, so we keep our options open. How do we sell? The economy is bad, and the neighborhood is depressed. Would we even be able to get our money out of the house?"

"I wouldn't try to sell the house, at least not yet. We'd rent it out first."

"And where would we get the money for a down payment on a new house?" I asked.

"Yes, well, time for more transparency. I have an *End-of-the-World* account with ten years' worth of income in it."

"What?" I asked, stunned. "Ten years of your income, or mine?"

"Ten years of combined income," Bruce said, sheepishly.

I had to get up and walk around the pavilion with that piece of news while Bruce watched me guardedly. "Let me make sure I understood you. We have ten years' worth of our *combined* income in an account somewhere?" I asked, screwing up my eyes at him.

"Yeah."

"Bruce, how could you keep something like this from me?" I asked, astounded. "How long have you had this account?"

"A little over thirteen years."

"So, when I was borrowing money from friends, and the church, to get to Germany, half out of my mind with fear and worry for you, we had money?" I shouted, gesticulating with my hands.

"Technically, *I* had money. The account is in my name only."

"What if you had died, Bruce?" I yelled, swelling with anger.

"Then, the money would have become yours. It's stipulated in the will Tony drew up for me."

"Tony knew about this money?" I fumed, eyes widening.

"Babe, he *is* our lawyer."

"I...I...I don't believe this!" I said, pacing. "I honestly don't know *who* you are anymore," I railed, tears stinging my eyes. "I need a break—I need a time out."

"Babe, come on..."

"No! Bruce, leave me be. I'll let you know I'm ready to continue when I sit back down at this table," I said, stalking away.

I walked, actually stomped, my way over to the "small patch" and speed-walked its perimeter multiple times while mulling over this last bombshell. I hated being blindsided! I didn't know which hurt more, Bruce punching me, or learning about this *End-of-the-World* account. I was angry again, only this was a tasteless, white-hot anger. Thirteen plus years he'd had this account. That meant he started it not long after he met my family—Tony, to be more precise. Granted, we weren't that serious at the time, but he should have told me once we were married. I tried to rationalize all of this, but every road led to the same destination: mistrust. Bruce did not trust me. I'd rather be gut kicked than believe my husband did not trust me. What should I do? How should we fix this and move on? I was working up a hard sweat coming to terms with this can of worms. I practically jogged the perimeter five more times non-stop before I came to a halt and a decision. There was nothing else to be done. We were going to have to sit down and verbally duke this out.

I must have walked and jogged several miles around the "patch." I was winded, sweaty, tired, and thirsty. Slowly, I made my way back to the pavilion and patiently waited for Bruce to also return. Fifteen minutes elapsed before he came around the corner of the house carrying two huge glasses of sweet tea. I was thankful, but I wasn't going to let him sweet talk his way out of this. Nor was I going to let him mesmerize me with his charm, or seduce me. Not this time.

"Hey, babe, I brought you some tea," Bruce offered with his *come-hither* look and *won't you take your drawers off* smile.

"Thank you." I gulped down his liquid offering.

"Lettie, I just want to tell you…"

"I think you should wait for your attorney before you speak, Mr. Jonson," I said with as much coldness and stiff formality as possible.

Right on cue, Tony came around the corner of the house, pad and pen in hand, striding as if he were walking into a courthouse for an arraignment. Sitting down, he asked, "Have you started yet?"

"We were just beginning," Bruce mumbled. "Lettie, I know you're angry, but—"

"Angry? No, I'm way past angry," I said, holding up one finger in his face. "I've moved on to the 'Land of Hurt', Bruce Jonson."

"All right, let's back this buggy up," Tony said. "Lettie, what, exactly, is your complaint against my client?"

"My *complaint*, is after almost thirteen years of marriage, your *client* doesn't trust me!" I exclaimed. "That's my complaint."

"Lettie, that's not true or fair," Bruce deflected.

"Fair? Who told you life was fair?" I spit back.

"Knock it off! Both of you," Tony ordered.

"No! I will not."

"Lettice!" Tony shouted. "You will shut your mouth, open your ears, and listen," Tony demanded.

"Lettice?" Bruce murmured to Tony.

"Long story, tell you later," Tony whispered in his ear. Turning back to me, he said, "Okay, you're angry, you're hurt, I get it. Now, climb down off that cross and listen to what I have to say. Thirteen years ago, closer to fourteen, when the family first met Bruce, I could tell he was stone serious about you. As your big brother, I wanted to know what kind of man he was, just like when the family recently interrogated Jimmy. When I was fully satisfied he meant business, I discussed setting up an *End-of-the-World* account for him. I explained that under no circumstances was he to talk about it or touch it for at least ten years. His job was to forget about it completely and let me manage it. The initial investment was his, now, both of yours. My contribution was moving monies around to get the maximum return on the investment. The account took a big hit when the market crashed, but we've stayed the course, and it came back two-fold. I'm recommending we further diversify," he said, looking at Bruce, "to insure your money continues to grow and not diminish."

"What do you get out of it?" I snidely asked.

"The joy of seeing my only sister well cared for," Tony snapped back, giving me the look of a shark in chum infested waters. "Bruce did his job well because he truly forgot about the account. I reminded him a few months after he returned home from Afghanistan, and I informed him of the balance in the account. So, you see, it wasn't about him not trusting you, it was all about him being a good soldier, and following orders, *my* orders."

I sat glaring at them, wiping away the tears that wouldn't stop falling, as I processed Tony's explanation of the account.

"Thanks, Bruh, for breaking all that down," Bruce whispered to Tony. "I don't think she would have believed me if I had said all that."

"No problem. I know you said she was upset, but damn!" Tony whispered back.

Bolstering my wounded pride, I spoke. "I don't know what to say, except, I'm sorry, Bruce. I should have allowed you to explain, but with everything else we've been through, this pushed me a little over the edge, which still is no excuse for my behavior. Please, forgive me," I said, mollified.

"Before you two get started making-up, or whatever straight people do, *I* have some questions. Why didn't you come to me, Lettie, when you needed help getting to Germany?"

"I didn't come to you because Bruce is *my* husband, and it was *my* responsibility to come up with the funds," I sputtered.

"I would have given you everything you needed and more. You did not need to borrow from anyone."

"But, I…"

"But nothing! Your pride stood in the way," Tony accused. "Let me say this clearly, to the both of you, so there is no misunderstanding.

We," he gestured between the three of us, "are family. If family cannot come together to aid one another, what good are we? I don't care how big, or small, your need is when you require help. I expect, as your attorney, to be the *first* person you call in the future. Have I made myself clearly understood?" he asked, looking first at Bruce, who blinked and slightly nodded, then to me.

"Tony, I appreciate all you've done, and what you're saying, but I will not call on you unless it's the last resort." Unapologetically, I added, "Just as every man has to stand on a footing of his own, so must I."

"As long as you call," Tony replied, looking at me hard. "Now, as your attorney, is there anything else we need to discuss?"

"No, Bruh, I think we're good," said Bruce.

"No," I said.

"Well, there is one more piece of business I need to conduct. I'd like very much if you two would be in my wedding," Tony said with a broad and happy smile.

"I'd be proud, man," Bruce smiled, slapping Tony's back.

"You know I'm in," I said. "But, you're going to have to pay for my dress because Bruce and I are going on an austerity plan."

"What? Wait, I don't want to know," Tony said, waving a hand in my direction.

"When's the date?" asked Bruce.

"We haven't fully worked out the details. We should have solid information to share after Christmas. How do you all feel about plaid?"

"Which tartan?" I asked.

"Jimmy's family tartan is black, gold, and red, but we've chosen a conservative Blackwatch," Tony answered.

"Love it," Bruce and I both said in union.

"Excellent! Let's go get some lunch and tell Jimmy the good news."

Lunch was vestiges of yesterday; leftover turkey made into turkey salad sandwiches with cranberry dressing, potato chips, and fresh fruit. Bruce and I hurriedly ate, so we could get back to the discussion table. We left Tony, Jimmy, and the children still eating.

Walking out the front door, Bruce proposed we take Daddy's suggestion, and walk a while in the pasture. Rather than wait for Bruce to collect me with the Gator, we went to the shed together. The day was one of those picturesque postcards of late autumn in the South. Many trees retained their leaves, and they were a glorious splash of burnt orange, sienna, rust, red, and brown. As we got closer to the northwest pasture, we came upon a tree break, which was comprised of long, tall, pine trees, their pitch fragrant in the air. Riding through the trees and over the rise, the pasture opened before us. We beheld the bucolic scene of lush vegetation with light green shoots of Bahia grass and patches of white clover. It was too bad Mama and Daddy didn't raise cattle because the pasture was ripe for raising fat bovines. Bruce played the gallant as he took my hand and escorted me out of the Gator. We decided to take a leisurely stroll around the pasture's perimeter.

"I know I began first at the pavilion, but I'd like to speak first again, if it's alright with you," Bruce said.

"By all means," I replied.

"Lettie, I can't give you children."

"How do you know, Bruce?" I asked, maintaining my thespian ambitions.

"Babe, I got tested three months after I came home."

"What did the test say, exactly?"

"The results came back as *void*," he said. "There was absolutely no sperm to count. You know how there's usually millions upon millions of little soldiers swimming around? I had zilch."

"Are they sure this isn't temporary?"

"Yep. Real sure."

"Bruce, why are you broaching the subject of children now?" I asked.

"Babe, I knew the possibilities of you becoming a widow were all too real. I've had to write those letters to widows with families for fallen comrades. I never wanted that scenario for us. If I had kids, I wanted to be around. The only way that could happen was me getting out of the army, which I didn't want to do. I know when we first got married we said we'd take our time, get to know each other well, and then think about a family. But the longer it was just us, the more comfortable I was simply being a couple. Maybe I'm a little selfish and didn't want to share you with anyone else."

"How do you feel now? Do *you* want children?"

"I think all men, at some point in their lives, want a mini me."

"I'm not asking all men. I'm asking you."

"Babe, you're not making this easy."

"Bruce, let me help you. I have never wanted children," I said, bluntly.

Bruce stopped dead in his tracks and stared at me, slack-jawed.

"Don't look at me like that. If you had wanted children, I would have gladly bore them for you. But, if given a choice, I choose none. I wanted a career, first and foremost. My mother was right. I don't have a maternal bone in my body. I consider babies little mucous and puke factories. If we had had any, I'm sure I would have loved them dearly because they were a part of you. But, we haven't, so back to the original question. Do *you* want children now?"

"Well, babe," Bruce hesitated.

"Bruce, are we being transparent here? Or are we just walking in a pasture? I truly *need* for you to communicate with me."

"I guess, my answer would have to be no," he said.

"I don't want a guess, Bruce," I pressed. "I want absolutes. Are you one-hundred percent sure you do not want children?"

"Yes."

"How do you know?" I pushed, harder.

"I know. Being with family this week has solidified my decision. Please don't think ill of me, but being around Chester's brood is tiring. I realized that when I come home, I want to relax, not react to, or diffuse some piece of drama. I like the thought of sleeping through the night, when I'm not having nightmares. The constant riding herd, babe, I don't want to do that. The crying and whining, put that down, don't touch that, leave that alone, stop looking at him, put that back, don't hit her—I'm tired just thinking about it."

"So, we're agreed—*we* are family and we won't let others shame us, cajole us, or otherwise dictate how *we* choose to lead our lives?"

"Yes, most definitely, we are agreed," Bruce said, sealing it with a kiss.

"Good because I'm stopping birth control tomorrow!"

"There is one more request I need to ask of you."

"Oh?"

"I would like to augment our family by one," Bruce said.

"Pray, tell," I said, it now being my turn to freeze in my tracks.

"Babe, I want a dog," he announced, sliding his eyes towards me sideways.

"A dog! What kind of dog?"

"A big, rambunctious, puppy," he said with a wide grin.

"Bruce, a puppy is like having a baby. It may not manufacture snot, but it cries, it pees, it poops, it pukes, and it chews up everything, shoes in particular," I frowned.

"I know, babe, but we could train it not to do those things."

"We? Huh-uh! Your puppy, your responsibility. You know our back yard is too small for a big dog."

"Oh, he'd live in the house," Bruce declared.

"Ix-nay! I will not have some hairy beast, which sheds when you look at it, taking over my house, my couch, or trying to sleep in my bed. No, no way."

"The dog would be crate trained, babe," he explained.

"Bruce Jonson, we have been married nearly thirteen years and this is the first time you've *ever* mentioned wanting a dog. Why now?"

"Well, in truth, it was yo' daddy's idea. He said we could keep burglars and creepers at bay with a big dog in the house. He does have a good point, you know."

"What if we got a small dog?"

"Ooooh, uh-uh! I will drop kick an ankle biter myself. And they won't instill any kind of fear into a would-be intruder."

"Bruce, neither will a puppy," I reasoned.

"Yeah, but a puppy will grow into a big dog in no time. Size intimidates."

My response could only be summed up by the sound, "Uhmh!" That sound is called, a *sister's phoneme*, and it is usually employed when a response is needed or expected. It conveys an air and attitude of disgust or incredulity, without a true verbal commitment. It is usually accompanied by a raised eyebrow, sucked teeth, pursed lips, and/or, possibly, an akimbo stance, complete with hands on hips. A *sister's phoneme* is effective. It relays, with extreme clarity, just how entirely stupid, senseless, selfish, trifling, ill-thought, or crazy a statement was in regards to its utterance.

"I want it as clear as Waterford crystal—this will be *your* dog. I will not be tending to it, getting up with it, walking it, feeding it, bathing it, taking it to the vet, cleaning up its poo, vacuuming up after it, training it, and it sho' nuf better not ever chew on my house, my furniture, my clothing, or any, and I mean any, of my shoes. Agreed?"

"Agreed!" he said with a huge grin.

"Bruce, if you cannot handle stupid, how are you going to deal with a dog's willfulness, disobedience, or stupidity?" I asked, giving him a worried look.

"You let me deal with that."

"Hear me, husband," I said with all seriousness, "the first time you hit or hurt this animal, it's gone. Just because I don't want anything to do with it, doesn't mean I will tolerate cruelty."

"There you go again, frettin' over something that may never happen. Did yo' daddy wrestle Tony down to the altar?"

"No."

"Did he try to cast demons out of Jimmy?"

"No."

"Then have a little faith in me, please."

"Bruce, I'm deadly serious."

"I know you are, babe, but we don't have a dog yet. Stop creating situations where none exist," he smiled.

"What kind of dog do you want?"

"I'm thinking a mutt. Purebloods are too neurotic and pretentious. A mutt knows it has to earn its keep," Bruce laughed.

"Whatever you decide upon, I insist that it get spayed or neutered because..."

"You don't want no babies," he finished.

"Damn straight!"

We walked exactly half of the perimeter before Bruce asked another question. "Babe, what did yo' mama say to you at the pavilion on Tuesday?"

"Why is that important? You gonna tell me what you said to Bucket? Or what you and Daddy talked about?"

After a pause, Bruce slowed our walking pace. Then he stopped to face me. "Yes."

"Yes, what?" I asked.

"Yes, I'll tell you the gist of what I told Brett, and I'll tell you what Pops and I talked about."

"Why?" I asked, eyebrow raised.

"Transparency, remember? I want no secrets between us. You and I are a unified front from now on," he said, caressing my cheeks.

After a long pause, I spoke. "To begin with, Mama wanted to know why I never talked about your PTSD."

"What did you tell her?"

"Bruce, I consider our hell, private. It's embarrassing," I confessed, "and I don't want *anybody* thinking you're crazy and I'm *crazier* for staying with you."

"You're not crazy, Lettie. You're one of the strongest, bravest, persons I know," he said, taking my hand and nudging us along.

"Mama told me about Daddy's PTSD. I never knew. She told me how one time he beat her badly during one of his spells. It was right before I was born. Did you know that?" I asked, searching his eyes.

"No. He told me he got pretty wild, but he never went into any details. Wow! Mama Jewel truly loved him to endure that kind of physical abuse. No wonder he calls her his rock."

"You know, when we were kids, we'd see Mama and Daddy kiss, sometimes passionately, and I knew, watching them kiss, they loved us. I was so secure in that knowledge." Looking Bruce in his eyes, I told him, "I want you to know, that's the kind of love I strive to practice with you."

"And I'm so thankful. Please, don't ever stop."

"Mama then wanted to know if you had hurt me," I informed.

"Did you tell her?" he asked, staring straight ahead.

"I did, but I made sure she knew you were not yourself."

"What did she say to that?"

"Not much. She asked if we knew what triggered your attacks. I told her no, at least not yet. She says once we figure that out, we'll be able to heal and put this past us."

Bruce was quiet, with that faraway look in his eyes.

I was unsure if he was mentally with me, so I poked him. "You still here? Or are you in *that place*?" I ventured.

"I'm still with you. But Mama has brought up an interesting question. Up until now, I've never thought about what triggers my nightmares. Lloyd has suggested regression therapy, but I've been too afraid to try it. *That place*," he shuddered, "just the thought of it chills me."

"Baby, I don't want you to do anything you're not ready to do, including regression therapy. Take this slow so there is no relapsing."

Bruce patted my hand and nodded as we reached the three-quarter marker. "Did Mama say anything else?"

"Yes. She told me I had changed. I wasn't the same person anymore. She accused me of hiding. Can you believe that? She even called me dull."

"Yes, I can, and in some ways, she's right. You have changed, and part of that lies at my door."

"What are you saying to me, Bruce? Are you telling me I'm no longer the vibrant, sexy, intelligent, generous, gorgeous woman you married?"

"Complete transparency, right?"

"Right," I said, warily.

"Wait here." He suddenly sprinted off to the Gator. Driving back to me, he motioned for me to get in.

"We're going to need to sit down for this," he said. My stomach felt heavy as stone with those words, and my face must have registered my emotions. "Babe, I don't want you to get upset with what I have to say, so I need your word you will remain calm. Will you do that for me?"

"Speak your mind, Bruce," I said, evenly.

"Lettie, we all change as we travel on this journey. God knows, I've changed. But what I think yo' mama was talking about is the fact that some of your vibrancy *has* dulled. Babe, it's not you, so much, as it's what you've had to do. When you married me, you sacrificed your executive career goals to be an army officer's wife. That was a lot of pressure, but I knew you could handle it. You performed admirably, above and beyond the call of duty most often. Your interpersonal skills aided and enhanced my career and promotion within the ranks. Without you, I may not have advanced as quickly as I did, but there was a cost. You had to always be on your guard in your speech, your actions, and comportment, even in how you dressed. You had to play the game, and the role dulled you a bit. You weren't free to speak your mind, and you had to always be on top of your wit, and control your tongue."

"Mama says I don't take the mask off anymore."

"I think she's right. It's time you came from behind the mask to be the freakin', awesome, fabulous woman I know you to be, and the woman I fell madly in love with. You are no longer held to a military standard of life. It's time for you to be you again."

"That means sarcasm and snark may be living with us. You sure you can reside with those twins?"

"Yeah, I can handle those heifers," he said, chuckling. "You're only mean-spirited with Brett," he said, giving me a direct look.

"Since you brought it up, tell me what you said to Bucket."

"I'll tell you, like I said I would, but I need a concession from you first."

"What concession?" I sighed.

"From this point forward, you will call him by his given name. Deal?" I paused, inwardly debating how badly I wanted to know the details of their conversation. "Lettie? Do we have a deal?"

I sighed, languidly, before I begrudgingly said, "Yes."

"What's his name, please?" Bruce questioned.

"Brett. Mama named him Brett Alexander Stanton. His name is Brett, but if I slip and call him Bucket, don't jump down my throat. Old habits are hard to break."

"Woman, bullshit somebody else. This is me you're talking to."

"All right," I said, rolling my eyes, "dish. What did you tell him?"

"Nothing he didn't already know. We talked about respect, what it is, and how it's earned, not given. Talked about his lack of respect toward Mama and Pops. Talked about what it means to be a man, and what was perceived masculinity. I talked about what the Bible had to say about honoring parents, manhood, and even threw in some stories about other cultural rites of passage. Then I became Socratic with him, so he would do some self-inspection. Finally, I told him how proud I was to be his big brother-in-law, and I would always be there as a listening ear. That's it!"

"And that's what caused the change I've seen?"

"Babe, I am, was, a leader of men. I know how to motivate without manipulating. All I did was give the boy some sandpaper and a mirror. I admit, he is spoiled, but he is also a much deeper person and a much profounder thinker than you give credit. Lettie, I believe Brett *is* on the verge of hitting it big in the video gaming world. The boy is not shiftless."

"Jimmy was telling me as much. He truly shamed me yesterday and caused me to do some soul searching regarding Buck, uh, Brett. He asked me when was the last time I had an honest conversation with him, and I couldn't answer because I don't really know," I said, looking at Bruce shamefaced.

"What is it with you and Brett, anyway? Do you hate him?"

"No, I've never hated him. I hated having to forever clean up behind him. Mama and Daddy allowed him to do, seemingly, any and everything. They never held him accountable for any piece of dirt he did, and I confess, I've resented him. Our relationship was fraught with tension from the day they brought that boy home. But I now acknowledge the sin isn't his. It's mine. I need to forgive Bucket, sorry…Brett, as well as Mama and Daddy. I fully intend to resolve all tensions with Brett before we leave."

Bruce sat quietly studying me. "Lettie, I believe you, and I've never been as proud of you as I am right now," he said, holding my face in his hands.

We sat a while longer, content to hold hands, appreciating the beauty of the pasture. The wind began to pick up, and the sound through the tree break wailed a low moan. A formation of ducks flew overhead, quacking sporadically.

"Are you ready to finish our walk," Bruce asked, breaking our silence.

"Not yet. There is one last piece of business we need to work through."

"Really? I thought we'd gotten through our list."

"We have, but this is an addendum," I said.

"What's on your mind, babe?"

"Bruce, who is Mr. Hyde?"

"Mr. Hyde?"

"That's what I call him. I've never met him until you came home from Germany. I see him flash behind your eyes, often. He manifests himself when you're in the midst of your nightmares. He's cold, indifferent, and hurtful. He's rough, and he scares me—truly. He's also the best lover I've ever had. Can you explain him to me?"

"Okay, time to walk."

"Bruce, really?"

"You want to know about Mr. Hyde, as you call him? Then, raise up," he said, getting out of the Gator and resuming our walk. Ten paces away he turned to see if I was following.

I started this and had to finish it, so I got out of the Gator and made my way over. "I'm here."

"Lettie," Bruce started as we walked again, "I am not a schizophrenic, first of all, and I'm sorry I scare you on occasion. Every one of us has a *Mr. Hyde* inside of them. A warrior needs, and depends, on Mr. Hyde in order to kill. Think of it as the embodiment of courage. Any man who says he doesn't experience fear on the battlefield is a damned liar. Mr. Hyde helps me channel my fear. He's always been a part of me, but I've been more adept at controlling him in the past. My PTSD has compromised my ability to limit his appearances," he said, falling silent.

"I'm not sure I know how to deal with Mr. Hyde, Bruce. He's radically different from who you've been during our marriage."

"Mr. Hyde is me, and I am him. He came out to play while on my job. My men knew Mr. Hyde and seldom got to see Mr. Jonson. You don't need to fear me, babe."

"Can you shed light on Mr. Hyde's lovemaking? Baby, you are an amazing lover. You tend my garden well, but our last two sessions were nothing like we've ever done before. Have you…been practicing with someone else?" I asked, nervous I may have stepped over the line.

Bruce stopped mid-stride, turned, and faced me. "Woman, I never said I was pure when we married. You came to me as a virgin, and I've never taken that gift for granted, nor have I ever betrayed your love and trust or our vows. I admit I've been tempted, but that's only because I was far from you, lonely, and hungry for your touch. Learning or demonstrating new sexual techniques does not mean I've practiced with anyone. I paid attention to advice some old salts gave us young troops, and I stored that information away for the right time."

"What kind of advice?"

"Woman, I could tell you everything that was ever said, but that would spoil the fun, now wouldn't it?"

"Maybe, maybe not."

"Patience is a virtue. Besides, you ambushed *me* that first night, remember? I did not plan for things to go as far as they did."

"Are you sorry things went that far?"

"Hell no!"

"But…"

"No buts. That night in the shower, I've never wanted you as much or as badly as I did. I couldn't get enough of you. I couldn't get far enough inside of you. It was as if I had to possess you, all of you, body and soul. I was fearful but withered and parched. You flooded my soul that night and watered my dry and thirsty world." Wondering, Bruce asked, "Was I too rough? Did I hurt you in any way?"

"I had no complaints then, and I have none now," I smiled. "Can I expect Mr. Hyde to show up more often in our bed?"

"Why?"

"Transparency, right?"

"Right."

"I want to see, feel, and experience more of Mr. Hyde. He's exciting and unpredictable."

"I'll make sure he's in attendance from time to time," Bruce said with a rakish smile.

"I think, now, our list is done," I said as we walked hand in hand toward the last fence post.

The sun began to descend on the horizon when we completed our promenade of the pasture. The wind picked up, the temperature dropped, and I had no sweater.

"Let's head back to the house, baby. I'm starting to get chilly," I said.

"Sure thing. Let's cut across the field back to the Gator. Be careful, there are a lot of gopher holes out here. I don't want you turning an ankle."

We walked at a brisk pace, silently meditating about everything we had spoken to each other. I was deep in thought when Bruce interrupted.

"Babe, what's that?" he asked, slowing our pace considerably.

"What?"

"Do you hear that?"

"No," I said with all honesty.

"Walk back with me a few paces."

"Okay." We retraced about fifteen steps before stopping.

"Now, let's walk forward, slowly, toward the Gator." We took three steps before Bruce said, "There! Do you hear it now?"

Listening carefully, I finally heard it. "Sounds like a mewling or whimpering of some sort."

"Help me find that noise," he said.

"Sure." We found the sound, actually the hole from where the sound emanated, within a few minutes of searching.

"Something's down there," Bruce said, getting on his knees.

"You are *not* going to stick your hand down there, I know."

"I'm not, Mr. Hyde is," Bruce said, grinning.

"Baby, you don't know what's down in that hole. It could be anything, and it may bite." Before I could speak another word, Bruce was up to his elbow in the hole.

"Whatever it is, it's furry," he said, pulling his arm out of the hole. In his hand was a muddy, yelping, puny, puppy.

"Oh, my God," I mumbled.

"Let's hurry back," he said while examining the animal. "This puppy's in distress."

"I'll drive," I said, remembering my mother's words all the way back. *Be careful what you throw out to the Universe. Irony is just one of the Lawd's many tools.*

Bruce held the puppy inside his shirt to keep the wind from hitting it further. I kept my eyes on the road to keep from looking at Bruce. I pulled up to the house so Bruce could get the animal indoors. Mama, the critter lover she was, would immediately know what to do and how to help the puppy. Daddy was on the porch when we drove up and offered to put the Gator away for me.

"How about we ride to the shed together, Daddy?" I suggested.

"All right, Baby Girl. How was y'all's trip to the pasture? Purdy, wasn't it?"

"Yes, it was beautiful and relaxing, right up until Bruce found *that* puppy. Daddy, I need to talk to you," I said, killing the Gator's motor once I parked in the shed.

"Baby Girl, what's troublin' you?"

"Daddy, why does it have to be trouble?"

"Baby Girl, you've always shared joys with yo' mama, but yo' burdens you've always shared with me."

I thought about that a moment, and once again, my daddy spoke truth. "Now that I think about it, I guess you're right. Does it bother you that I only come to you when I'm in trouble?"

"Baby Girl, it would bother me if you didn't. Now, what's on yo' heart?"

"First, I need to tell you, Bruce and I have talked through everything. The PTSD, his nightmares, future plans, kids, his talk with Brett, your discussion, everything."

"And?"

"And, we're good," I smiled.

"Chi'ren?"

"We aren't having any. You already know he cannot sire, but, more importantly, I don't want any."

"Baby Girl, you sho' 'bout this? Completely sho'?"

"Yes, sir, completely sure, and we're good."

"What 'bout relocation?"

"Daddy, you know if Bruce decided to live in a hut, that's where I'd be; I love him that much. Besides, you know I like to travel, meet new people, and learn about new places. Relocating won't be hard. Losing my walk-in shower is going to be the hard thing," I chuckled. "We've agreed there will be no secrets between us. Total transparency, as Bruce calls it, is our aim."

"That's good, real good," Daddy exclaimed.

"There are some questions I need to ask you, and some things I need to say to you."

"Go 'head."

"Mama told me about your PTSD after the war. She also told me how you beat her badly one night when she was pregnant with me. What happened that night? Do you remember?"

"Baby Girl, to this day, I am ashamed of what I did that night. You got to understand, back then, the Klan was kickin' up a ruckus every chance they got. I cain't tell you how many times they tried to burn us out, just 'cause. But back then, like now, there was mo' of us than them, and we'd fight 'em off, every time. One night, yo' granddaddy was tusslin' with the ring leader and managed to pull off his hood. We found out right then who was stirrin' up the mess. That's when we decided to go on the offense, and start our own campaign of terror."

"Daddy, what did you all do?"

"Baby Girl, you ain't gon' believe me when I tell you. Firs', I got to say I wasn't walkin' as close to the Lawd as I am today, otherwise I wouldn't have been comfortable doing what I did. Peckerwoods back then were a scary bunch, so we used Hoodoo against 'em."

"Daddy, you believed and practiced Hoodoo?"

"No, but they believed in it. We jus' used what they feared is all," Daddy laughed. "Them people was so ig'nant, it was almos' child's play. We started out by leaving *Devil Catchers* in strategic places on their land, like the wells, chicken coops, in the middle of their crops after we sewed salt all around it. Made it look like the ground was cursed so they'd start frettin' 'bout their crops. Then whenever we could, we'd put *Devil Catchers* near cattle pens, or feed cribs. One time," he said, snickering, "we snuck up and put one next to the back do' of their church, along with a voodoo doll with pins in the head and gut. As it so happened, there was a bad flu epidemic that year, and lots of the white folk came down with it bad. They all seemed to have right bad pains in their heads and stomach. So, when we was 'round them at the sto', post office, 'round town, and such, after speakin' we'd whisper 'You gon' die tonight!' You've never seen people as scared as them ig'nant white folk," Daddy said, laughing hard.

"We had an old sister livin' back then named Miss Maggie. She not only looked like a Hoodoo woman, but she acted like one too. She got so bold, she would point her bony finger at someone we knew was Klan and would say real loud, 'So-in-so, the Lawd requires yo' soul this night. Get on yo' knees and pray, 'cause the demons be ridin' tonight!' Then, she'd let loose this cackle that could loose yo' bowels. One time, the sheriff tried to mess with her. That's when she really cut up. 'Harvey,' she said, 'God don't like how y'all been treatin' us. He don't like ugly. Said he gon' take you firs' to prove what I say be real. You gon' die, tonight!' And do you know, he did! Them white folk ran to Miss Maggie beggin' her to lift the curse. She said she'd do it only when they started treatin' us better and leaving us alone. Otherwise, mo' would die. The next night, another Klansman up and died. Next mo'ning, mo' white folk came to her beggin', pleadin', crying, and such. Some even gave her money. Her answer remained the same. In short order, the Klan quit trying to terrorize us, and the white folks became better neighbors."

"Daddy, are you pulling my leg?" I asked.

"I'm tellin' you the gospel truth!"

"And the Klan stopped trying to burn you and Grandpa out?"

"They sho' did."

"So what made you beat Mama the way you did?"

"I was not a well man back then. I was twisted with hate for the Klan and fear from my memories."

"The concentration camps?"

"Yeah, the camps. What y'all learned in school, barely cut the surface of what them folk endured. When we got there, the Germans had left, but then again, they hadn't. I cain't convey the degradation them folk suffered. I didn't think people could be that inhumane, but they could and still are. That's why Bruce is suffering now."

"But, Daddy, how could you beat Mama up like that?" I asked, getting him back on topic.

"During my spells, I was never the liberator. I was always the captive. That terror, along with what the Klan was doin', enraged me.

When I beat yo' mama, I thought, dreamt, one of them peckerwoods was trying to beat on me. Well, I wasn't havin' it! He was gon' die that night. I didn't know I was beatin' yo' mama 'til yo' grand-daddy started whoopin' up on me."

"That woke you up?"

"I'll say! Nobody could hit harder than my daddy. I've seen grown men sit down and cry after only one good punch from him. Yo' grand-daddy was no joke. When I realized it was Jewel I beat, I broke open, couldn't stop cryin'—so scared," he whispered looking into my eyes, "scared I killed my own child, and maybe even made it so we couldn't have no mo' chi'ren. I fell on my face before God, and begged him to forgive me. I pleaded for yo' life that night. Sunday mo'nin' found me on the Mourner's Bench. I kept asking God to heal me, to heal my mind. I prayed, and prayed, and prayed. Prayed he'd give me a loving heart. Prayed for a forgiving spirit. I sought the Lawd, plumbed his Word. The more I sought him, the fewer nightmares I had. By the time Chester got here, I seldom had them. I was so thankful he blessed us with another chile, I could hardly contain my joy."

"Did somebody have to hold your mule?" I teased.

"You better know it," he laughed, heartily. After our laughter died down, I asked a harder question.

"Daddy, did…do…you love Brett more than the rest of us?"

"Baby Girl, no! I don't favor either one of you over the other."

"It felt like you did. Brett was never held accountable for his mess. It seemed like you and Mama made all kinds of excuses for him, but you held the rest of us to a higher standard," I said.

"I confess, by the time Brett came into full adolescence, I didn't ride him like I should have. I was too soft, and I let Jewel have her way too often."

"Daddy, I need to ask your forgiveness for the way I've treated Brett all these years. I was resentful, and at times, jealous of his relationship with you and Mama. Please, forgive me. I am sorry."

"Baby Girl, if anyone needs to ask for forgiveness, it's me. I'm the patriarch of this clan. I should have seen what was happening with you and your brothers. I, ask *yo'* forgiveness."

"Daddy, I forgive you, and I love you dearly," I said, reaching over to hug him.

"Thank you, Baby Girl, I love you more than you could ever know."

"I'm beginning to understand that love," I said. "Also know that I'm going to make things right with Brett. All my hatchets get buried before I leave."

Looking at me as if his chest would burst, Daddy asked, "Any mo' questions for me?"

"Yes, sir. Knowing you, and what the church teaches about homosexuality, how is it you've accepted Tony and Jimmy?"

"Baby Girl, the Book of Proverbs, chapter 6, verses 16 – 19, talks about the seven things detestable to God. Nowhere on that list is sex, of any kind, mentioned. I don't believe homosexuality is something that can simply be chosen. I've watched yo' brother grow up, and I've always known he was different. I don't believe he had a choice. He is *my* son; bone of my bone, and flesh of my flesh. *I will, in no wise, cast him out.* If he has found true love, how could I not accept that? It's no different than when you decided to marry Bruce, or Chester choosing Clarissa."

"How are you going to deal with the gossip?"

"Folk been talkin' 'bout me for a long time now. Let them talk! They don't know nothin' 'bout me or mine."

"You know, I was worried about how you'd react when you found out, and I've got to say, you surprised us all," I said.

"I bet you thought I was gon' wrestle him down to the altar, didn't you?"

"Yes, sir, I sure did," I said, laughing along with Daddy. "So, are you and Mama going to the wedding?"

"Nothin' but death would keep me, or yo' mama, from goin'. I proudly stand with my chile."

"Daddy, you are amazing, and I love you more now than ever," I said, squeezing his hand.

"We bes' be getting' back to the house. Don't you want to see yo' new dog?"

"Oh, Lord, I forgot about that mutt. Why did you encourage Bruce?"

"Baby Girl, if things are as bad as he says, y'all gon' need that dog. Love that animal, and it will protect y'all with its life. Count on that."

I found Bruce on the back porch with Mama and the puppy. They had found a good-sized box and lined it with newspaper and an old quilt. Mama had put a hot water bottle underneath the covers. They were gently shampooing the puppy in warm water. There was no telling how long the puppy had been in that hole, but it was long enough to be caked with earth. Slowly, a clean and fluffy coat appeared. To my eye, Bruce got his wish. It was a mutt. She had finally stopped yelping, and began to feel comfortable with Bruce's handling. Mama had one of Suzie's old bottles she filled with warm milk. Wrapping up the damp puppy, Bruce bottle-fed her.

"Well, baby, looks like you've got your mutt. Any idea what you'll call her?" I asked.

"Not yet. I need to study on it a while."

"Son, I called my vet and we can get her in first thing tomorrow morning," Mama said. "My vet's real good, and I bet he'll be able to classify this dog."

"That will be great, Mama, Thanks. What time?" Bruce asked.

"8:00 a.m."

"We'll be ready."

"When you say *we*, I'm assuming you mean you and the dog, right?" I asked for clarity.

"Yes, I mean me and the dog."

"Just checking," I said.

Bruce was up, dressed, and drinking coffee by 6:30 a.m. Little furry madam was hungry early, and Bruce's foray into surrogate fatherhood started with a bang — a 4:00 a.m. feeding. Out of sheer curiosity, I got up, dressed, caffeinated myself, and waited for the crew to emerge by 7:15 a.m.

"Baby, are you going with us?" Mama asked.

"Yeah, I'm curious to hear what the vet has to say."

"Woman, you need to come clean," Bruce interjected. "Go on and admit it. You find the puppy adorable, don't you?"

"It's a mutt!"

"Uh-huh," said Bruce, sucking his teeth.

Arriving at the vet's office, we sat a short five minutes before they called us back. We were all allowed to go into the examination room.

"Well, let's see this baby," the vet said. "My, my, what a pretty little girl you are. Okay, this baby is clearly underweight. She appears to be nearing eight weeks. Is she still suckling?"

"Yes, we fed her via bottle last night and this morning," Bruce said.

"Can you tell us what breed of dog she is?" asked Mama.

"She's definitely a mutt," he said, smiling, "but she plainly has some German Shepherd in her. Where did you find her?"

"In our northwest pasture, deep in a gopher hole," Mama said.

"Were there any other siblings? Or carcasses where you found her?"

"No. She was the only animal I could feel in the hole," said Bruce.

"Hmm. It's possible, since she's small, she was the runt of the litter. If mama was traveling with her pups and this one slid down a hole, she probably wouldn't have known it was missing for some time. She wouldn't have tried to find her with other mouths to suckle either. Other than being under nourished, this pup looks good. I'm going to clip her dew claws and give her the initial immunization shots. She might need to be wormed as well. Play close attention to her stool. You'll definitely know if she's got worms."

"What about fleas?" Mama asked.

"I'd recommend a simple flea collar for right now. Let her get a little older and a tad heavier before giving her topical or oral flea meds. Do you plan to spay her?"

"Yes."

"Good answer. I recommend you get that done no later than three months from now. This is going to be a big dog. You'll need to have her spayed before her ribcage gets too large," the vet advised, clipping the dew claws.

"How big a dog do you think she'll be?" I asked.

"That's hard to say because we don't know what she's mixed with, but if she takes after her Shepherd genetics, you can expect her to top out between seventy to eighty pounds. Guard against over feeding her. Too much weight on a large frame is going to lead to trouble down the road. I also recommend that you begin obedience training as soon as you get her home. I cannot emphasize how important it is to establish dominance quickly with a big dog. Can I assume," the vet asked, turning to Bruce, "that you're going to be alpha dog?"

"Yes," Bruce confirmed.

"When you go back to your mother-in-law's, start training her. Don't allow her to walk into the house before you. Make her follow you at all times, so she'll know who the pack leader is. Teach her to respect your wife, or she'll run her. I recommend you both read everything you can get your hands on regarding dog training and everything about the German Shepherd breed. These animals are highly intelligent and highly territorial. They protect their pack and their territory. They do well with little ones, especially if you raise them together."

"We don't have any children," I informed the vet. "She will be the baby of the house."

"Well, whatever you do, don't spoil her. You need to be intentionally regimented with this breed. Love her, yes. Spoil her, no."

Driving back to the house, Bruce cradled and loved on the puppy something fierce. "Bruce, do I need to be concerned little

Miss Thang is going to be my competition for your affections?" I asked.

"Woman, please. Nothing comes between us, not even this puppy," he said.

"Son, I have a spare extra-large crate you may take back home with you. It was Brutus', so I know it will house this pup once she reaches maturity. When we get back to the house, we'll scrub it down with some bleach water, so it'll be disinfected for your dog. Now, y'all need to listen to what I'm about to tell you. Love this animal like you would a child. Praise her often, especially when she obeys commands. Chastise her harshly only when you catch her in the act. Dogs have short-term memories when it comes to actions. They get confused when you correct them after the fact. Praise her often and she will strive to please you constantly. Don't put that dog in your bed, unless you intend on her sleeping there. Dogs are den oriented, and truly do want to call the crate their home. It provides her a sense of safety and security. And put the dog out of your room when you're making love. The smell of sex will arouse her."

"Mama? Is there something you'd like to share with us?" I asked, teasingly.

"I've shared with y'all all I'm going to share," she said, tight-lipped.

Bruce and I snickered, and soon we were all laughing aloud.

"Lettie, I know you don't want anything to do with this dog, but you're going to have to get involved," Mama advised. "This dog will need to obey you, as well as Bruce. So, when y'all start training her, do it together as much as possible. You want this dog loyal to *both* of you, not Bruce alone."

I sighed and shook my head.

"What's the matter, daughter?" Mama asked, looking in the rearview mirror.

"Mama, I hate it when you're right."

"I know. It's a mother's prerogative," she said, hitting Bruce's arm and laughing maniacally.

"Give me strength," I muttered.

As we pulled into the driveway, I noticed Willa's car. I was glad to see her at the house, and hoped I could get some one-on-one time with her. "Mama, will you need help with supper tonight?" I asked.

"No, sweetie, Peaches and Luther have decided not to leave till tomorrow, so she'll give me a hand. Besides, all we're going to do is rehash Thanksgiving supper. By the way, all that dessert cannot stay here. Decide what you both want, and take it back home with you."

"Mama Jewel, you're trying to make me fat," Bruce accused. "I may have to take a bit of everything."

"Long as it leaves my house," Mama said. "Okay, I need to check on my grandbabies," Mama said, getting out of the car. "What do y'all plan to do now?"

"I was going to invite Willa and Brett to spend a little time with us at the pavilion," I said.

"What did you say?" Mama asked, spinning around. "Did I hear her correctly?" she asked, looking at Bruce. "Did she just say 'Brett'?"

"Yeah," Bruce said, grinning.

"Well, do tell," Mama said, "will wonders never cease? Whatever will she say next?"

I found Willa and Brett in the den and invited them to join Bruce and me out at the pavilion. Willa gladly accepted, but Brett was understandably suspicious. Upon reaching the pavilion, Willa went crazy over the puppy.

"Ohhhh, such a sweet puppy. When did y'all get her?"

"Yesterday evening. Bruce and I were walking in the northwest pasture when we discovered her in a gopher hole. Bruce is the one who rescued her really," I explained.

"She is sooooo precious, just adorable," Willa cooed while cuddling with her.

"Figured out what you're gonna name her yet, Bruh?" Brett asked.

"Not yet, but I'm thinking something regal," Bruce said.

"I guess 'Mutt' won't work, huh?" I offered.

"No, it will not," Bruce said, giving me a rather jaundiced eye.

"How about 'Lady' or 'Princess'?" Willa asked.

"Too common," said Brett. "She needs a name that will stand out."

"There's 'Duchess', 'Countess', 'Marchesa', 'Queen', or 'Sultana'," Willa mused.

"How about 'Reina'?" I suggested.

Bruce looked at me and considered my offering before saying, "Let's see what the puppy likes." He took her to the far end of the pavilion then sprinted back to us. He called her by every name we thought of, but she only responded and came to one—Reina. "I guess Reina it is," Bruce said, winking at me. "A queen by another name."

"As long as it's understood, I am the one *true* queen in our house," I said.

Soon, we were all petting, fawning over, or playing with Reina when one by one, Chester's brood found us and the puppy. Everyone, including Tony and Jimmy, got a chance to hold or pet Reina. The poor puppy got so tuckered out, she crashed.

That's when Thomas unceremoniously plopped her in Bruce's lap and said, "Uncle Bruce, it's dead," and wordlessly walked away.

Bruce shook his head, chuckled, and tucked his baby in the crook of his arm. We all laughed at Thomas' honest, if not misunderstood, observation. I watched my husband closely. Bruce would have made a wonderful, loving, and protective father. I was amazed at the softness and tenderness he exhibited toward a puny runt that surely would have died had we not found her. I was equally astonished at the impact our lives experienced already in only a day of Reina coming to us. We left home as a couple, but would return as a family of three.

Chester came to the house around lunch time. He sat and ate with his children, assuring them Clarissa was well. He told them only what they needed to know about their departed baby sister. After lunch, he made his way out to the pavilion where the rest of us were still gathered.

"Hey, everybody," Chester greeted.

"Chester," Bruce stood to embrace him, "good to see you. How's Clarissa doing?"

"The Lawd be praised, she's doing so much better. I came to give the family an update."

"Come sit down," Tony said, bringing him a chair.

"What's the doctor saying?" Willa soberly asked.

"The doctor believes she's gon' be just fine," Chester said, smiling. "There hasn't been any more bleeding, her color's up, bowels have moved, and she's eatin' good. She's mighty weak, but the doctor says that's to be expected. She'll be able to come home Monday."

"That's great," we all chanted.

"Chester, please give Clarissa my best. I know I should have gone out to see her, but I figured with her mama and sisters at the hospital, she didn't need us taking up any more space in her room. Let her know we're praying for her, too," I said.

"I will, Lettie. Bruce, Willa, I want to thank y'all, from the bottom of my heart, for all you did for Clarissa. Willa, if you hadn't got Buddy to clear the roads for us, I'd have lost both my babies," he said, choking back tears. "Bruce, just bein' there with me, you don't know how much that meant," he said, now fully in tears. We all went and surrounded Chester with a huge group hug as he softly cried.

Willa and I were moved to sympathetic tears, but the men remained stoic.

After collecting himself, Chester said, "I don't know what I'd do without my Clarissa. She's the rock of my family. I know my chi'ren would suffer without her, even though they've got both grandparents, aunts, and uncles. Not having a mama would be hard."

"So, how're you doing?" Brett asked.

"I'm holding on. Actually, better now I know Clarissa's coming home. I'll be takin' the chi'ren with me when I leave today. See if we cain't get the house spruced up for her home-coming."

"Do you need any help?" Willa asked.

"No, ma'am. Between me, the chi'ren, Bernice, and my sisters-in-law, we'll be fine, but I thank you kindly."

As the conversation came to a lull, and before my courage failed, I spoke. "Chester, I'm glad you're here because I need to say some things that I want everyone to hear." I held all assembled in rapt attention. Bruce blinked and nodded slightly, giving me the encouragement I needed. "Brett," I called, turning to face him. "Baby brother, I want to publicly apologize to you for my treatment towards you these many years. I've resented you, probably from the day Mama and Daddy first brought you home. I was not a nice sister, and, I confess, I've only been critical of you. I have sinned against you, and I'm asking for your forgiveness. I was in the wrong. I want to get to know you better and to see you, acknowledge you, as the man you are becoming," I said, sliding my eyes toward Jimmy, who was smiling broadly. "Also, from this time forward, I promise to call you Brett, and only Brett, unless you want Alexander thrown in for good measure. Brother, do I have your forgiveness?" I asked, looking earnestly in his eyes.

Brett sat, utterly dumbfounded, slack-jawed, paralyzed, and speechless. We waited, patiently, for his response.

Tony decided to hasten him along. "Brett! Baby brother, did you understand the question? Does she need to repeat herself?"

Brett, flicking eyes between me and Tony, finally spoke. "Uh, yes, I mean, no, uh, I mean, wait." Brett clarified his thoughts, then turned towards me. "Lettie, I've always felt like you hated me. Nothing I did was ever good enough for you. Nothing! I think I intentionally antagonized you because of that, but I want you to know I've never hated you, and I'm real thankful you married Bruce," he said grinning, beating his chest, throwing make-believe gang signs, which were gestures of endearment, in Bruce's direction. "I guess my answer to your question has to be—yes—I forgive you. And I thank you for calling me by my given name, and meaning it," he said with all openness. "So, let's make this legit…bring it in," he said, motioning me to give him a hug. He embraced me, and I him in true sibling affection. "I love you, Lettie," he murmured in my ear.

"I love you too, little brother."

Pulling away, he held me at arm's length. "When I become a millionaire, I'll let you call me Bucket again, only it should be plural."

"Why plural?" I asked.

"Because of all the buckets of money I'll have," he laughed while cutting a high step.

"Boyfriend, please!" Tony quipped, while everyone else rolled their eyes and groaned, including Willa.

Walking back to Bruce, Tony and Jimmy reached out and gave me a crushing group hug.

"Lass, I'm proud of you," Jimmy said, kissing both my cheeks.

"That was extremely commendable, Sis. I'm proud of you too," Tony added, and hugged me again.

Getting back and sitting next to Bruce, he took my hand, with Reina still in arm asleep. Looking adoringly into my eyes he breathed, "Woman, you do me proud. God, how I love you!"

I had no clue Mama and Daddy witnessed my reconciliation with Brett until they both laid their hands on my shoulders. Looking up, I saw them smiling down on me.

"Heard that, did you?" I asked.

"Yep. Right proud of you, Baby Girl," Daddy said.

"I knew you couldn't remain bitchy for long," Mama added. "Glad to see you've come to yo' senses and buried yo' hatchets."

Our last supper together was like celebrating Thanksgiving all over again, sans Chester and family. The fare was supplemented with wicked good mashed potatoes, Marsala gravy, and scalloped apples. Uncle Luther eclipsed his first eating attempt, and did offend his Maker this round. Uncle Thadd made sure to bring that bit of information to everyone's attention. Uncle Luther actually unbuttoned his pants at the table, which brought much mirth to the family.

"Luther, how on Earth did you get to where you could eat like this?" Uncle Thadd asked.

"Guess I got it honest," he said, rubbing his belly. "I'm told my grand-pappy Wade could do the same thing. I remember hearing tales 'bout what a glutton he was. One time, my great-grandma sent him to carry dinner to a friend who was sick. Back in them days, folks used handled tin buckets, like yo' syrup used to come in, to pack take-away food. Well, he was spotted coming up the hill toward the friend's house, crawling on his hands and knees. Folk ran to see 'bout him thinkin' he was hurt. They asked, 'What's wrong, Mr. Wade?' and he said, 'Nothin' wrong.' Then they asked, 'Why is you crawling?' and he told them why he was there. When they asked where the dinner was, he said, 'I was nosey an' took a peek. It smelt so good, I jus' had to taste it.' Turns out he ate every spoonful and almos' busted a sorry gut doing it."

"Luther, you need to stop lying on the dead," Aunt Peaches chortled as we all laughed at that story.

"But, Uncle Luther, don't you ever get sick eating like this?" Brett asked.

"Boy, I only abuse my belly when I know I can lie down after. If I was still working, I wouldn't eat so heavy. But, I do declare, my Peaches can make a man forget and hurt himself," he said, smiling at Peaches.

"Don't forget about me, Luther," Mama quipped. "I helped to bust yo' britches, too."

"Jewel, I do have to give credit where it's due. You sho' can burn some pots and pans."

"Aunt Peaches, Uncle Thadd has told us some tall tales about you and Aunt Cherry this week. Can you tell us any stories about him?" I asked.

"Child, don't I wish. We were the babies. I've got no dirt on Thadd."

"And never will!" Uncle Thadd assured us, cackling.

"All right, ladies," Mama announced, "let's get this table cleared. Y'all need to voice your choice about which desserts you want to take back home with you tomorrow. We'll pack them up if you tell us what you want."

"How much can we take?" Tony asked.

"As much as you want. They can't stay here."

"Awesome," Tony, Jimmy, Bruce, and Uncle Luther voiced in concert.

We women finished our duties in the kitchen. While we were working, the menfolk broke down the tables in the den, then carried them out and stacked them at the pavilion. Daddy assured the men he, Brett, and Chester would return the tables to the barn once we left.

We all gathered before a warming fire in the den and spent our last night as a family. We were content, and savored the love and closeness, marking this night as the beginning of better times ahead.

9

There and Back Again

Early Sunday morning, Aunt Peaches insisted on preparing a breakfast that would hold everyone over until they reached their final destination. It was a classic country breakfast: hot cakes, biscuits, grits, hot links, eggs, fried fish, okra, rice, two kinds of Mama's preserves, sweet butter, fresh fruit, and an abundant supply of rich, dark, coffee. To our surprise, Uncle Luther ate lightly. He explained he couldn't sit behind the wheel long on an overly full stomach.

"Guess that means you won't be driving long today?" Bruce teased.

Amidst titters and guffaws, Uncle Luther schooled Bruce. "Look here boy, I can out work and out drive *you* anytime, anywhere."

"Okay, okay, Uncle, I was just messing with you," Bruce laughed.

"Me too," he chuckled, looking over at Uncle Thadd. "Besides, Peaches is no good on long-distance drives. I promise you, she'll be 'sleep 'fo' we can reach the interstate good."

"As hard as she's worked this week," I said, "she deserves to sleep all the way home."

"Amen," said Mama.

As we continued to eat, I reached over and took Jimmy's hand. "I'm so glad you came this week."

"Me too, lass," he smiled.

"I wonder if I could impose upon you for a favor."

"You just name it, and it's yours," he assured.

"If it's no trouble, would you keep an eye out for any positions for security supervisor or security consultant? When Bruce is ready, he's going to need a job, and we're ready to relocate from the D.C. area."

"Of course, but do you mind if we talk to him about this now? I wouldn't want him to think we're conspiring behind his back."

"You're so right. Please, go ahead and ask him."

"Bruce, I've got some questions for you if you don't mind," Jimmy said, catching his attention.

"It's only fitting that I answer some questions after the interrogation we gave you," Bruce said, snickering.

"Now that you're no longer in the army, what do you plan to do with yourself?"

"That's a good question, Jimmy. I honestly don't know."

"Well, man, what do you do best?"

"I kill people," Bruce said, stone-faced.

"Now there's a skill," Jimmy breathed, eyes widening. "Can you make people completely disappear without a trace? 'Cause if you can, I could sure use you in my line of work. You have no idea the number of irritatin' gits I have to deal with on a daily basis."

"Last I looked, there were no legitimate openings for hired assassin. But if you just need me to do a drive by, we might be able to work something out," Bruce grinned. "How much you paying for this gig?"

"The sky's the limit," Jimmy said, holding up both hands to the ceiling. "You know my pockets run deep," Jimmy hooted.

"Mr. MacLeod, make sure you leave your business card. I may have need of it someday," Bruce said, pointing his fork at Jimmy.

"All levity aside, I'm currently a head hunter. Maybe I could broker some type of employment for you when the time's right. I'll give you one of my cards, and I expect you to call me, anytime, understand? And *not* because I'll be making an honest man out of your brother either," he said, patting Tony's arm. "I'd be pleased as punch to do something meaningful for you."

"Thank you, Jimmy. I'll keep you in mind."

"I'm serious, man. You call me now," Jimmy said, winking at me.

"Oh, by the way, this is for you," Tony said, sliding an envelope toward Bruce.

"What is that?" Bruce asked, guardedly.

"Remember what we talked about at the pavilion regarding your portfolio?"

"Yes."

"This is just a small advance on your share of the dividends. I thought you both could use it now instead of later."

"Tony, you don't need to do this, really," Bruce said.

"Brother, this is *your* money. I'm simply managing it, remember? And I meant it when I said I'm the *first* person you call whenever you and Lettie are in need. Got it? Now, take this. There's no more to be discussed," he said, pressing the envelope upon Bruce.

"Thank you, Tony," Bruce said as he passed the envelope to me. "Please, put this in your purse, babe."

I nodded and put it in my shirt pocket for the time being, then continued my conversation with Jimmy.

"Actually, Tony, there is one more thing to be discussed," Bruce said, *sotto voce*. "What's up with Lettice? You said you'd tell me, but you never got around to it."

"Oh!" Tony chuckled, wiping his mouth. "When Lettie was born, or so the story goes, Mama wanted to name her Lettice J'Nay, but Daddy kept pronouncing it Lettuce. Every time Mama tried to correct Daddy, he'd say stuff like Bib Lettuce, Boston Lettuce, Red Lettuce, instead of I don't like the name Lettice. Mama really didn't want to name her Lettie because it was too close to the name of an old girlfriend of Daddy's—a girlfriend Mama didn't particularly care for. Somehow, they managed to make a compromise. Mama would let him have Lettie, if she could have J'Nay."

"So, why do you call her 'Lettice'?"

"Because she can't stand it. Calling her Lettice is the same as her calling Brett, Bucket. You'd have thought she would have figured that out by now. At any rate, when I need her undivided attention, I call her Lettice."

"Smooth. I'll keep that one in mind."

"Oh, no, Bruh, don't try it. She will give you the beat down for sure. Save yourself and your marriage. Just keep calling her what you do," advised Tony.

"That's sounds like good advice from my attorney," Bruce acquiesced.

After breakfast, Bruce and I excused ourselves from the table and went to our room to finish packing. Since we traveled light, we didn't have much to do. I took the envelope and dutifully put it in my purse unopened. I decided to let Bruce be the one to show me its contents since the account was still in his name only. We stripped the bed of all its linens, and I placed them in the laundry hamper. Bruce had taken our bag out to the porch and began pulling Reina's things together. With a little help from Brett, Bruce loaded her crate in the SUV. He lined one corner of the crate with plastic and covered it with newspapers where she could relieve herself, and in the other areas, he put various old towels and blankets that were on hand. Mama gave Reina an old water bottle so she would be warm and comfortable on the trip home, as well as Suzie's old baby bottle. Once the car was loaded, we spent another two hours on the porch with the family.

"Mama, remember you said you were going to show us what you could do with alpaca fleece? Can you show us before we leave, please?" I asked.

"Indeed, Mum, I'd like to also see what you do with the hair from those magnificent beast's as well," Jimmy added.

"Wait right here, I'll be back in a flash."

Mama was gone for five minutes. When she returned, she was pulling a tall cylindrical woven basket behind her.

"All right, children, get ready to turn into a puddle. Y'all have never felt anything as decadent as this," Mama bragged. She pulled out of her basket skein after skein of one-hundred percent alpaca yarn, and it felt like butter in the hands, as soft as pure cashmere. They were all natural colors, but what a variety of hues she had. Then she showed us a scarf she had knitted from the alpaca yarn, followed by a pair of socks. Next she produced a simple crew neck sweater. Behind it was a V-necked vest. Then a multitude of hats, fingerless gloves, mittens, etc. All of it was an orgy for the senses. Jimmy and I couldn't stop squeezing, stroking, petting, or ogling everything Mama showed us. Even Bruce was impressed.

"Mama, did you knit all this up?" I asked.

"I sure did. Now that my nest is empty, the nights tend to get long. So I occupy myself. You know that idle hands…"

"Are the Devil's workshop," we all recited in unison.

"Mama, would I be imposing too much to ask you to knit a sweater for me out of this stuff?" asked Bruce. "I don't care about the color. I'm looking for something simple, like a pullover."

"Son, I would be proud to knit one for you. How about you, Lettie? Want a sweater too?" she asked.

"Yes, ma'am, since you're asking," I said. "You know my tastes, Mama; simple, clean, and understated. But, unlike Bruce, I'd like mine in this light fawn color. Will that be a problem?"

"Not at all. I never took you up to the attic where I have all my processed fleeces. It is just a matter of me spinning up enough yarn to do what I need to do. Lucky for you, I love spinning yarn. You know, I'm truly looking forward to retiring. After this year with the *Children of the Corn*, I'm ready to let it go and do some creative things that feed my soul and not consternate it," she said.

"How about you, sons?" she asked Jimmy and Tony.

"If I can have a sweater as fine as this, could you make mine a cardigan?" Jimmy asked. "Color doesn't matter. I just want to be able to snuggle in ridiculously indulgent softness and warmth."

"Not to sound demanding," said Tony, "but if you make me a sweater, could it be a raglan pullover in a smaller gauge?"

"Of course. Do you have a color preference?"

"I prefer blue, black, or grey—conservative neutrals that can go with anything," Tony said.

"Done. All y'all need to give me some time to fill these orders, hear? I'll treat them just like my prayer shawls. Every time I pick them up to knit, you'll know you've been bathed in my prayers," Mama smiled.

We talked a little while longer before Daddy gathered us together for parting prayer. "Chi'ren, y'all know I have enjoyed having my family back home, and Jimmy we're real blessed to welcome you into our hearts. Peaches, Luther, y'all know it's always a treat to see you. Now, let's join hands and pray."

"Gracious Master and our God, thank ya for such a marvelous Thanksgiving season. We praise you fo' yo' many blessings. We thank ya for Clarissa's life and ask that ya bring her back to good health. We thank ya for reconciliation, a strengthened marriage, and the beginnings of another. Protect, oh God, and give safe traveling mercies to all driving. Keep them safe from others, and others safe from them. Make homes safe upon return, and guard over them 'til we meet again. In Yo' Son's name, we pray, amen."

Bruce, Reina, and I settled into the car, prepared to get underway. We had hugged and kissed, kissed and hugged, yet Mama still wasn't ready to let us go. "Son, don't forget what I've told you. That's a baby you've got back there. She may not travel well, so stop often and check on her."

"Yes, ma'am."

"Remember to put one of yo' musty T-shirts in her crate to help keep her calm through the night."

"Yes, ma'am," Bruce smiled.

"And make sure you get her on a feeding regimen quickly. Help her regulate her bowels and potty runs by using a clock. Her bladder will soon mature where you won't have to be so hands-on."

"Yes, ma'am."

"And don't forget to love that baby, the both of you."

"Yes, ma'am," Bruce nodded.

"Yes, Mama. Anything else?" I asked.

"Yes. I'm gon' miss you two. Be good, and good to each other. Son, you know what I'm talking about."

"Yes, ma'am," Bruce said, sliding his eyes in my direction.

"Jewel! Let them chi'ren go," Daddy chided. "Bye, you two. Call us when y'all get home. Now, git!"

"Thanks, Pops," Bruce hollered, already in reverse. He honked, and I waved as we pulled off and headed for home.

The drive to D.C. was, mercifully, easy and uneventful. We stopped three times to give Reina some time out of her crate. She did remarkably well; no motion sickness, and no accidents in her crate.

We navigated off the interstate onto the city streets, and turned onto our street in our pitiable neighborhood, and into our driveway not long before sunset. Rallo wasn't there, so we went directly into the garage. The house appeared safe, sound, and clean. I expected it to look like a bachelor's pad, but Rallo was impressively neat. Immediately, I called home to let the folks know we had made it back safely. Fortunately, Daddy answered the phone, so our conversation was blessedly short.

"Baby, we need to decide where Reina's crate is going to stay," I said.

"I'd like to start her in the den near the kitchen, next to the sliding glass door. This way, we can train her quickly to let us know when she needs to go out."

"Okay, I can work with that," I said.

"Babe, I am so glad to be home. I've been looking forward to sleeping in my own firm, roomy bed all week."

"Ditto. I'm looking forward to all that *and* more. You know what I'm talkin' about," I said, imitating my mother's voice.

"Ha, ha, ha, very funny."

"I'm going to take a shower, while you, Daddy, feed your baby girl."

"Make sure you put on something sexy when you come out," he said in a dusky voice.

"For you or for Rallo?"

"Oh! I forgot he's coming back tonight. Check that, wait for him to leave."

"You sure?"

"Go. Get sexy."

My shower was bliss, and I took my sweet time. Afterwards, I slipped on a flowing caftan and dabbed on some expensive perfume. Walking back to the kitchen, I saw Rallo had returned. He was aggressively playing with Reina, who was truly trying to growl at him.

"Sister Lettie!"

"Hello, Rallo," I said, greeting him with a hug and kiss.

"Welcome back. I'm glad to see you brought this baby home," he said, pulling at Reina. "She's going to be a real asset to you two. As I was telling Bruce, they're coming. I had to call the cops twice this week over small gangs breaking into two of the houses nearby. I hate to be the bearer of bad news, but you all need to think about moving soon."

"God help them if they break in here and hurt my wife," Bruce said in a low voice.

"I know, man, but baby girl here is your organic alarm. Did you hear how she was growling at me? Give her a couple of months, and she *will* make folks back up," Rallo said, laughing.

"That's the plan," said Bruce.

"Rallo, can we offer you anything sweet to eat? Mama sent us home packed to the gills."

"What 'cha got?"

"Stop me when I hit your poison. Pecan pie, peach cobbler, Mississippi Mud, 7-Up cake, pineapple-upside-down cake, jelly cake..."

"Stop! Yo' mama sent some jelly cake? That's my poison. Hook me up, sister!"

"Would you like some milk with that?"

"Yes, ma'am. I bought a fresh gallon yesterday." Digging into the healthy slice I served, Rallo immediately began grunting. "Umh, umh, umh, yo' mama sure knows her way around a jelly cake. It's been too long since I've had one this good. Bruce! You eat like this all week, man?"

"Better, Bruh! I was ready to sell my clothes. Glory can't be better than my mama's table."

"The next time you all go home, take me with you," Rallo said.

"You are a mess," I laughed.

"Yes, ma'am," he said, chewing the last bite and draining his glass of milk. "I hate to eat and run, but I've got the early shift tomorrow, and I need to get some shut-eye. See you all at church next week?"

"Yes, sir," Bruce said.

"Aw'ight, peace out," Rallo said, grabbing his jacket and walking out the front door.

Alone at last, I sidled up to Bruce, and ran my hands over his chest. "Are you ready for me?" I asked.

"Not quite. I need to take baby girl out in the backyard for a bit. Give me fifteen minutes."

"Take your time. I'll be—resting—in our spacious, firm, bed," I said, looking over my shoulder as I walked back to our bedroom.

Bruce cut his quality time with Reina short. He was in and out of the shower ten minutes later. Sliding next to me he began to cuddle.

"I've missed this," he said.

"I thought Daddy told you to blow your pipes out before we left?" I ribbed.

"Babe, you know…"

"Yes, I do. I've always been uncomfortable having sex in my parent's house."

"Babe, we've been married for some years now," he reminded me.

"Yes, I know, but I'm still uncomfortable. I don't feel I can be *expressive* when I'm at Mama's house."

"You mean loud."

"Especially when it's good, yes!"

"Well, we're home now, so prepare for your world to be rocked," he said, nibbling on my ear.

From my ear, Bruce moved to my neck. As he started to pass my collarbone, Reina started whining.

"Your baby's crying," I said.

"Ignore her. She'll stop."

Moving to my left triceps, Bruce kissed and swirled with his tongue to excite the extraneous erogenous zones. As he reached my left nipple, Reina barked, and scratched at the gate of her crate.

"She's escalating," I said.

"Yeah, I hear," Bruce sighed.

"Did you put an old T-shirt in the crate?"

"No."

"Hot water bottle?"

"No," he sighed. "I'll take care of it."

Bruce lingered a little longer, and Reina began a pitiful moan as she tried to howl. Reluctantly, he got up to tend to his baby. Children and puppies—they are effective and proven birth control, not to mention, mood wreckers. By the time Bruce had settled Reina down, I was nearly asleep. I pretended to be dead to the world when Bruce returned because I had to be in the office early the next morning. Sensing he had lost the moment, Bruce was content to cuddle before rapidly falling asleep himself.

The alarm rang at 5:30 a.m. The hour came before I was ready for it. I was spoiled during my vacation by rising late. I knew by past experience it was going to take all this week to get back into my usual routine. Bruce awoke at the same time I did, but instead of sharing bathroom time, he immediately went to check on Reina. She was still asleep, so he slipped into the shower with me.

"Morning, wife," he said, caressing me from behind.

"Morning, husband," I said, reciprocating his affection by grinding on him.

"Can I start your day with a smile?"

"No, but you can sure relieve my stress this evening," I huskily answered, leaning against his strong body. "Unfortunately, I've got to get into the office early. There's no telling how many fires I'll have to put out before the boss gets in."

"Then, prepare to be transported to the land of sensual delights upon your return this evening."

"And will we have a baby sitter?"

"You leave Miss Thang to me."

Lingering only long enough to arouse my husband, I quickly jumped out of the shower and finished getting ready for work. I neglected to set the coffee pot the night before, so my mug of joe would have to be procured on the way in to work. As I was slipping on my pumps, Bruce emerged from the bathroom.

"Have a good day today, babe."

"Thank you, I'll try. What are your plans for today?" I asked.

"Oh, a little of this, and a little of that."

"Okay, I'll see you tonight," I said, pecking him on the lips. Making my way through the kitchen to the garage door, I called back, "Your baby's awake!"

"On my way," Bruce hollered back.

My day was exactly as I had feared. Why was it the shorter work week always seemed to be the most troublesome? Apparently, *Mr. Murphy* took up residence while I was on vacation. Whatever could go wrong, did. By quitting time, I was more than ready to leave, anxiously anticipating Bruce's tantalizing threat of sensual delights.

The drive home took longer than expected due to multiple accidents. Every year the scenario repeated itself. We were now entering the *Season of Fools*. Drivers who were used to dry roads completely forgot how to drive on icy or snowy roads. They were lulled into a false sense of security and believed if they had 4-wheel drive, they could command the roads. In their arrogance, they forgot 4-wheel drive only worked to their advantage if the wheels actually *had contact* with the road. Ice negated that particularly flawed logic. Consequently, the drive home was jacked-up for everybody.

I arrived an hour later than usual. Entering through the garage door, I was greeted with the welcoming aroma of dinner. Bruce met me with a loving embrace and kiss. Reina nipped at my heels, begging to be included in a group hug. Picking up the animated ball of fur, she eagerly tried to lick my face before pleading for Bruce's attentions.

"Rough day?" he asked.

"Like no other," I replied.

"Dinner's ready. I've been keeping it warm for you. Would you like to sit down now or grab a shower first?"

"I'm famished. Let me kick off my shoes and wash up."

"I'll have it on the table for you when you come back."

Sitting down to dinner with Bruce was heaven. He was no stranger in the kitchen, but I could tell he went to extra efforts for this meal. And he made sure my winter wonderland was in full blaze upon my arrival. This was the Bruce I married—considerate, thoughtful, striving to please for love's sake. It was nice to see *him* again, and I hoped it was not for a short time.

"You've already heard a sampling of my day, how was yours? What did you and Reina do?"

"Reina had her first ride in Brewster today, and she didn't throw up at all," he proudly boasted.

"How did you manage that?" I asked.

"I rigged up a way to keep her strapped down until we could get to the pet supply store. Once there, I got a halter for traveling where she'll be safely strapped in. I also bought some toys, leashes, and other stuff to make our lives good. Then, I found a reputable vet not far from us and got baby girl established at that practice."

Smiling at Bruce while he unpacked his day caused him to ask, "What?"

"It really is just like having a child, isn't it?" I shot back. "Next we'll be enrolling her in school," I laughed.

"Funny you should say that," Bruce continued. "I did exactly that today as well."

"Obedience training?"

"Yes and no. We signed up for the basic obedience, but I'm going further. I'm going to train Reina to be a guard dog."

"And that's different, how?" I asked.

"It's much more involved than simply sit, stay, and come. We, as in you and me, are going to be able to communicate through sign or hand commands. She's going to have to be desensitized to noise and other distractions that could allow an intruder in our home. She's also going to be trained how to bite to effectively bring down an intruder. I Skyped a buddy of mine who trains dogs for the army, and he's given me some good advice and recommendations for schools in the area."

"How much is all this going to cost?"

"To begin, about $1,000."

"Bruce, where are we going to come up with an extra $1,000 right now?"

"Go get that envelope from Tony. Let's see what's in it."

I went to my purse, retrieved the envelope, and immediately brought it back to the table.

"You didn't open it?" Bruce asked, surprised.

"No. This account is in your name only. I figured if you wanted me to know, you'd tell me."

"Wow!" was Bruce's sole comment when he opened the envelope. Looking at me wide-eyed, he slipped the envelope to me. To my shock and disbelief, the check was $25,000 made out to Bruce *and* me.

"Please get this to the bank first thing tomorrow on your way in."

"Done and done. I'll deposit it into our checking account, and once we've made some plans, I'll transfer the bulk into our savings. Agreed?"

"Agreed," said Bruce.

"How long do you think it's going to take to train her?"

"Every dog is different, so it's hard to estimate. I can tell you this, Reina is an extremely intelligent pup. I don't think it will take her long. Maybe a full year to get the real hang of protecting us. She'll have basic commands in a matter of weeks."

"Let's hope our creepers can wait that long," I said.

"Let us pray, not hope."

"Amen."

"Babe, I don't want to weird you out, but Reina and I are going to be near inseparable while we're training. I don't want you to feel like you're being shut out – you're not. Nothing comes between us, not even the dog, but in order to achieve the results I'm looking for, she and I will have to be in close proximity for a while. I want very much for you to bond with her, too. That means all of us are going to have to spend some quality cuddle time together."

"*Where* is this happening?" I ask with raised eyebrow.

"Here in the den, on the floor," he laughed. "I'm not proposing she come into our bed. I'm paying close attention to what yo' mama said," he assured.

"I suppose I can support the notion," I said. "We're not beginning tonight are we? Because I've been looking forward to my night of splendid delights all day."

"I was hoping you were. Finish eating while I attend to Reina. I'm going to make sure she doesn't disturb us tonight."

"I'm almost finished. I'm going to take a leisurely shower once I'm done. Will that fit into your plans?"

"Mos' def'. Help yo'self."

After eating, I rinsed our place settings and stacked them in the dishwasher before heading to the shower. Daddy was cradling his baby and lovingly bottle feeding her while gently stroking and speaking to her. She was pure putty in his lap.

I made my way to our bedroom. Hanging up my clothes, I decided to lay out tomorrow's choices so, if necessary, I could rinse, slip on, and run. The hot and steamy shower felt marvelous to my tied up neck and shoulder muscles. I would let Bruce have a shot at these muscles while he was loosening up other parts of me. I intentionally skipped my normal exit routine of dabbing on perfume, and opted for the fresh, clean, natural scent of me.

Bruce lay in wait for me to come out of the bathroom. As soon as I opened the door and turned off the light…

CLAP – CLAP

...Our bedroom became a whimsical, twinkling playground. Our bed, covers drawn and pooled at the foot of the bed, was laid with a rubber flannel backed sheet festooned with fresh rose pedals. There were three covered boxes of various heights on the left side of the bed. One displayed multiple scented pillar candles all ablaze. Another one held a platter of sliced pineapples, whole strawberries, honeydew melon balls, maraschino cherries, big, fat, red seedless grapes, and two cans of whipped crème, regular and chocolate. The final box held our Bose radio/CD player with Branford Marsalis playing the *Eternal* album. Seeing all this, my stress levels almost bottomed out to zero. I smiled at Bruce as he held out his hand to escort me over to the bed.

"If madam will allow," he said while romantically kissing my hand, "may I take the liberty of briefly massaging your stress zones?"

If madam will allow? "Madam would be most grateful," I said.

Bruce, who was appropriately dressed for the occasion in only his six-pack abs and light man-musk, sat down near the head of the bed. He then lay my head in his lap where he slowly massaged my temples with lavender, sweet orange, and sandalwood infused oil. After ten minutes, Bruce rolled me on my stomach and began massaging my neck, shoulders, and upper back. The massage and the ambiance reduced whatever stress I had to nothing.

Turning me over on my back, Bruce asked, "Are you ready for dessert?"

"Yes, please."

"Which fruit would you like to start with?"

"Grapes, please."

Sensuously, he first slid one grape over my lips before allowing me to bite. Next, he took a fat strawberry, crowned the end with chocolate whipped crème, and held it where only my tongue could gather the crème. Once I lapped up as much as he'd allow, he teasingly brought the berry to my lips. It was luscious, juicy, and flavorful. I must remember to ask where he purchased these.

Bruce put a cherry between his teeth, and while planked above me, leaned his torso down inviting me to take of it what I could. He remained motionless in that position for a long while, which impressed the hell out of me. His mustiness was intoxicating and arousing. His musk ignited my pheromones and stimulated my garden. Slowly, I nibbled at the cherry making sure my tongue swirled around the inner circumference of his lips. My man was steel, continuing to plank unmoving above me. Consuming the first cherry, Bruce deftly reached for another, supporting himself with only one arm and a six pack.

"How are you doing that?" I breathed with wonder.

"I have incentive," he smoothly answered.

Leaning down again, Bruce offered up his dazzling smile, and I playfully sucked and pulled at his lower lip. I taunted his steely abs by feathering my fingernails across his flanks until he flinched. Swiftly, I pulled him down onto me, smothering his mouth with mine. Languidly, I released him confident the cherry was now mine.

"Husband, what are you having for dessert?"

"I hoped you would ask. Shall I show you?"

"Yes."

"Stay right where you are," he said, reaching for the regular whipped crème. Boyfriend used the whipped crème as his brush, more fruit as his palette, and my body as his edible canvas.

His first brush stroke was circling each areola with crème creating a cup where cherries sat atop each nipple. From there, he drew a wiggly line down to my navel where he created a crème nest for a trio of melon balls. He continued by painting primitive glyphs on the bikini line embellished with slices of pineapple. Bruce placed one jumbo grape in the nook of my garden's gate. Satisfied with his finished masterpiece, he commenced to erasing his canvas. Hovering above me on hands and knees, Bruce leisurely ate his dessert. With tongue only, he manipulated the pineapple and crème glyphs, savoring every mouthful, allowing some juice to fall as an excuse to go back over cleared ground. Moving to my navel, he inhaled the melon balls much like a vacuum sucks up ping-pong balls. He slurped the navel's nest until there were spotty remnants. Then his tongue washed and tickled me as he probed the recesses of my belly button. Traveling upward, Bruce confidently licked the line leading to my breasts. There, he took his time swirling his tongue in the crème. My desire to remain a static canvas shattered once he enveloped nipples and areolas in search of cherries. Shivers gripped me as moans escaped my lips. I didn't think I could endure the sensations any further when Bruce abruptly shifted gears and headed for my garden's gate. Oh, my lord! The tingling was magically in sync with the twinkling ceiling. I was nearing the cliffs edge when suddenly he purposefully slid his manhood inside me and touched off a firestorm of orgasmic titillations. Each slow thrust methodically sought my sweet spot. Faster and faster the search continued until my unabashed cries confirmed he had not only found it but owned it. The last of the fireworks, like a huge Roman candle, elicited shrieks of surfeit from us both. Panting, glistening, and slightly sticky, we collapsed upon each other.

"Oh, my God," I breathed when I finally caught my breath.

"Yes, ma'am," he drawled.

"That was incredible, husband. Thank you."

"It was good, wasn't it?"

"Uh huh," I agreed as afterglow was transporting me toward sleep.

"Happy to be of service," Bruce said as he gathered me in his arms, where together we slept for hours. At midnight, Bruce gently shook me awake. "Babe, wake up. Go shower and let me clear the bed. You can go back to sleep afterwards."

"Okay," I mumbled. Drowsy, I made my way to the shower. I washed quickly, thinking I would help Bruce clean up, but he was done and waiting for me as I came out of the bathroom. My husband was efficient, like no other person I knew.

"That was awfully quick," I commented.

"Anything is simple if you know what you're doing and have planned well."

"I'm truly impressed and blessed," I whispered, kissing his forehead.

Kissing my hands, he said, "Go back to sleep; get your rest. I'll be up with you in the morning to care for Reina."

"What about your VA appointments? Will she be alright in her crate that long?"

"I'll be taking her along. Don't worry, it's all been worked out. Trust me," he said, looking in my eyes, "it'll be okay."

"I trust you, and I trust you have everything well in hand."

CLAP – CLAP.

Acknowledgements

The story of the Jonson family is an epic that was born out of my imagination, and warped sense of humor, but I could not have presented the credible realities without input from vital and reliable sources. I wish to thank Col. John (Jack) Trepagnier, US Army, Ret., a dear friend to my late father, and also a good friend of mine, for all his insight into the trappings, workings, and failures of the VA system today. It is with deep appreciation and sincere thanks to him for allowing me a peek behind the curtain of army command structure, and for being brutally honest in his opinions and life experiences. I could listen to his war stories—literally—without end.

Likewise, I must acknowledge and thank Sharon Luke, former Associate Professor at the University of Mount Union, Alliance, OH, former Department Chair and Physician Assistant Studies Program Director, for her graciousness and patience with my endless health related questions. Sharon can break down the most complicated terminology so that an idiot can understand with clarity.

Special thanks to my sister and friend, the Rev. Dr. Gloria A. Johnson of Atlanta, GA, for the sharing of her expertise in the field of Pastoral Psychotherapy. According to Gloria, anyone as crazy as I am needs all the help she can give.

I extend a heartfelt thanks to my road sisters: Jennifer, Marty, Bonnie, Deb, Peggy, Eva, Judy, and especially, Amy, who gave tirelessly of her professional time and talents, without whom I could not have completed this work. I thank them all for being my endless readers and guinea pigs who never feared to challenge me on every level. They are an amazing cadre of strong women with whom laughter, meals, and drinks were succor for my soul.

To my brothers: I thank Frank for all his support, honesty, professional advice, and for encouraging me to just "do it" and write while the spirit was upon me. Thanks to my Boo, Justin, for always being willing to provide an alibi at a moment's notice along with a ginger martini. A big thanks goes to the love of my life, I. Lee, who resisted running and screaming naked in the street when I would ask to read to him "just this little bit" for the umpteenth time. Baby, I love you to bits!

Finally, I praise my God for *all* His blessings and for the mother He blessed me with. Thanks, Mom, for your unwavering support and for always being my biggest fan and cheerleader.